THE ARTEMIS KEY

The Agency of the Ancient Lost & Found Book 4

JANE THORNLEY

PROLOGUE

D*elphi, Greece, 392 AD*

SHE HAD RUN AS THOUGH THE ARMIES STILL BURNED AT HER HEELS, RUN as though her feet knew not how to stop, how to rest, how to heal. When she had finally reached the coast, the remnants of her people—terrified men and women who, like her, had watched their temples burn—helped her escape across the sea. Only twenty could fit into the single boat so the leader chose six of the strongest men plus their wives and children.

The way was long and tortuous. Apollo had cast such feeble light across the waves that it was as though he bled pale blood upon the swells. Was the god truly dying? She could not find him or his sister, Artemis, anywhere. The men had called for Poseidon—they had always used the old Greek names when they could—to grant them speed for their escape, but the Pythia remained silent. They were dead, all dead. The mighty had fallen. Even the priests could not deny it.

"Honored Pythia," the woman huddled beside her had asked, "what have we done to anger the gods so? Why have they forsaken us?"

She had not the heart to answer. "Nothing" was not something her people would understand. To them, she had always held the answers and would speak them without hesitation. How could she tell them that the time of their gods had run aground, that the power they had once believed so absolute had been replaced by another?

In Delphi, she had sensed the change coming in the voices of the soldiers passing through, heard word that the might of Rome trembled upon its very foundations as the priests whispered among themselves. A new emperor had appeared—Constantine—and with him came another god. Once the conqueror, now the conquered—such an old, old story. She had sat in the temple to request guidance and the answer had come by way of total darkness, a deep, all-consuming void. Before, there had always been swirling colors, sparks in her vision, scenes rolling across her inner gaze. Now nothing, nothing. How could she journey into nothing? And yet she must.

Long ago Rome had conquered Greece—her home, her people—and now the same threatened them. New conquerors brought a new god, razing sanctuaries and their deities to the ground. Now she finally understood how destroying gods was even possible. Once the temples were gone and the believers dispersed, the gods withered like wheat in the burning sun.

And she could not find in herself to honor another, even if the soldiers would permit her to live, which they would not. To them she represented all that must be abolished. The Voice of Apollo must be strangled and his priestess raped and butchered to make way for the new god. They slaughtered the priests first, believing the oracle spoke through them and that the Pythia was merely their tool, but while they writhed, she escaped, taking the key with her. They would never have guessed that she even possessed such a thing because most believed the oracles were a hoax. Most were, she knew, but she, the last Pythia, held the true key.

So she ran, holding her gods and goddesses close to her heart, hoping for one last word, for a single sign from her once-protectors. Her ultimate haven was more journey than destination. The gods would find her in their final sanctuary.

"I must go there," she had whispered to her boatmen after drawing a map in the sand.

"But, Pythia, we do not know this place," the leader protested.

"I will guide you." And she did, using the signs that had appeared long ago, signs sketched into the floor of the temple that no one but her had understood. After many days of hiding from the warships, clustering on beaches of distant shores, the tiny island finally came into view, the sharp peaks gouging the gray skies.

"Honored Pythia," the man had cried, "what place is this? No one can survive here! Nothing but cliffs all about!"

"You will find a small beach on the other side where you will leave me. Take me there."

They resisted, of course they did. "We will not abandon you!" the leader shouted, a chorus of others joining in, but she could see the fear in their faces when they trudged up the shale beach. A more forbidding place could not be devised by Hades himself.

"What is this place?" a woman asked.

"An ancient temple lies hidden at the mouth of the labyrinth," she told them. "Do not be frightened for only I will enter the darkness. You will leave me there. Follow me."

So they followed her up the scrabbled path, between the rocks and into the first cave, their torches burning acrid smoke into the darkness. The goat they had brought bleated in protest while the children cried one after the other. Then gasps of awe broke out as the flames picked out the shape of dancers painted on the walls.

"Behold," Pythia called, turning, "this is the mark of our people, painted here by our ancestors thousands of years before. They lead us to the sacred temple of Artemis. There you will be safe until you find your new home."

The corridor widened into a huge cavern with even more paintings, more dancers, and the golden image of the goddess Artemis running with her hounds. Her people surged towards the statue, bowing and crying in supplication, begging for her protection. Everywhere there were gold and precious objects lay scattered about, long-ago offerings their ancestors had left behind, enough to buy them food and clothing wherever they landed. Pythia turned her gaze to the tunnels opening up on all sides. She had not anticipated so many.

"Honored Pythia," the leader cried, "you have delivered us to safety!

We will hide here and sacrifice our goat to the goddess and you this night. We will feast in your honor!"

"Yes!" the others agreed, many still sobbing at the cella's feet.

"Thank you," Pythia whispered for her voice was hoarse from crying, "but I do not require a feast. Instead, I implore you to use the goat—" she pointed toward the bony animal held by a starving child as if it were a pet "—to feed your people one final meal. Apollo and Artemis wish you to feast in their name before you escape to your new home." In truth, she had no idea what either deity wanted anymore but this was what she wanted. "As for me, I ask only that you leave me to walk alone into the labyrinth beyond while you escape in the morning for Delos. You will be welcomed there."

He shook his head, aghast. "The labyrinth, honored Pythia? But..." His words faded as she pointed to the blackness yawning there.

"This is our last sanctuary. You must never speak of this place to man or god. It must die on your lips."

The man bowed and the others followed. "As you wish."

"There is no time to waste," she continued. "Even now, ships hunt me down. They will arrive on these shores within days and kill the weakest and force the strongest into slavery." There was no point in hiding the truth. "You must escape tomorrow at dawn, for if they find your boat, they will find me, and this sacred place, then all will be lost. Feast now. You will need your strength." With that, she turned and walked past the statue of Artemis frozen in her headlong flight to forever, past her people with their weeping children and grief-stricken faces, straight toward the sixth tunnel moving east.

A woman rushed behind her holding a torch aloft. "You cannot go into the darkness without a light, Pythia," she gasped. "There are monsters down there."

Pythia turned and smiled. "The only monsters lie beyond these walls and they will not accompany me on this journey. Hold the torch for me only for the first few steps and then I shall continue alone."

The woman nodded, hoisted her tattered robes in one hand and stepped into the tunnel behind Pythia, holding the torch as high as she could. Around them, the ancient dancers strode bravely on, the colors of their tunics still glowing in the light while her living people gathered at the tunnel's mouth to watch.

"Can you hear the music?" Pythia asked after several steps.

"No, mistress."

"Listen."

The woman tried with all her might but the only sounds she heard were of a baby crying behind her and the endless bleating of the goat.

"Clap your hands and sing for me, my friends!" the Pythia called. "Do not let the monsters frighten you, for as long as you seek the light, they cannot harm you."

She glanced up at the image of the priestess of long ago holding a torch above her head, the other arm pointing into the darkness. *Yes, my sister, I understand.*

Pythia beckoned for the woman to stay behind, then held the hem of her robe in one hand and stepped alone into the darkness.

I

S he ran with a white stag under a full silver moon. Her short white tunic, gold sash, and the quiver of arrows thrown over one shoulder pegged to be the Artemis, guardian of animals, queen of the hunt, and protector of young women. The small poster was definitely Art Nouveau in style with the tack holes in each dogeared corner implying that it had graced multiple walls in its time. At that moment, it sat under a brochure featuring a ruined marble temple.

"What's this?" I asked. "I mean, I know what it is just not why you've put it here."

"I thought you needed a bit of inspiration for your Grecian vacation," Zann replied as she lounged near one of our light tables in the lab. "I used to pin that pic onto my walls back in the old days. Thought it was so inspiring. Everywhere I went, it went with me. As an archaeology student, I thought of myself as the huntress of buried objects, kind of what you are now. You can take it with you along with the brochure, if you want."

Zann Masters the rogue archaeologist who I had extricated from a snake pit of trouble weeks before, hadn't stopped causing our agency more of the same since our return to London. When she had announced in Italy over live TV that she was working for the Agency (which she wasn't) and that we were hunting down the master art thief and my former lover, Noel, (which we weren't), that in itself should have been enough for me to close the door. But we didn't. Correction—I didn't. I had promised to help untangle her legal woes and that's what I did, which meant her presence remained a constant irritant in our lives for weeks too long. Thankfully, she'd be on her way to the United States to visit her father the next day and I'd be off on vacation, so relief was in sight.

Despite everything, I liked her which explained why I'd requested that my colleagues put up with her while I worked on her behalf. And, besides, most of the time she meant well.

I took a deep breath. "Thanks, Zann, but a vacation in the Greek isles is inspiration enough, don't you think? It's just a sailing holiday so this brochure is not really relevant."

"Not relevant? Are you kidding me? Brauronia is the site of one of the most important temples to Artemis in the ancient world, after Ephesus, that is. I mean of the known temples. There are plenty of others around, too, but the most important one is yet to be discovered. Just thought you might be interested in a side excursion," she said while pulling up a chair across from mine. Typical of Zann to consider finding a lost temple to be a day trip. "I mean, you'll be so close, being in Greece, and Artemis is such a goddess powerhouse."

I nodded. "Thanks but this isn't a working holiday, just a holiday." Actually, I had an ulterior agenda of my own. I'd been streaming film in my imagination where Evan joined me aboard this tall ship sailing across an impossibly blue sea. He'd proclaim his love to me and I to him, all while violins played and we gaze lovingly into one another's eyes. That alone was enough to activate my own inner goddess, powerhouse or not.

Okay, so I had booked in a bit of agency business in Athens on the side but only a day's worth so it didn't count.

"Just so you know, I've worked on a few digs in Greece in my time and there's this rumor going around of a hidden temple of Artemis buried on a Greek island somewhere."

I studied her, taking in the freshly pressed striped shirt, the navy pants, the tweedy jacket. She had ditched the disheveled look from our Florentine traumas weeks earlier in for something more tailored and preppy. She'd even sheared her hair short.

"When you were working for Baldi, you mean?" The topic of the now deceased arms dealer and his possible replacement, my ex, had finally subsided as everyone's topic of choice around here. We had agreed that we were in the business of retrieving lost art and artifacts, not tracking down arms dealers, no matter how strong the emotional ties. For now the matter had been laid to rest.

"Yeah, may he burn in hell. Anyway, my point is that I've excavated a few digs in Greek and Turkey so I know what I'm talking about. This belief in a lost temple is, like, everywhere. Imagine if we could find it?"

"We? Zann, please understand that you are not part of the Agency so there is no 'we.'" I'd lost count of the number of times I'd told her this in a variety of ways, from strident to gentle. Plus, we have no compelling reason to go off on a hunt for a lost temple. Lost temples aren't our business."

She leaned forward. "Listen up: I was in Greece poking around once and kept hearing the tale of an ancient temple that had been hidden in anticipation of an invasion, maybe back when Xerxes invaded Attica circa 480 BC or when one the other ancient hotshot conquerors decided to invade. All the archies have been looking for it for eons but can't find it but they didn't have you, the lost art sniffer dog, on the team."

Why, oh, why had I coined that expression let alone voiced it aloud? "'Archies'?" I enquired.

"Archaeologists. Just think of the possibilities?" Zann continued, her enthusiasm swelling. "Everybody thinks it's a myth along the lines of when Troy was believed to be just a tale, that is until Schliemann proved them wrong."

And destroyed an archaeological site while plundering ancient treasure. Given her history, I could see why Zann revered him. Passing back the picture and brochure, I smiled. "And I love a good myth as much as anyone else but right now I'd love a good vacation more." My phone buzzed in my pocket. "Excuse me."

I jumped up and headed for the toilet, which was about the only place I could escape Zann for a moment's privacy. Leaning against the door, I pulled out my cell.

It was a text from Peaches: *Are you and Ev still going on vacation together?*
Me: *That's the plan. Why?*
Peaches: *Because I'm your bodyguard and your body shouldn't be going*

anywhere without mine guarding it, obviously. But if Ev's coming, I'll let him take care of said body. He'll do it in ways I won't. Bet he's good at it, too. Just sayin'.

Me: *Glad you approve. Enjoy your own R&R. Got to get back to keep an eye on Zann before she rifles through my drawers.*

When I emerged later, it was to find Zann sitting at my desk accessing one of the stolen art databases. "Think they'll ever find that heisted Gardner museum loot?" she asked without looking up.

"I have no idea. I keep hoping they'll hire our agency to take on the case but until then...Look, I have to talk to Max about something," I said heading for the elevator. "Coming?" Anything to get her away from our work stations.

"Sure."

Up in the main floor showroom, Max and Serena were studying the mid-16th century Persian niche rug, our newest acquisition, now hanging in a prime location close to the front windows. The gallery was open by appointment only but we still had plenty of window shoppers drifting by.

"I believe I have a sale for this already," Max said, catching sight of me. He shot Zann a curt nod before continuing. "In fact, most of our best pieces are now sold so I expect to be in full bidding mode at Sotheby's next month." Our rare textile and ethnographic artifact gallery really was booming which served as the perfect front for my side of the operation, the Agency of the Ancient Lost & Found. Max had washed his hands of that part and preferred to concentrate on the gallery.

"Great," I said, admiring my godfather's handsome physique that proved that the image of the declining seventy-five year old belonged to another generation. "Will you two be fine holding down the fort by yourselves while everyone's gone?" Of course they would. That was more for Zann's benefit in case she felt compelled to volunteer her services again.

Max grinned, dapper as ever in his silk waistcoat and jeans, his thick silver hair gleaming in the halogen lights. "Naturally, darlin'. Rena and I will have a grand old time, won't we Reni?" He put an arm around the diminutive Serena and drew her near, a gesture that plucked at my heartstrings, romanticist that I was. Love at any age was such a thrill.

Serena, affectionally known as "Rena" beamed, the picture of a woman who had at last obtained her heart's desire after a long spell of longing. Now that she and Max were an item, it's as though nothing could wipe away her glow. Even the colors in her kimonos had grown more vibrant. "We will keep the fort going, Phoebe. No need to worry. You enjoy your vacation and forget all about work."

That was the plan. The agency calls were being routed to Rupert currently renovating his ancestral pile in the country while Evan was away attending a museum opening on our behalf in Berlin. With Peaches visiting family in Jamaica, the agency was taking a bit of a hiatus, which we all badly needed and justly deserved.

"Well, I'll just be off now," Zann announced, gazing at each of us in turn as if hoping someone would implore her to stay. No one did. "I might catch you later, then. My plane leaves tomorrow afternoon," she added.

"Have a very good flight," Serena said. "I will walk you to the door."

"Don't hurry back," Max called.

Linking Zann's arm with hers, she steered the woman towards the front, chatting away about long plane rides and the weather.

"Bye, Phoebe," Zann called over her shoulder. "Remember what I told you."

Once Zann had been dispatched, Serena returned to cast a disapproving gaze at Max. "You were not kind."

Max looked up from where he had been checking off the carpets he planned to bid on from a catalogue, me peering over his shoulder. "But I was't unkind, either. I just didn't want that one to keep making herself at home around here. She's always underfoot, asking questions, pestering the bejesus out of everyone, especially Phoebe here."

"She is very curious," Serena said. "She asks intelligent questions. I like her."

"Me, too," I added quickly. "She's a trained archaeologist with an inquiring mind."

"And an irritating disposition," Max countered. "She's poking her nose into everything and seems obsessed with you."

"Perhaps she has—what do they call it?—a 'girl crush'," Rena suggested.

Max grumbled, nudging me as he circled a particularly stellar Persian rug in the catalogue. I nodded my agreement with his choice. "Anyway, I was tolerant for awhile, seeing as she'd once known Noel but that soon wore thin since she couldn't say a good thing about him. Where does she get off calling my son a crook and thieving scumbag when she's hardly unblemished herself? One way or the the other, I'm glad she's gone."

I was desperately hoping that Noel's name wouldn't come up but I should have known better. Now that Max realized that his son was still alive, relations between us had improved significantly. I could no longer be accused of killing him. Still, it wouldn't take much for tensions to erupt again, especially since I didn't share my godfather's relief in my ex's continued existence. Besides, I had a few names for him of my own.

I will not engage, I told myself. *Walk away.* "Right, well time to finish packing. I love your carpet choices, Max." I said, heading for the elevator and to my top floor flat. "Catch you later."

I hadn't make it to the doors before noticing the brochure and Artemis picture sitting on one of our display tables.

***

ATHENS HIT ME IN UNEXPECTED WAYS. THE ACROPOLIS, PERCHED ON ITS ancient rock, was gleaming white marble in the sunshine. It dominated the city just as I had imagined, but the graffiti on the urban walls glimpsed in passing hit me as jarringly modern. But that was misguided thinking, right? If Greece was the undisputed birthplace of democracy, why shouldn't the current citizens express themselves in bold spray paint colors? Everyone had plenty to complain about these days.

But the Acropolis was once home of the gods, the largest known conglomeration of temples to the ancient Grecian polytheism with the namesake Athena queen of the mount. That deserved a measure of respect across the millennia so I fervently hoped I'd never see the day when modern graffiti sprawled across ancient ruins.

Dr. Nickolas Christpodoulopoulo, a new employee of the esteemed Acropolis museum, was to meet me in the lobby. Based on a bit of preliminary research that included museum staff lists, I knew that he had been hired exactly two months prior. I figured that if a junior historian had been assigned as my welcoming committee it was probably because I was not considered high enough up on the VIP ladder to warrant being greeted by a top dog. That suited me. Top dogs often needed their egos groomed and I wanted this process executed as simply as possible so I could get on with my vacation. Besides, it wasn't like I was repatriating the Elgin Marbles.

All I needed was to officially sign over the helmeted head of Athena which had been gazing at me from my shelf for the best part of a year. We had shipped her over weeks before and my role was to formalize the repatriation process with a signature and be done.

But I was going to miss her. Sometimes the marble eyes of the goddess of wisdom seemed to either caution or chastise me, usually the latter. I had often warned myself to approach difficult situations with wisdom...and often failed. Whatever the case, the absence of Athena's head would leave a gap on my headquarters shelf with no one able to caution me with a stony glance.

At first we didn't know exactly where our disembodied Athena belonged. Greece had thousands of Athena bits floating around, remnants of an ancient empire that had spread across the Mediterranean and beyond when warring civilizations had been bent on decapitating its splendor. And yet the Acropolis museum was the only facility willing to bring this one home.

"Phoebe McCabe, this is a great honor." I looked up from where I had been gazing down through the glass floor at the museum's archaeological dig to see a young curly dark haired man approaching from across the foyer of the impressive modern space. Attractive in a boyish way with short curly hair and a neatly-trimmed beard framing a round face, I liked him immediately. A few inches taller than I and probably several years younger, dressed in a suit jacket with a tieless shirt and big grin, Dr. Christpodoulopoulo shook my hand with unabashed enthusiasm.

"I'm excited to be here, Dr. Christpodoulopoulo." I had even taken the time to practice pronouncing his name with the help of a Greek restaurant owner in London. "Thanks for accepting my homeless goddess. I was surprised at how hard it was to find her a place. The last thing we wanted was for a deity of wisdom to end up decorating somebody's living room or to remain stuck on a shelf somewhere. Imagine the ignominy?" My gaze shifted to his neck. He wore an amulet that looked for all the world to be an ancient talisman of some kind.

"Perish the thought," Dr. Christpodoulopoulo exclaimed, clutching his heart and gazing upward like an actor seeking his stage. His ancient countrymen would have approved. "And call me Nick. I only inflict my full name on arrogant foreigners which you are not." He grinned, dipped a tiny bow, and lifted his head to hold my gaze seconds longer that necessary. "By the way, I have witnessed a 3rd century Hellenic bust acting as a pedestal for a coffee table in a holiday home once. Almost brought me to tears. But tell me, Phoebe, how could Athens refuse to grant Athena residence in her namesake city?"

"Yes, how could you?" Okay, so Nick had dramatic flair, but I loved that enthusiasm. Give me flair over dry scholarship any day.

We laughed as he lead the way down the light-filled hall lined with marble statuary and friezes towards a group of figures bathed in light. A majestic headless robed female figure stood surrounded by by a pose of supplicants, one hand bearing a spear, the other a shield with Medusa's head incised on its surface. I stared. "Do you mean that this may be her missing body?"

"If not, it's a close enough to make a perfect fit. The lab is currently assessing the piece further but it does appear to be of the same period and marble source. At one time, she would have been painted and her accessories gilded in pure gold, as you probably know. Time does bring one down a peg, doesn't it, Phoebe?"

"Yes, it does, Nick," I whispered, gazing up at the exquisite form, the folds of her marble robe draping the goddess in the dignity she deserved.

"Would you sign the papers, please?"

I took the metal clipboard and briefly scanned the document which acknowledged that my bust—accurately described and accompanied by a photo insert—was hereby officially repatriated to the Acropolis museum on behalf of the Agency of the Ancient Lost & Found. I signed in the space provide and passed the clipboard back.

"Thank you. The question is how did our goddess's head wander so far away from home?" Nick asked, his accent faint but pleasing.

As if I was going to mention my brother and ex's art heisting ways here. For the next two weeks, I'd banned them from my lips. "I have no idea. If only Athena could talk."

We chatted all the way through the museum and up the steady incline towards the Acropolis itself where I was given a private tour that almost left me mute with wonder. To stand below the Parthenon and gaze up at the glory of the ancient world was such a thrill. To think that thousands of years ago, some of the greatest names of ancient philosophy and science had trod those very steps.

"How much of their knowledge had been lost while our civilization presumably advances?" I remarked while gazing up at the monumental ruin.

Nick turned to me with quickening interest. "How much indeed? I often ask myself the same thing as I seek esoteric knowledge which the modern world with its narrow definition of science would consider irrelevant or even fantastical."

I nodded. "The Greek legacy has given us so much—the foundation for mathematics, science, drama, architecture and art, to name but a smidgeon, but what's been lost along the way? What are we still missing? It's like the further the modern world advances, the more we leave a profound understanding of ancient knowledge far behind. We don't know what we don't know." As a favorite topic of mine, I relished the opportunity to expound.

"My belief exactly," he said, one hand resting on his heart. "We are indeed kindred spirits, Phoebe, which does not surprise me in the least."

Kindred spirits? Perhaps. Nick certainly was an amusing and knowledgeable companion, a combination which I enjoyed, and we were hitting it off splendidly. He lead me across the remains of temple complex, weaving around the the tour groups with their guides explaining the history in several languages. After admiring all the temples, we ended up taking a breather in front of the sanctuary of Artemis, now no more than a few broken columns and a collection of monumental rubble.

Sitting on a rock before the temple breathing in the amazing ruin scape all around, I just had to ask: "So, is it true that there may be an intact temple of Artemis buried in Greece somewhere?"

Nick smiled and it occurred to me that he was very attractive, not as attractive as a certain other individual but a close fifth. "So they say, Phoebe, but the scientific community asks how can that be? Temples were built above ground, they say. How can one hide something that large beneath the surface? Meanwhile, I say that anything is possible if we just look with our whole being instead of with just the intellect. The Greeks were a complex and advanced civilization. Why not bury a secret temple below ground? The Romans who absorbed so much of the essence of ancient Greece had secret underground temples."

"Are you referring to the Roman cult of Mithras?"

"As one example, yes. The Mithras sanctuaries are probably the best known underground sanctuaries but who says that they're weren't others just because we don't recognize them as such? Most Grecian deities had many cults with differing practices of worship." He was staring at me intently. "Is this the real reason why you have come to Greece, to locate a hidden temple of Artemis?"

Now that was an odd question. "I'm here on vacation and to do a bit of agency work on the side which I just completed, by the way. I'm certainly not on the hunt for a lost temples or treasure. Besides, lost temples are a bit out of my league."

"Nothing is out of your league from what I understand, Phoebe, and here you are in a veritable playground of ancient buried treasure—art, artifacts, *temples*. Phoebe, consider this: throughout the ancient world countless rumored sites have vanished. To me that says that they only await the right alignment of the stars to locate and require a different kind of tool other than those used by historians and archaeologists to find."

That struck me as an odd comment coming from a historian. I also noted how he seemed to say my name at every opportunity while holding my gaze seconds too long. Disconcerting but soon forgotten when gazing around at this ancient panorama.

"Did you know that the name 'Phoebe' originates from ancient Greece and is the feminine form of Phoebus from Apollo meaning 'bright'?" he asked. "In Greek mythology, Phoebe was associated with the power of prophecy and the moon. As sister to Apollo, god of the sun, she was originally a Titan, a goddess among gods."

I smiled. This was getting weird. "I did know that but I admit to having forgotten much of it."

"And here you have come to Greece bearing the head of a goddess. Perhaps you are part of an ancient prophecy?" He spoke lightly and yet I sensed tension behind his words.

"Right!" I laughed, deciding to take this as a joke. "I've just blown in on Apollo's chariot to do a moon dance in his honor!"

"Exactly!"

Sometimes I can be so obtuse.

Along the way, I learned that Nick had grown up in Athens and in various island holiday homes scattered across Greece. His father had been very well-off but they had disagreed over an important point when Nick was a teenager and hadn't spoken since.

"Seriously?" I exclaimed. "That must have been quite an argument."

"It was," he acknowledged, his expression grim. "When a line is drawn, a man must decide whether to cross it and succumb to that which he vehemently disagrees or to go forward to live his truth. I chose the latter. My father disowned me and I him."

"Wow." Wouldn't I love to know what line was crossed there but I sensed it was deeply painful so decided not to prod. "And your mother?"

"A wonderful woman but now, sadly, passed."

I gave his arm a squeeze. "We are both adult orphans, it seems."

So, it happened that after the tour, Nick invited me to supper and I accepted because that's what I thought official museum visitors did. Not having much experience in the dignitary department, and not being much of a dignitary, anyway, I thought that it would be rude not to accept. That's how I came to be sitting across from Nick sipping wine and devouring the best calamari I had ever tasted in a candlelit restaurant that framed the spotlit Acropolis in near 360 degree views.

"So, Phoebe, I understand that you have amazing proclivities for locating lost or stolen art and artifacts," he said while gazing at me with a smile.

"Me?" I swallowed a bit of calamari followed by a sip of wine. "I don't know where that rumor came from. I've had extraordinary luck, that's all, not to mention expert help, and an ability to put the pieces together. I'm a dot-connector extraordinaire. No mystery there."

Nick's smile widened. "Perhaps you are too modest, Phoebe, and I object to your terminology—dot-connector? Never! That's too prosaic a term for your abilities. I see before me a woman of extraordinary talents, one who can find objects the world believes lost. You possess a rare gift, an ability the ancient Greeks used to revere in their oracles and champion accordingly."

I gulped back my last bit of calamari. What had I waded into? "Seriously?"

"As a seeker of anything lost or hidden, you would indeed be considered a daughter of Artemis."

I stifled a laugh. "How extraordinary—me a child of Artemis. How about a 'Lost Art Sniffer Dog', instead? Brings it more down to earth, don't you think?"

But Nick was honing in on the topic I began to believe had been the ultimate point of the entire evening. "Have you ever heard of the Artemis Key, Phoebe?"

"No," I said wondering how I could escape before the main course arrived.

"Think of it as the ancient Greek's version of the sacred chalice, or the Philosopher's Stone, or even the Ark of the Covenant. Nearly every civilization, religion or belief has some kind of sacred object which its believers are encouraged to seek to achieve enlightenment. The ancients believed that the Oracle of Delphi once possessed the Artemis Key and when faced with invading forces, the last Pythia buried it it in a secret temple of Artemis to keep it safe. It has yet to be found. I believe that you are meant to find it, Phoebe."

Oh, hell. "Only I'm not a believer so am hardly a likely candidate to go after this probably mythical object or the temple it's supposedly buried in." Frankly, I was growing annoyed. "What is the Artemis Key, anyway? Is it an actual key?"

"No one knows but it does exist, I can feel it in my heart and your arrival in Greece can hardly be a coincidence: a woman named Phoebe, named after a Titan, arrives in Athens to return the head of Athens missing for thousands of years. Admit it, it sounds mythic."

Crud. "That doesn't mean that every seemingly synchronous event is significant. Besides, the only thing important to me now is to relax and enjoy the start of my vacation."

"I'm sorry. I've annoyed you. Forgive me. We'll change the topic." He smiled and nodded, one hand inching across the damask tablecloth towards mine. "So, tell me, Phoebe, where are you off to next?"

I snatched my hand away long enough to dip a wedge of bread into the lemon and rosemary infused olive oil, taking such a big bite that I couldn't respond at first.

"I'd be delighted to take you around," he continued. "Tomorrow being Saturday and with the entire weekend at our feet, I could show you the wonders of the ancient world, take you for a drive to Cape Sounion, visit the Aegina, tour the venerable Corinth."

His eyes were luminous in the candlelight as if he was suffused with some kind of inner glow. I was beginning to realize that wine mingled with the setting had slipped our relations far too south of warm. It had been so long since a man had hit on me—well, technically only weeks ago but under much different circumstances—that I had failed to recognize the signs earlier.

I swallowed quickly. "That would be lovely, thank you, but tomorrow I take a flight to Santorini for an overnight stay before catching a high speed ferry for Mykonos where I hop a tall ship to sail around a few islands. I realize that means going backwards since Santorini is after Mykonos but the ship didn't drop anchor at Santorini and I wanted to see that, too."

"Which ship?"

"The Sylvan Seas," I replied without thinking. "It's one of those modern clipper ships which I hope will recharge my old sailing fever. It only has 25 cabins so is very exclusive. It actually spends the first week traveling in a big circle and barely sails more than 30 kilometers a day with a focus on archaeological sites. It's perfect!" I'd booked a cabin with a bed plus a pullout couch in the lounge portion, my splurge of the decade. "This is the start of my vacation and I plan to meet up with my boyfriend along the way."

I didn't technically have a boyfriend but how else was I supposed to frame this—tell him that I hoped the trip would make the man my boyfriend? "I've been longing for a real vacation for so long and what could be better than two weeks sailing the Greek Isles?" I was in full babble mode. "I had planned to rent a sailboat on my own but decided that true relaxation was to let someone else do the work while I just sit on deck and read or knit." Yes, I was that woman backpedaling her way out of a predicament by tossing out superficial banalities—not my finest hour.

"You have a boyfriend," he said, not hiding his disappointment. "I hadn't heard."

"Why would you have?"

He didn't have an answer for that so I filled in the awkward spaces by rambling on about absolutely nothing until desert was delivered and the evening officially wound down.

Later, Nick had recovered admirably and walked me back to my hotel with apparently no hard feelings. "You can't blame a man for trying," he remarked while giving me a hug goodbye. He smelled of some delicious spicy aftershave, something like rosemary mixed with lemon. For a moment, I had the ridiculous notion that he'd dosed himself with marinade.

"Do you believe in fate, Phoebe?" he called as I strode up the path to my hotel.

I turned. "Yes and no," I replied before calling goodnight and dashing for the door.

Twenty minutes later, I was sitting in my hotel room chastising myself for stupidity above and beyond the call of ridiculous. I was so busy reviewing where I had gone wrong that I almost missed Peaches text that popped up on my phone seconds before I engaged the intruder app.

Peaches: *Where is Evan?*

I thumbed in my reply: *In Berlin opening the new room of the Zentrum, why?*

Peaches: *No he isn't. Have you checked lately?*

Me: *I'm not into stalking him, remember? I'll leave the mother hen thing to you. The last time he messaged me, Berlin was his location.*

Peaches: *Check the group map. He appears to have left the planet.*

I quickly opened our agency global GPS positioning app on my super phone and scanned the green dots. Rupert's was centered in Wilshire, Peaches' in Jamaica, mine in Greece, Nicolina and Seraphina's on the Amalfi Coast, and Evan's was....nowhere. Alarm pinged. There's only three ways that Evan's signal would go dark: either he had lost his phone (highly unlikely); he had left the planet (even more unlikely), or he had deliberately taken himself off the tracking grid. Possible.

Me: *Why would he shield his signal?*

Peaches: *Didn't want us to know what he was up to, obviously. I though you were going to invite him along on your vacation for a romantic interlude?*

Me: *I'm waiting until Santorini before extending the invitation. I didn't want to sound too eager.*

Peaches: *And then what? the guy's supposed to just drop everything and come running to your side like a lovesick puppy?*

Me: *Exactly.*

In my defense, he had pledged his undying devotion but when I said that I needed more time, he had responded by remaining out of my orbit for weeks, in fact since we returned from Florence. I assumed my request was the reason for his absence.

Peaches: *When did you last hear from him?*

Me: *Two days ago. He had just arrived in Berlin. When I didn't hear anything further, I figured he'd become busy.* But now that I thought about it, that wasn't like Evan. I added: *Going to text him now. Check with you tomorrow.*

Evan usually respond to my texts within minutes, sometimes seconds. I typed: *Evan, sitting here in Athens thinking of you. Where are you?*

Nearly an hour passed with me staring at a blank screen before I finally dragged myself off to sleep.

❧ 2 ❧

When Evan still hadn't responded by the next morning, I texted Rupert. Since those two seemed inexplicably joined at the hip, I thought he'd have some answers.

Rupert: *Phoebe, the lad doesn't inform me of his whereabouts every second of every day. I understood that he was on Interpol business, the details of which I'd rather not know seeing as I am involved in the tiresome matter of completely gutting my baronial hall and, therefore, not on the job, so to speak. The rain last spring wrecked havoc on the old timbers and the one of the chimneys in the east wing crumbles as I writhe—write. Blast this auto correct! I must get the brickwork shored up before winter descends. Alarming business seeing one's roof disintegrating before one's very eyes.*

Ask Rupert a simple question... I interrupted what I feared might become another windy text by phoning him.

"Good morning, Phoebe. What a surprise," came his droll greeting. "Aren't you on vacation?"

"I am but, Rupert, Evan has taken himself off-grid and is not responding to either phone call, text, or email, which is so unlike him. I can't help but be alarmed."

"Alarmed by what exactly, Phoebe? Is this an emergency?"

His question stopped me short. What was I doing? "I'm worried, that's all."

"Worried about a man trained to be an undercover operative who currently does odd jobs for Interpol? That sounds very peculiar, indeed. Fear not, Phoebe. The lad will reenter our orbit once the time is right. In the meantime, he is obviously at work on a sensitive matter not formally an agency concern and therefore not ours. Now do run along and enjoy your vacation. I will forward a mockup for my proposed agency badge the moment it settles down around here. I still favor the Medusa image. it holds a certain gravitas. Do catch some sun and enjoy the Greek Isles for me in the meantime. I wouldn't be averse to a tan line myself about now."

After he hung up, I stood baffled. Why *was* I so keen on knowing Evan's whereabouts? Looking out over Athens through my hotel window, I reminded myself that being involved with someone romantically did not mean becoming controlling or needy, two things I despised in others and even more so in myself. That man had become my emotional Achilles heel.

I vowed not to check the group map again unless it was absolutely necessary. Obviously, I was doing this trip solo which is all that I deserved considering that I hadn't properly invited the man—another sign of my continued ambiguity. Meanwhile, it was time to practice being on vacation. Obviously, I was no good at it.

The flight from Athens to Santorini took 55 minutes, almost an hour of gazing down at an impossibly blue Aegean sea dreaming of sailing across the waves and putting heists, gangs, guns, and violence far from my personal shoreline. History and art, however, remained very much in my viewfinder.

I had chosen Santorini as my first stop because the pictures of the caldera encircled by the stony volcanic outcrop had always struck me as so extraordinary. I had been disappointed when the Sylvan Seas did not include the port in their itinerary so I decided to spend one night there. The island was the site of one of the largest volcanic eruptions in recorded history, powerful enough to collapse the Minoan civilization about 3,600 years prior and the island still held remnants of the largest Minoan site outside of Crete.

That was my main destination—Akrotiri—after I had booked into my luxury room, that is. The site of the Cycladic Bronze Age settlement had been on my bucket list forever. Forget that view looking down on the caldera's circle of intense blue; forget the glimpses of the sapphire-hued domed churches amid the whitewashed buildings; forget the infinity pool, too. No matter how stunning the backdrop or the amenities, I could never stray from history or art for long.

The fact that the site may also have been the location of Plato's Atlantis was a bonus. I booked into my room and changed into capri pants, a loose t-shirt, and stopped by the gift shop to purchase a straw hat and grab a tube of sunblock. Looking totally unlike my usual self, I set off for the day.

Minutes later, I was strolling the white cobbled streets that climbed the side of the caldera cliffs heading towards the bus stop. The sunshine smiled overhead, the streets brimmed with day visitors from the cruise ships and I could see why Greece just might be the land of the goddesses.

Somewhere after the second pause to take in the view and the next stop at a little boutique to purchase a bracelet I didn't need and would probably never wear again, I hit the vacation zone. All my worries dried up in the late October warmth. Two hours of roaming the archaeological site at Akrotiri, studying the frescos, some with evidence of weaving, and gazing at the almost lyrical design elements of the Minoan civilization, the modern world slipped away entirely.

The massive excavation site, which consisted of streets and partial houses under a roofed enclosure was totally absorbing. I ate lunch in a kind of relaxed haze and caught the bus back to the town in the same state of mind. Sleep came quickly that night after a quick supper in a little restaurant a few doors down from the hotel.

Even my internal stalker alert had relaxed, which explained why it wasn't until I was on the ferry to Mykonos the next day that I confirmed that I was being followed. I didn't expect stalkers while on vacation, not that I ever went on vacation. In London I was used to it, in Italy, too, but not on this holiday island populated by leisure travelers with fanny packs. Still, I had trained myself to notice things even on an unconscious level.

On Santorini, I thought I might be imagining things. In a busy port town where tourists climbed up and around well-trod paths on a regular basis, it wasn't uncommon to bump into the same person over and over again, especially on narrow paths.

That guy with the shorts, sunglasses, T-shirt, and the cross-body man bag who always seemed to be taking phone pics nearby was a case in point. He cut such an ordinary figure that he instantly blended into the background while hanging out with a clutch of cruisers and sporting the same lanyard as the rest. That he appeared in Akrotiri wasn't such a shock, either, since the site was on the day trip route for the cruise ships but his lack of distinguishing features raised a flag. Most people want to be individuals as well as part of a pack. This one seemed to want to disappear. There were probably other indicators communicating to me below the surface, too. Call it instinct.

When I spotted him on the ferry to Mykonos the next day, I took his presence seriously. The guy had changed his broad sunhat for a straw fedora and now wore a windbreaker and yet I recognized the shape of his body, the way he stood partially hunched over while always looking off into the distance. He was stalking me. I pretended not to notice while plotting a trap. By this time, I wasn't concerned so much as annoyed, very annoyed.

My time on Mykonos may be brief but I was too irked to let that stop me. After I dropped off my luggage and registered at the Sylvan Seas office, I took off for an hour of exploration through the town. Boarding the clipper didn't begin for another hour so I had time to spare.

Mykonos hugged the harbor with vacation properties and restaurants set against a dry, rocky backdrop. Under ordinary circumstances I might be wooed by the many old blue-dome churches or the famous windmills seen in the distance but the town's reported party atmosphere was not my scene. Apparently it rocked after hours so I vowed not to spend a single night there and had planned my itinerary accordingly. I knew that the famed archaeological site of Delos lay not more than a 20 minute boat ride away but that was on the Sylvan itinerary so I was good to wait for that. Instead, I'd make a quick pass through the town, trap a stalker, and board my ship in that order.

Mykonos made it easy. Though the town still swelled with daytrippers and visitors even this late in the season, parts of the brilliantly white-washed streets overhung with punchy magenta bougainvillea offered pockets of brief solitude. All I had to do was turn a corner and in minutes I'd be alone, which offered the perfect opportunity to enact my plan.

While I stood angling my phone pretending to get a selfie shot, the stalker appeared behind me right on cue looking as though he was admiring the little step-roofed church at the end of the lane. I set my phone's stun app on mild, turned as if taking a selfie shot, and zapped him between the shoulder blades. He stumbled against a building and slid to sitting, back against the wall, bony legs splayed.

In seconds, I was kneeling before him. "Who the hell are you and why are you following me?" I demanded. "Tell me or I'll zap you again, only this time with a charge strong enough to pop out your eyeballs." I loved sounding tough.

He mumbled, fixing me with a slack-mouthed stare as his fedora rolled to the pavers. Early forties, darkly-tanned complexion, regular features, thin straight hair combed over a balding head. While he gaped, I pulled his wallet from his pocked and checked his identification: George G. Baros with an address in Athens. I stuffed his wallet back into his pocket and slapped his face. "Who are you working for, bozo? Tell me."

But the man couldn't yet speak...yet. Damn it. I had to tell Evan to work up a lighter charge on the sliding stun spectrum. I'd used a mild zap and it still was too debilitating.

At that moment a family of five entered the lane—parents and three kids. "Is everything all right?" the man said with a British accent, striding towards us in a take-charge attitude. I knew the type: they loved nothing better than to take control of any situation. The world kept ticking along thanks to these guys.

"No," I exclaimed, acting flustered. "I think this man had a heart attack. I was just walking along and he collapsed."

"Is he your husband?" the man asked while checking the guy's pulse. Mrs. Samaritan gave me a reassuring squeeze on the shoulder.

"Never seen him before. He was just standing there taking pictures and then fell over! Think he's okay? Could you wait with him while I get help?"

"Of course," Mr. Samaritan assured me while offering George a sip of water from an extra bottle in his knapsack.

And so I left my dazed stalker in their care and retreated down the lane to enter the nearest taverna. "Quick! Call an ambulance. A man collapsed up the street. It could be a heart attack!"

That prompted a flurry of activity—a phone call, a man running out with me while I pointed him in the right direction and in the midst of all the commotion, I disappeared into the crowd. Soon I was on my way to the harbor to board a skiff to the clipper Sylvan Seas which cut a stunning picture moored in the harbor.

With pleasure I watched as my tender approached the magnificent tall ship which held steady with its five stately masts, imagining it in full sail with those white wings swelling with sea breezes. Not only luxurious, it promised the ideal way to cruise the Greek isles as the itinerary included many archaeological sites, talks by an expert, an optional diving trip, and plenty of romantic possibilities with (still hopefully) the companion of my choice. For me, this was the ultimate luxury. If one must go a vacation, it may as well be in style.

The captain was there to greet me, standing by a little registration desk where a woman took my passport, proof of Covid vaccinations, and handed me brochures, maps, itineraries and menus. Captain Giannis Adamos was a sturdily-built, deeply suntanned man with neatly-trimmed graying hair who I estimated to be in his mid sixties. He insisted that being in charge of the Sylvan Seas was a dream come true for one who had once captained the big cruise ships.

"I know these islands like the back of my hand," he insisted and I believed him. He chatted with me all the way to my cabin telling me that a crew of 30 manned the clipper with an additional 80 staff assigned to various guest services. I did the math: that meant nearly 6 crew per passenger.

The map and schematic of the Sylvan Seas outlined a massive five masted ship sectioned into the top deck designed for promenading, lounging, and dining with a partially glassed-in dining area on the main deck. The level below featured guest services which included the largest dining area, another lounge, massage rooms, a games room, and a library, among other features. Guest staterooms and cabins were spread at the back half of the ship on all three upper decks with the launch deck on the fourth level along with the crew quarters below that.

At the door of my stateroom, Captan Adamos introduced me to my room valet, Artino Andino, who I was to call by his first name. Artino was to be my personal butler, I was told, and had already provided a steamed towel for me to refresh myself with as well as an iced lime cocktail. All I had do was call, Artino assured me, and he'd be there tending to my every comfort. I started with a pot of tea, plenty of bottles of cold water, and another one of those cocktails. So far, I believed this would be the ultimate escape with or without male company.

An hour later, I was nestled in my deluxe suite with its balcony facing away from the island, enjoying a cup of tea while knitting the first row of what I'd decided to name my Salty Rose wrap. Azure blue, white and touches of coral pink would be my colors for this one and luckily I'd packed just those yarns with the intention of making a gift for somebody, recipient as yet undecided.

Between periodic sips of tea, I savored the cocktail, hoping to dilute the alcohol with medicinal oolong, or at least that was the theory. Meanwhile, I couldn't help but feel self-congratulatory for disabling this George Baros character even though that brought me no closer to understanding why he was ghosting me in the first place. At least he couldn't follow me onboard this exclusive yachting experience that would become my home for 12 days.

After scanning the cabin for surveillance devices and finding none, I felt as though I had battened down the proverbial hatches and all I need do from here on in was to enjoy myself.

With my feet propped on my balcony railing, I was finally relaxed, gazing out at the boats and cruisers plying the waves in Mykonos harbor. By supper time at 7:30, the ship would be sailing into what could only be imagined as a glorious sunset every bit as magnificent as those the ancient mariners had experienced centuries before. I'd even brought a copy of Homer's *Ulysses* in case I needed a setting enhancer. One way or another, I was feeling amazingly content. So this was a vacation? Why hadn't I tried one sooner?

My phone buzzed on the cabin table behind me where it lay charging. Should I answer it or should I not? I considered ignoring it but conditioning ruled. I put aside my knitting and stepped back into the cabin to stare at the screen.

Evan: *Hello, Phoebe. Who did you stun in Mykonos at 4:46 this afternoon?*

For a moment I was thrilled to hear from him. That lasted seconds. Picking up the phone, I thumbed in a response. *Where have you been? I've been trying to contact you.*

Evan: *I've been offline for awhile. Why are you in Greece by yourself?*

The question was irksome. Me: *I'm on vacation. I did mention that I'd planned to take a couple of weeks off.*

Evan: *I remember, but alone?*

Me: *Alone unless you have a better idea...*

Evan: *Why isn't Peaches with you?*

That wasn't the better idea I'd been considering. Me: *Why don't you join me?*

A long pause...I counted the seconds. Fifteen, in case you're wondering.

Evan: *As much as I love to, I'll be tied up for awhile longer.*

Me: *Tied up with what?* Or whom, I thought.

Evan: *Meanwhile, you shouldn't be anywhere by yourself, Phoebe. I thought we'd made that point clear. Especially now. You need a bodyguard. Call Peaches immediately or I'll do it for you.*

Try telling me that you can't pick up on tone in a text. So I picked up on a tone that set my teeth on edge.

Me: *Peaches is visiting her family in Jamaica, as you know since you can see all of us on the grid. How did you manage to go offline while the rest of us can't? And at no time do I recall anyone saying that I require a bodyguard 24/7. Why now? And don't give me orders.*

Actually, I knew I needed a bodyguard. It's just that I expected it to be him. Yes, poor planning.

Evan: *You need protection 24/7 because of who you are and what you can do. You're famous, Phoebe, and if you used the stun app you already have proof.*

That didn't lessen my irritation. I had expected him to join me, in which case I wouldn't be alone, would I? As it was, I'd just have to take care of myself.

Me: *Signing off now. I have a sunset welcome dinner to enjoy. Too bad you can't join me.*

Evan: *I'll call you as soon as I am able.*

Me: *I'm putting on Do Not Disturb.*

I turned on the feature and headed for the shower, steamed before I even hit the water. Why was he being evasive? Why had I even let myself care? Wasn't this exactly the kind of emotional entanglement I'd been trying to avoid? Yes, I was overreacting but that's what happens too easily between men and women when emotion is involved. It's why I had sworn off male/female entanglements for so long.

An hour later, fluffed, refreshed, and wearing a silk skirt and a full poet style blouse with my new leather and copper bracelet, I swept into the long dining room feeling a bit like I was onboard a floating Orient Express— only without the handsome suitor awaiting my arrival.

The decor had that turn-of-the-century grandeur while hinting at a thousand years of sailing history. Deep blue carpets, brass brightwork gleaming, round tables draped in snowy linen on either side of a grand wrought iron stairway, reproduction frescos adorning every wall. Several mariner antiques had been mounted here and there including a massive brass steering wheel that must have come off an original clipper. The decor was extraordinary and a nod to the sailing past while also capturing every modern amenity. True luxury surrounded me and now I needed to work extra hard to feel joy in any of it.

Because I was sailing solo and realized that was probably going to be a permanent state for this vacation. Blame the imaginary streaming movie I'd been replaying in my head but that's not how I had envisioned this trip. My exchange with Evan had sucked the wind from my sails.

I had booked all of my dinner reservations in advance, each of them changeable with 24 hours notice. The private nook tucked behind a potted palm positioned by porthole windows was unnecessary now that I was alone. The romantic ambience was painfully inappropriate. Next time, maybe I'd join in a couple of group dining experiences in order to meet new friends or grab a buffet on the top deck to take in sunset dining at its best. In other words, only two days into my vacation and already I was lonely. It would be just me, Homer, and my knitting, after all.

Of course, I didn't blame Evan for making other plans, considering that I had failed to inform him of mine. I was more annoyed by his secrecy, not that that made any more sense. In fact my roiling feelings made no sense, period, which just made me angrier.

Looking around, I noted that 10 of the approximately 20 tables had diners, including couples and groups of 4 or 6. There was much clinking of glasses, laughter, and conversations in progress. One older couple held hands across their cozy little table. A young couple appeared to be either on their honeymoon or deep in the flush of new romance, leaving me feeling lonelier by the minute. Apparently there were 23 passengers listed and I'd never felt more alone in my life.

The maitre'd sat me at my table for two and passed me the wine list saying that my server would be along shortly. I stared across at the sparkling silver and glassware towards the empty chair across from mine. I had neglected to say that no one would be joining me. Now I was doubly irked, unreasonably for sure, but that didn't change my mood.

Still, if I thought I was annoyed before, it paled in comparison to the moment when Nick Christpodoulopoulo slid into the empty chair across from mine and beamed across the table at me.

❧ 3 ❧

"**Y**ou followed me?" I half rose from my seat.

"Phoebe, let me explain," he began.

"Make it quick."

He was wearing a crisp white tux with a natty little bowtie, hair neatly combed back, every inch of him groomed to the last speck. "I'm convinced that you arrived in Greece for a greater purpose other than to simply enjoy your vacation, I mean. All the signs are there. Please hear me out."

I slid back down into my chair, my whole body rigid. The server came by. "Nick, nice to see you again. May I offer you and the lady something to drink?"

Nick caught my eye but I made no response. "Bring us a bottle of your best Naoussa Xinomavro, Damon, and put it on my tab—room 19." He grinned. "Two doors up from stowage."

Damon beamed and took off.

"And they even know you by name here?"

Nick held up one hand. "Let me explain: so when you said that you had booked on the Sylvan Seas, I checked a few details. I've worked the circuit on these cruises as a guest lecturer before so I know the contacts. It turns out that the guy slotted for the Greek history lecture and ground guide series came down with laryngitis." He caught my expression. "Hey, not my doing—another coincidence, honestly, though not for a minute do I believe in coincidences. There are many connective forces in our coming together, Phoebe, none of them circumstantial. This is but one."

"So the guy came down with a mysterious throat problem...."

"And the fleet's event planner contacted me after I left a message and, lo and behold, they were scrambling to find a replacement so here I am. For a nightly lecture coupled with playing the tour guide on a couple of the archaeological tour sites plus odd jobs here and there, I get free room and board in a cabin the size of a shoebox."

"A miracle,' I said dryly. "What about your job at the museum?"

"Ah, well," he dropped his gaze. "Forgive me but that was pure subterfuge. My name is not Nickolas Christpodoulopoulo but Nickolas Pallas but I happen to be friends with Nick Christpodoulopoulo which is how I came to hear about your arrival. I've been reading about your exploits with great interest, saw your podcast interview, and desperately wanted to meet you. I begged my friend, the other Nick, to let me greet you, and since he was trying to juggle too many balls the other day, he gave in. It's a new job, he's still scrambling, plus I can be very persuasive." He grinned.

I didn't know whether to be offended or outraged and settled on a bit of both. "Are you even a historian? 'Hateful to me as the gates of Hades is that man who hides one thing in his heart and speaks another.'"

He looked as though he wanted to lunge across the table and hug me. "From the Illiad? Phoebe you are extraordinary!"

"Are you even a historian?" I glowered at him.

"I certainly am a historian, educated at the University of Athens and graduated with my PHD in 2016 but I work freelance. I've written several books on investigative history as it relates to the exploration of alternative hypotheses for ancient civilizations, specifically Grecian. Surely you've heard of my *Unlocking Ancient Voices with Your Mind?*"

Before I could respond, Damon arrived with the wine and performed the little sommelier ritual of waiting for Nick to approve the first sip. After our glasses were filled and he had retreated, I leaned over and said. "*Unlocking Ancient Voices with your Mind* is not unlocking any recognition with me."

"Ah, well, it's not a bestseller or anything but it's doing quite well, especially when I nab a few promotional gigs."

"Meanwhile, you've lied your way into my holiday and are trying to convince me it was all 'fate'?" I added air quotes for good measure. "Don't get me wrong, I believe in fate, just not nefarious finagling kind."

"It is fate, Phoebe, which doesn't negate human intervention when warranted. Try the wine. It's a bright crisp white that pairs beautifully with our local seafood."

"Will you just get on with your excuses?"

"They are not excuses, Phoebe. You of all people should recognize the signs: a woman named after a Titan moon deity, which is also an epithet for the goddess Artemis, arrives in Greece bearing the head of Athena saying that a friend urged her to find a lost temple. That same Phoebe has gained a reputation for finding lost or stolen art using unexplained powers. If that's not a sign from the Universe, I don't know what is. It's practically mythic."

I took a sip of wine, actually more like a gulp, and leaned forward on the table trying to collect my thoughts.

"I sense you're a believer, too," he added.

"A believer in what?" I was just buying time.

"A believer in elements beyond traditional science's fixation on solely empirical-based knowledge. The ancient Greeks married both the soul with a quest for the truth, the heart with the intellect. Science uses the intellect as the road to discovery but there's always a leap of consciousness along the way, one that doesn't fit neatly into the constraints of conventional proof and, therefore, something which science prefers to explain away."

"Intuition," I said.

"Exactly." He smiled. "Intuition is the great leap that everyone experiences yet rarely trusts. Why is that, I ask? Why have we become such slaves to empirical knowledge and measurable fact at the expense of our inner compass?"

Wearying of playing the devil's advocate, I sat back. "Yes, why have we? Why don't we accept what we know unless someone else confirms its existence with a string of measurable facts? History is always difficult to verify at the best of times since past recorders and narrators often had politically-motivated points of view or, at the very least, saw things through their own social construct." Hell, I sounded like I was on his side.

"Precisely so. And yet intuition is the great unclaimed fount of knowing. Artemis the huntress was also the goddess of finding lost objects and missing truths. The Artemis Key is said to have instilled the goddess's powers to seek what is missing, hidden, or lost as well as to foretell the future. She was the ultimate hunter, the finder of everything lost or missing as well as the nocturnal huntress of wild animals."

"And she was also a myth."

"Was she?" he asked with a wry smile. "Do not all of the great religions say the same thing about another's gods?"

"You're not seriously saying that Artemis, Zeus, Poseidon—all the Greek gods—were real?"

"Not exactly."

I took another sip of wine. "Well, that's a relief."

"But it depends on how we define reality. Look, let us change directions for a moment: consider the fact that your involvement has led to the retrieval of countless pieces of art and artifacts all over the globe."

"Yes, so? I used professional help and a base of research. Science definitely played a part along with a trail of bread crumbs we might consider clues."

"And?"

I sighed. "Okay, and intuition."

He nodded, still smiling. "Science aids insight without usurping it. Don't tell me that you aren't a believer in insight, Phoebe. I heard that interview you gave regarding a certain Tuscan chapel fresco where you expounded on a theory you had gained from reading the signs found in a Boticelli portrait, a few letters, and the fresco itself. You began by stating that you could prove very little of your story concerning the painter Filippino Lippi and a seamstress—"

"Designer."

"Sorry, *designer* named Gabriella, but that you *knew* your story to be true. You went on to say that you refuse to defend your story. Let others prove or disprove it as they will, you said, but that to you the story was completely authentic despite its missing parts."

I closed my eyes. I should never have given that interview but I needed to formalize my position. Tired of being refuted by esteemed historians picking apart my every statement, I resolved not to defend my insights to anyone ever again. Instead, I'd just tell the stories as I felt them and let my listeners decide for themselves.

"The menus, my friends," Damon, interrupted, seemingly oblivious to the atmosphere. Handing us letter-sized cards printed on fine parchment with a compass rose at the top, he asked how we were enjoying the wine before slipping away.

"What do you want from me, Nick?" I asked, as if I didn't know the answer.

"Participate in my research, Phoebe. All I request is that I have the opportunity to study your intuition when faced with the remnants of the ancient Greek civilization we will visit on this voyage. Let us see whether we can locate the Artemis Key using your gifts. Be my oracle, Phoebe. I promise not to ruin your vacation. In fact, I vow to enhance it. I just want to ask how you experience these ancient sites we visit, observe what happens to your mind and being. I'd like to, if at all possible and you agree, use some of this research for my next book. All you need do is to be at my side as we sail around the islands visiting archaeological digs and tell me what your feeling. That's it."

"Look, I'm not like some fleshy divining rod that vibrates when around hidden treasure. My gift doesn't work that way."

"How does it work, then? I'd like to understand. By the way, I recommend the seafood platter."

"Fine but no octopi. I've developed a deep appreciation of the creatures following a documentary I watched not long ago. Anyway, my insights don't come to me in a sudden eureka! effect, or at least not at first. In the beginning, I gather clues, immerse myself as much as possible in the history and culture of the period, maybe touch something that belonged to a person connected to the lost item."

"All signs of divination but we won't linger on that point for the moment. All I ask is that you keep your mind open and let's see what happens. Will you do it?"

What did I have to lose? It wasn't like his hypothesis wasn't of interest to me. I'd always accepted my insights as just the way I worked but maybe the time had come to investigate my gifts further. Why not now when my vision of a romantic vacation had become toast on the proverbial back burner? "Fine, but I'm not happy with how you snagged me, just for the record."

He placed one hand over his heart. "I'll make it up to you. I swear."

"Okay, I'll do it. And what are we looking for exactly?"

"Probably the lost temple of Artemis."

"Probably?"

He leaned towards me. "It could be either the Artemis Key or the lost temple. The two are interconnected."

All I had to do is look at this idea from another angle and come up with another response. "This is crazy."

"Think with your whole being instead of just your intellect, Phoebe. When you asked me about the temple back on the Acropolis, I knew you were the one. You came here with that in your mind's eye, whether you were conscious of it or not."

"Zann."

"Pardon?"

"Zann, the archaeologist I was telling you about, is to blame for planting Artemis in my head."

"She was merely playing a role in the greater design. Cheers!" He raised a glass across the table and we clinked our glasses. "Here's to new partnerships!"

It really was very good wine and I did enjoy his company, if not his methods. "Cheers! Oh, look, we're moving." I gazed through the porthole window at the brilliant sunset where I could see the edge of cliffs moving past. The ship rumbled as the engines engaged which would probably continue until the wind caught its sails. For a moment I felt that thrill of expectation and imagined all my stalker minions left far behind on shore. Free at last.

A salad of the Greek variety landed before me which I dug into with gusto, savoring the black olives, the feta cheese, the fresh oregano. It paired nicely with the wine which I was thoroughly enjoying, too. I briefly forgot about stalkers and by the time I remembered, our main meals had arrived.

An aromatic blend of everything fresh from the sea swimming in a light tomato-infused broth with a sprinkling of herbs, it looked delicious but I realized in an instant that I was already full. Besides, a few creatures appeared as though they were still wiggling which made me slightly queasy. I sipped more wine.

What had we been thinking about? Oh, yes, stalkers. I stabbed a shrimp, the only thing I immediately recognized, and smiled. "Nick, I must warn you that hanging around with me can be hazardous to your health. Already somebody's following me. I zapped him on Mykonos, a one George Barros from Athens. Do you know him?"

"No, why would I? Why is he following you and what do you mean by 'zapped'?" The dark eyes widened in the candlelight.

I struggled to muster my wine-soddened brain. "As to the first question, just a stab in the dark in case you mentioned my arrival to someone. You're the only one outside my circle who knows my itinerary. As to the second question, that's what I need to find out—who and why. I mean, it happens all the time but I didn't expect it here."

He gazed at me. "You're always being followed?"

"Various people stalk me on a constant basis, yes, but I have no idea who this guy is and why he's on my heels. As I said, my destination was deliberately kept a secret with no one outside the agency and its immediate affiliates knowing where I went. Believe me, that network is private. I even booked under an assumed name. I'll be Phoebe Baker, by the way. Anyways, that should in theory remove all the usual suspects. As for question number 3, it can wait." But the wine couldn't. More followed.

As I dabbed the rich broth with a piece of bread, I realized Nick had fallen silent. I looked across the table after a few seconds to find him gazing at me with his mouth half open. I laid down my fork. "Who did you tell?"

"In my defense, I didn't realize your arrival was a secret."

"Who. Did. You. Tell?"

"There's a network of fellow alternate ancient civilization theorists who I chat with online regularly. We are always sharing ideas, finds, keeping each other apprised of our investigations, that sort of thing. It's a closed group but not exactly private. Nothing on social media is private."

I swore and took another sip. Okay, so I was on vacation, wine's permitted, even encouraged. "Listen up, Nick, from here on you tell no one, understand? Put the lid on your social media discourses. Shut the door and slam the book on your alternate ancient civilization theorists." That was a mouthful after wine, believe me.

"I hear you."

But I wasn't finished. "This is a dangerous business I'm in. Hundreds of criminals, syndicates, and just plain greedy bastards are out there looking for something ancient and lucrative at all times. I'm now a prime target, the goose that lays the golden egg or at the very least—no, wait. I think I jumbled up that analogy. Oh, hell, I mean I'm the one that leads the bastards to treasure. Look at you. Not calling you a bastard exactly but you've cornered me for a variation of the same reason, get it?" I was waving my fork around for emphasis.

"I do and I'm so sorry. I just had no idea but it makes complete sense, of course I should have been more cautious. I'm such an idiot."

"Agreed but try to assess the risks from here on in. Realize that this is a dangerous world you've maneuvered yourself into. Now we must assume that somebody, or somebody who knows somebody, in this ancient civilization alternate history theorists network of yours—" I took a deep breath, "Can't you make up an acronym?—is on my tail." I took another sip "and may kill to get what they think we're seeking." I paused, trying to decide if that even made sense. Probably not. I shot him a quick look. "Did you tell your alternate history theorists what you thought I was seeking—were seeking, that you thought I'd be seeking?" Yes, I was getting drunk.

He swallowed. "Unintentionally. And they know your itinerary since this ship's route is on their website."

"Damn, I forgot about that. Still, if George Baros is any example, the efforts are pretty amateur so far but the word may get out to a more dangerous group of treasure hunters. Could a lost temple of Artemis or this Artemis Key be valuable other than for historical purposes?"

"Definitely yes," he said. "If an untouched temple were ever located, well it defies description since nothing like that has ever been found—tombs, yes, plenty of tombs—but not an intact temple. These were as far as we know, above ground structures, remember, and centuries of invasions, religious fanatics from one doctrine or another not to mention time itself, has raised them to rubble."

"But the value part?" I prompted.

"Most ancient Greek temples reportedly had a gold statue of the god or goddess—the cella—at its center plus a treasury of gifts to the deity. If such a place were ever to survive intact and be discovered, it would have immense monetary value, yes, but historically speaking, it would be totally priceless. It could rival King Tutankhamen's tomb, the find of the century. As for the Artemis Key, that would be like finding the Holy Grail in our time."

I sat back, my appetite plummeting, the room swaying. "This is bad, very bad." I stared at my plate which now struck me as a lumpy platter of blood-drenched bait. I gnawed at my bread. "I'll need my bodyguard for sure."

Nick, who appeared to have broken into a sweat, croaked. "Bodyguard?"

"That's okay," I waved my hand to reassure him and gulped water. Best to dilute the alcohol. "She'll be on her way by now. The agency's network reacts pretty quickly. Actually, the man I thought would be my bodyguard on this trip is actually the same man I'd hoped to stage a romantic rendezvous with. That didn't work out—poor planning on my part. Actually, no planning. Lesson learned. Still, I'm not without a few skills of my own." I hoped I was still making sense. "Now I'll have Peaches?"

"Peaches? Do you want dessert?"

"Peaches, as in my bodyguard. Her real name is Penelope. And not as in Ulysses' Penelope so don't go there. She's a trained engineer with plenty of defensive maneuvers plus a few other skills."

Before Nick could comment, Damon arrived to refill our glasses. "Enjoying your meals?"

"Actually", I said, gazing down at my plate. "I don't think I can eat this. It's delicious but just too much food. So sorry. I hate to think that all these sea creatures may have died in vain but would you mind taking the plate away?"

"I'll take it." Nick said quickly, extending his hand. At that moment I realized that his dinner had stopped at the salad.

"Sure," I said, stunned. "I barely touched it."

Once Damon disappeared and Nick was digging into my seafood plate, I leaned forward. "Did the bottle of wine drain your onboard resources?"

He smiled sheepishly. "Completely. My dining credits don't cover alcohol and only two courses per meal, otherwise. Phoebe, about this bodyguard—"

"On the way, I'm guessing, but in the meantime, you need to become extra vigilant. If these alternate ancient theorists of yours include rabid treasure hunters, you've just landed us both in the crosshairs of some very dangerous stuff. Welcome to the club." I toasted him and grinned.

The rest of the evening passed in a blur. There was definitely too much wine involved, especially after I ordered a second bottle, plus dessert followed by an above deck stroll. I was hanging onto Nick's arm by then only because I was afraid my sea legs would fail to engage post vino. Besides, I liked the guy as a friend and overall was very relaxed in his company, despite recent disclosures.

"And so you'll be taking this sailing excursion without your intended boyfriend," he said as we continued our promenade passed other passengers.

"Even a fool learns something once it hits him," I mused.

"More Homer. I'm amazed by your repertoire," he said with a grin.

"If it gets too tiresome, just shake me. I've been immersing myself in all things ancient Greek in preparation for this trip. It's amazing how at these quotes are so apt the human condition in general."

"Isn't that just so? My ancestors have greatly influenced our existence."

"So, give me an example of an alternative ancient civilizations theory," I asked.

"Atlantis," he said with a smile. "We believe it really did exist, maybe not exactly as described in the myths but still a powerful and advanced maritime civilization."

"Related to the Minoans?"

"That's one theory."

I was gazing off the starboard side towards the blur of hills silhouetted against the horizon. "Oh, look at that blue." I was easily distracted by then.

"That's Naxos, part of the Cyclades islands which we are sailing through at the moment. We're heading to Paros first which is nearby but we will return. In fact, we'll make a big circle. We passed Delos which is only a 30 minute boat ride from Mykonos but the ship will be dropping anchor near there for two days eventually. There are 50 islands all together in this grouping but the Cyclades were one of the three main branches of Aegean civilization."

He said much more about Aegean civilizations, none of which I remembered. Admittedly, my brain was skimming over the historical details just then. "Wow. It's so gorgeous with the shade of smoky purply blue. I'd love to knit that."

"Pardon?"

"Never mind. Tell me more abut the Cyclades. No, wait—forget it. My powers of retention have taken a nosedive. I want to learn more, though. Most of my studies have been focused on Renaissance European art history lately. I need to refresh my ancient art databanks, though I did a little preparatory research before I came."

"I'd be happy to enlighten you further but it can wait for another day. So there really is a boyfriend?" he asked as we leaned against the railing, allowing the breeze to play with our hair. To be back on the ocean again after so long a time nearly brought me to tears. Probably the wine again.

"There really is," I said, glancing in his direction, "but we've yet to make it official. I'm recovering from a bad relationship—actually no relationship with steamy interludes—and have been hesitant to recommit but I'm getting there. What about you?" Really, I usually don't disclose so much personal information but with the alcoholic assistance...

"I continue to await the goddess of my dreams. In truth, I thought it might be you, Phoebe." He was leaning against the balcony gazing at me intently.

"Sorry." I turned away to stare down into the mesmerizing surge of dark water, my stomach rolling along with the waves. "Think I'd better get to bed—alone," I added just in case.

He walked me down to the end of the second level deck corridor where my stateroom was located, one of two occupying the end of that deck. Courteous and gallant every step of the way, he bowed at the teak door of my quarters. "A goddess deserves one of the best cabins on the ship and I see she has just such accommodations."

I grinned. "My big extravagance, half of it paid for my my godfather as a birthday gift. The birthday was many months ago, by the way, and don't ask my age but I'm guessing I'm still older than you by a few years."

"A woman's age is irrelevant, her spirit being all that matters." He looked very dapper in that tux. Before leaving me at the door, he asked: "May I join you for breakfast tomorrow?"

"Sure."

"Great. Let's do the buffet on the upper deck. The first port tomorrow will be Paros. Pretty little island with plenty of beaches. It's more of a recreational destination than an archaeological one but history is everywhere on these islands."

"Perfect," I said just before entering my cabin, I spewed another Homeric quote: "*Sleep, delicious and profound...*"

"*...the very counterfeit of death,*" he finished off for me. I hadn't planned to voice that part..

Moments later, facing my luxurious quarters with the turned-down bed, the chocolate on the pillow, the bouquet in the bracketed bowl on the side table, the little brass captain's lamp, I sighed. Twelve days of luxury, relaxation, respite from worry and fear had just became even more interesting. I preferred to focus on the *delicious and profound* part.

Pulling my phone from my pocket, I skimmed the multitude of messages: Max asking how I was enjoying myself, Evan inquiring as to when was the best time to call, and Peaches telling me that she'd booked her flight for Greece the next day. All of them could wait until morning. I didn't trust myself to speak or type another coherent word that night, anyway. Too much effort.

Despite the cognitive stumbling, I still engaged my intruder app, preformed my nightly ablutions, latched the balcony door, and plunged into the smooth sheets, dropping off that velvet cliff of sleep almost at once.

Sleeping at sea is like blending a lullaby with several streaming videos spliced together by a drunken editor. The rocking seems to shake up the brain cells while the wine drowns them. I was riding a dolphin in downtown London waving at the red buses as I went. Then I was hosting a party with the goddess Artemis as my special guest while Peaches offered her wardrobe advice, as in one goddess to another. Artemis preferred something long and diaphanous to Peaches' stretchy leggings and we didn't have anything else on hand when suddenly a Minotaur began banging on the door. Banging hard. He wanted to come to the party.

I sat up and blinked. "Go away!" I called. Wait, where was I and why was the room rocking? I checked my phone on the night table but no red intruder alert was flashing. Only I was sure that banging was real. Probably a drunken passenger at the wrong door. And I was thirsty.

It was 3:15 A.M. Then I remembered the ship, the vacation...

Grabbing my phone, I used it as a nightlight to locate the mini fridge with it's selection of cold water. After a long drink, I was heading for the bathroom when my light flashed against something on the floor. Backing up, I beamed the phone full on it and a chill hit my spine.

A tarot card lay face up on the carpet, the High Priestess gazing out at me as if from another dimension.

4

"This was shoved under my door in the middle of the night." I sat across from Nick at breakfast while the other diners occupied tables along the open deck around us. To my right, the little island of Paros beckoned in the sunlight and the delicious-looking array of breakfast offerings lay on a long table nearby.

"The High Priestess?" He studied the card on the table between us, turning it over, a mix of emotions fleeting across his face.

"From the Rider Waite deck. As you know the artist Pamela Coleman Smith was commissioned by Arthur Edward Waite in 1909 to create the 78 card deck based on symbols and esoteric knowledge gleaned from the involvement with the Order of The Golden Dawn."

"Yes, I know and have studied the symbolism since I believe it may have roots in the Ancient Egyptian and Greek civilizations but this couldn't have been shoved under your door, Phoebe. The ship has sealed doors as a safety precaution in case of capsizing. Someone would have had to have placed this card in your room another way." He looked up, his excitement mounting. "It's another sign, Phoebe. Don't you see? Mystery, secrets, the future unrevealed—"

I leaned forward. "I see it as a sign that someone aboard this ship knows my identity and that I'm seeking something lost, though how they could know that when I didn't myself until last night is beyond me. It also in indicates that someone had access to my room last night but how could that be? I had my security app engaged." But what if someone opened the door just wide enough to slip in a card? My phone wouldn't likely pick that up.

"Security app?"

"Hard to explain. Let's just say that our agency has some handy gizmos." I sat back and scanned my fellow holidayers with the usual mix of international and local travelers. "I think it's also a warning, probably from one of your alternate ancient civilization theorist connections."

"But how can that be?" he protested. "Phoebe, that network is spread all over the globe. How could anyone get to Greece and aboard this ship so quickly?"

"You did." I pointed out.

He stared. "Yes, but I live here and have connections."

"I'm guessing so does he or she," I said. "And whoever this person is, they obviously have resources, too, not to mention access to this ship. The door is activated by a keycard so who else has that kind of clearance?"

"Just the steward and housekeeping services who have been carefully vetted."

"There are always ways, Nick. Look, the ship isn't even fully booked. I asked one of the staff when I came aboard. We have only 21 passengers on a ship with the capacity for 25. Somebody could have easily bought a last minute cabin or maybe wiggled into the crew the way you did."

He shot a furtive look over his shoulder.

I gazed around. "We need to be on our guard, check out everyone. You're part of the staff so you can check the crew signups while I work on discovering more about the passengers. See if you can nab a passenger list and identify last minute bookers." My bossy side was kicking in. Hangovers can have that effect.

He nodded, looking grim. "Definitely. They gave me a passenger manifest so I can learn everybody's names but I'll get their cabin numbers and shore trip bookings for you, too. I'll ask that man in the white jacket over there."

I looked in the direction he indicated to see an older man decked out in a crisp white short sleeved uniform with shoulder epaulets helping himself to coffee.

"That's the head steward, Leo Vitalis. He's in charge of everything related to passenger comfort and itineraries. If you need something, that's where you turn. He'll circulate among he guests making himself acquainted now. But look, Phoebe, if these people are on board, what's the worst they can do?"

I gazed at him sadly. So innocent the way I had once been long ago before life sucker-punched me again and again. "Actually, quite a variety of interesting possibilities there, none of them pleasant. International art thieves are an inventive bunch, not to mention ruthless. I'm going to get some breakfast." Actually, I had a headache and not much of an appetite but coffee was definitely in order. I wondered if they served a side of antacids.

The buffet spread was extensive and offered everything an international traveler might desire from rice dishes for our Asian travelers to eggs for the English and American voyagers plus everything in between. I'd spied fruit, yogurt and and endless assortment of fresh breads in passing plus chafing dishes of warm breakfast dishes. Maybe I could manage toast and coffee. I'd already dosed myself with painkillers.

Carefully selecting their breakfasts next to me stood a middle-aged Chinese couple, the Wongs, who smiled and nodded while I used tongs to pluck a croissant onto my plate. "Beautiful morning," I said. They continued to smile and nod which made me assume but that they knew little English. Maybe I'd scratch them off the suspect list. On the other hand, they made a perfect cover.

On my way to the coffee station, a family of five—mother, father and three teenage kids stood in line ahead of me. "Are you excited about today's shore trip?" I asked the young guy who couldn't be older than 16. Tall, tanned, with a mop of blond hair, he grinned down at me. "Sure am. Can't wait to hit the waves."

His mother turned around and smiled, another blond, natural by the looks of those grey-streaked tresses. "Luke hopes to go body surfing today and take his two sisters with him. Do they even do that around here, I ask? Forget anything historical. Hi, I'm Linda Jenkins and this is my husband, Rob. My brood are Luke, Andrea and Suzanne by order of birth". The two girls, also blonde, turned around to wave at me and grin as did her tall balding husband before he took off, mug in hand. "We're from Arkansas and you?" Linda asked.

"I'm Phoebe from London by way of Canada," I told her and we chatted about shore itineraries all the way back to our respective tables. They had booked months ago. The first suspects eliminated.

Nick was now sitting at our table before an ample selection of breakfast offerings including an omelet, a dish of roasted potatoes, fruit and bread. "There are twenty-one passengers on board spread among 18 booked cabins with the four most expensive staterooms like yours fully booked," Leo said between mouthfuls. "Turns out they had a sale for the last month trying to get the numbers up but there are still empty cabins." The guy worked fast.

"Any last-minute bookers?" I asked while buttering my croissant.

"Two of the cabins were booked within the last two weeks. I'll find out who booked what as soon as I can." He was gazing at me with that look I was beginning to recognize as thoughtful consternation. Meanwhile, I was thinking how outfitted for adventure he looked in his safari shorts and matching shirt and how young.

"Nick, be careful. Don't do anything to raise suspicions, okay? We don't want anyone to know we're sleuthing. Just go about your usual business and do your detective work on the sly," I cautioned. "As a historian, you know how to research and detective work is similar but much more circumspect."

"Of, course but, Phoebe, don't be offended when I say this, but I think this alarm excessive considering that the only thing that's occurred so far is a tarot card slipped under your door. Surely that can't be considered a threat? In fact, if anything, it's another sign aligned with all the others to which have alerted us to our quest and that guy on Mykonos might just be a garden variety mugger."

I gazed at him, sipping my coffee, wondering how to explain to one who appears to have lived a more or less normal life, albeit one populated by ancient alternate history theories, that the world is filled with very human monsters. "Nick, that card did not manifest in my room by magic. A human put it there for a reason."

"Yes but maybe that reason isn't anything nefarious. Perhaps we have an ally?"

I shook my head. "All right, this is my intuition talking, but putting this card in my room does not feel friendly to me."

Still eating—actually more like ploughing the food into his mouth—he nodded. "When your intuition speaks, I listen. The subconscious mind is one of the most powerful tools we have. What about your room steward?"

"Artino? Too obvious but I'll be checking him out."

He got to his feet. "Sorry I can't stay longer and must run. Even though I'm not on shore duty today, we're supposed to remain with the passengers as they go off on the tours. Today they are heading to the beaches, three little towns, and to Parikia by boat, the main town over there. Tomorrow at Delos we'll test your abilities. I'll be lecturing about the island tonight, by the way. What are you planning today?" He was half on his feet ready to dash.

"I'm not sure yet," I said looking up at him. "I may just wander through the town. See you tonight."

Actually, my vacation plans had been upended. I knew that by the time I'd arranged for Peaches to share my cabin, sorted out when and where we could meet up among these islands, most of the morning would be gone. So much for my relaxing vacation. Still, being in Greece made everything much better. Nick and I said our goodbyes and I watched as he dashed off to earn his keep.

It took over an hour to book Peaches in as my cabin mate. These things were complicated. I needed her passport info which I didn't have which meant I had to email her and wait for the response. In the meantime, she'd only be half registered and, of course, I had to pay for the booking which meant an e-transfer from London.

"Last minute decision," I told Leo Vitalis as we stood outside his office with my debit card in hand. He was being very accommodating while diplomatically informing me of all the difficulties involved in adding new passengers once the ship had embarked.

"Where's the best place for her to board? She'll be arriving in Athens at 12:00 this afternoon," I asked.

"Let us look at the map, shall we?" he said pointing to a map of Greece and its archipelagos painted onto the wall of his office. The islands scattered across the blue sea looked like schools of irregularly shaped yellow fish leaping through the Aegean waves.

Leo was always smiling. He smiled so much my cheeks hurt just looking at him and he smelled faintly of starch mixed with some powerful after-shave. "Here you see The Sylvan Seas itinerary."

I followed his finger tracing a broken red line around a multitude of islands.

"First we are here at Paros for the night and then we sail over to Delos tomorrow for two days but drop anchor at Rhenia island along the way for snorkeling and diving in the magical waters." He turned and beamed, if possible his grin widening. "Everything in Greece is magical, everywhere there is magic."

I wondered whether that included magically appearing tarot cards but generally agreed with him. "Looks like we're ambling about in an irregular pattern," I remarked,"kind of like a Greek key design."

If possible, his smile widened. "Like the Greek key—yes! We amble, yes, like fish we flow in and out, back and forth. I like this word 'amble'. We are a pleasure cruise so no need to hurry. From Delos we go to Rhodes and then sail to Crete—of importance, you will agree—and from there to Hydra and on to Athens. I think it best that your friend meet us on Delos, don't you agree? There are many quick flights from Athens to Nisi Delos and she can meet us in port. We will be docked there tomorrow afternoon and remain there for two nights."

I considered his suggestion which could mean another night onboard alone with my imaginary minotaur. "What if she meets up with us here this afternoon?"

"Ah, that is possible but perhaps not so practical?" He shrugged. "She arrives, collects luggage, buys ticket, flight takes 40 minutes if she can get booking. Sometimes flights are cancelled or are fully booked. Olympic Air has many flights but maybe she misses? This time of year it is not so regular. So many last minute cancellations and things to cause delays. This late in the season, the ferries are not so regular, either. I always think it best to err on the side of caution."

"Thank you for your help. I'm sure we'll work it out." For Peaches the caution part did not apply.

Back in my cabin, I zipped off a note to Peaches providing the pertinent information, knowing she'd already be on her flight and may not collect her mail until later. I was wrong. She responded in minutes along with her passport info thanks to in-flight WiFi.

Peaches: *Can't wait to land in Greece. Any bad guys for me to battle?*

Me: *Only minotaurs and a high priestess so far but it's bound to get more interesting.*

Peaches: *Good. BTW, Evan's back on the planet—France. See you soon.*

Peaches took everything in stride, including mythical beasts and goddesses. For my part, I'd be glad for her company, not because I was afraid but because I badly wanted a trained, experienced agent at my side as well as a friend. Nick's innocence unsettled me. As for Evan being in France, I pushed that info to the back of my brain.

Meanwhile, I admit to having been unsettled by the otherworldly aspect of this situation. I believed in elements beyond which I could see or hear and recognized power in all its forms, including that of the unconscious mind. That didn't mean I found it comfortable.

My views on goddesses and tarot cards notwithstanding, I'd always found that theorists and organized followers of anything arcane or supernatural to be an eccentric and sometimes fanatic bunch, even when I believed in their theories or didn't dismiss them out if hand. Stir into that a hunt for gold and valuable ancient art and the danger factor accelerates. Now I wished I'd never agreed to participate in Nick's little research project though it was possible that I'd be targeted, regardless. At the same time, I was as burning with curiosity to see where it all would end.

While Greece sparkled in the sunlight beyond my balcony, I spent a solid hour researching Artemis beliefs and cults and downloaded multiple books on Greek history, ancient mythology, and a book on tarot cards. I'd never have time to read it all but I intended to scan like mad.

An hour later, my phone rang. Evan.

"Phoebe." He spoke my name like an invocation. My heart did that ridiculous little flutter thing.

"Hi, Evan. I'm standing here on a clipper ship in the Greek isles gazing out at the Aegean wishing you were here."

"I'm wishing I was there, too, though it wouldn't matter how glorious the setting if I was by your side."

Sometimes he said exactly the right thing. "But you're in France so I'll just have to send you a postcard. Any requests?"

"Yes, hold on a bit longer. I'll fly to Greece as soon as I can—once I settle a few matters, that is."

What matters? It was a testament to my will that I didn't ask. "I'd save a place for you in my cabin but it looks like Peaches will claim your spot."

"I would never let a little thing like that stop me."

We bantered back and forth for a few minutes before I insisted that I had to catch the next boat to port, which I did. More to the point, I wanted to be the one to end the call, an effort to maintain some control in this blossoming relationship, I admit. Being the one everyone strives to protect can leave you feeling vulnerable in multiple ways.

By the time I'd grabbed my backpack and all the necessities for a day on shore, very few passengers were left onboard. I noticed an elderly couple taking in the rays on the top sundeck but I was the only passenger in the tender heading to shore that afternoon, everyone else having left already.

The ship contracted a couple of private shore-based water taxis to drop passengers off at key spots whenever they wished as well as employing one of their own. Giorgi, my driver, was one of the contracted ones and told me that all I need do was choose a destination and I'd be delivered. These taxis cruised around to all the major pick-up points approximately every half hour right up to curfew time at 11:00. Curfew was for passenger security, he assured me. After 11 the ship was locked for the evening, which made perfect sense.

"So, what's life like for you, Giorgi?" I asked as I stood beside him in the pilot house watching as he manned the wheel.

"Have good life right here on Paros," he told me, a cigarette wedged between his teeth. His deeply grooved face leathered from the sun, he struck a jaunty figure in his kerchief and captain's cap angled on his head. "Sometimes too slow," he said. "But better than for city people. You live in little boxes—too much concrete. I know. I was in Athens many times."

I didn't want to know how he knew I was a city dweller. I guess it showed. "So Paros is your home?"

"My home, yes. These ships hire me to take passengers. Good life, very good life—sea, nice peoples, fresh air, money." He rubbed his fingers together and grinned. I took that to mean that the tips were good.

"I bet you know these islands inside out," I remarked as I gazed out at the shoreline with its white houses hugging the sea below a low grey scrabble of rocky hills. There were few trees in this arid land and those that existed looked to have been planted deliberately, yet everywhere I sensed people lived bright, vivid lives unless that was just me romanticizing.

"I grew up here. My father fisherman. Yes, these waves are my home." Giorgi remarked.

"My father was a fisherman, too," I told him—a treasure hunting fisherman but he didn't need to know that.

My comment surprised him. In fact, it was as if I rose several degrees in his estimation. "Fishermen the best."

Minutes later, we sailed into the port of Parikia, a major hub for catamarans and ferries that plied the island, he told me. I asked him about the airport and he told me where it was located.

"I have a friend arriving later this evening and somehow she's got to get to the ship," I told him.

"You give your friend my number. I come and pick her up to take to ship. The boy they have working on board lazy," He handed me his card and I handed him a hefty tip. Giorgi was no fool.

By the time I disembarked in Parikia, a perfectly picturesque town crammed with tiny streets, it was 1:32 and I'd finally worked up an appetite. Finding a lunch spot in the labyrinthine town with its tangle of white-washed streets packed with cafes, boutiques, and restaurants was the easiest thing I'd done all day. I chose a little restaurant overlooking the bay and made short work of a plate of stuffed bell peppers, a side of dolmades, and probably the best bread I'd ever tasted. Alcohol was avoided in lieu of fresh lemonade.

While digesting, I checked on Peaches' status. She'd sent me a text at 12:30 to say that she'd arrived in Athens but that all flights to Paros were fully booked until the next day. Instead, she was hopping a ferry which should deliver her to the island early that evening and that she'd let me know when she had arrived. *See you soon. Love this place already*.

I smiled, sipped my lemonade, and studied the diners in my vicinity, all of whom seemed busy with their own lives, vacations, conversations... None of them were stalkers., In other words, I couldn't see a George Baros lookalike anywhere. That left me free to enjoy my holiday afternoon.

First on my agenda was the archaeological museum which turned out to be a magnificent site of diverse and interesting artifacts including frescos, a 6th century BC marble Gorgon that looked uncomfortably like me on a frizzy hair day, and an early headless Artemis figure in a lovely flowing marble tunic. I felt no sudden insight by gazing at any of them. Though the wonder of each hit me by right of age and artistry, I felt no tremors or any sense that the ancient past wished to communicate. It occurred to me then that maybe I should read NIck's book to see if there were some techniques I should employ.

Despite that, intellectually I was completely engaged. The island had been occupied by Cretans, Minoans, Ionians, Arcadians, Byzantians, Macedonias, and even the Romans, layering many civilizations and influences into the ruins which gave me plenty to absorb. Otherwise, I just enjoyed the sights, strolling the lovely little streets, poking around the boutiques, and buying things I didn't need but which so felt so right to wear in that setting.

By 4:00, I was ready for a spell of knitting and a bit of Homer on my private deck. I wandered down the harbor to catch my ride and on the way checked on Peaches again. She had messaged me to say that she'd caught the ferry but claimed that this ship seemed to stop at every port and that it would be a slow trip. She'd missed the high speed link, apparently. Her arrival time was anticipated to be 7:30. Meanwhile she was having a scenic overload and was starving.

I smiled, wondering if she'd like the sexy little Grecian silk wrap dress I bought her as a welcome present. I shot her off a text requesting an update when she was a few minutes away from Paros. Following that, an hour of knitting on my balcony, researching, and otherwise relaxing rounded out a near perfect afternoon.

That evening over supper, I told Nick about Peaches' expected arrival.

"So your boyfriend definitely isn't coming," Nick mused a bit too cheerfully, I thought.

"Sadly, no, but Peaches will be good fun."

He seemed to accept that and we compared notes. "According to Leo, an Italian couple booked last minute into one of the staterooms cabins, the Drs. Bergognones from Milan. Also, two men booked a less expensive cabin yesterday, both named Tsaoussis from Athens, brothers, probably. Leo insisted that the ship's fare reduction sale paid off and that's why the last-minute bookings. Everyone else has been registered for weeks, he says."

I was savoring a rice dish featuring capers and some tasty pungent cheese. "That's the place to start then. I'll get into their cabins while you're lecturing tonight and see what I can find out."

His eyes widened. "You're going to break into their rooms?"

Actually, I was hoping Peaches would arrive in time to give me hand there. She had excellent break-and-entry skills. I laid down my fork. "How else can we learn pertinent information?"

"Maybe by asking them questions and hoping they'll trip up?"

I shook my head. "That might work for Hercule Poirot who could grill suspects with impunity but not in our situation. Anyway, checking their rooms is a place to start."

"Who's Hercule Poirot, may I ask?"

"An Agatha Christie detective. Don't you read detective novels?"

"I have no time to read such things. I am always researching or writing. What are you looking for?" he asked. He seemed preoccupied, focused on eating and turning over whatever was on his mind.

"Anything suspicious—guns, a pack of Tarot cards missing the high Priestess..."

"Oh, excellent idea." He tapped his forehead. "I must learn to think like a detective."

"By the way, did you notice anything peculiar while you were out with the shore trippers today?"

He was cutting his moussaka into bite-sized pieces and spearing eggplant from a platter of roasted vegetables set between us. "Nothing suspicious though I'm not certain what to look for. The Tsaoussis guys were on the windsurfing beach group and the couple from Milan spent the day in the town shopping and dining. I struck a conversation with them when we were boarding earlier. The husband was laden with shopping bags of mostly food. They called themselves 'foodies'. Both are medical doctors, by the way, speak very good English, and seem very pleasant—Maria and Roberto, respectively"

"Good detecting. They don't sound like likely suspects but we can't rule anyone out. Do you have that passenger manifest and crew list for me?"

"I do." He passed me a thick wad of paper under the table which I slipped into my bag. "So, Phoebe, did you experience anything yourself today?"

I glanced at him. "You mean like a sudden message beamed into my cranium while strolling through the archaeological museum?"

He smiled. "Something like that."

"No, sorry, and Artemis didn't speak to me, either, but then the statue I saw was missing her head." I laughed at my own little joke. "Anyway, the occasional piece of ancient statuary that have passed through my hands in the past like Athena's head, for instance, never communicated, either. My previous insights have all come from the last seven hundred years. Perhaps my supposed gifts won't work past a certain century?"

"Do you believe that?" he inquired.

"No."

"Art regardless of the age affects you, yes?"

"Of course, art affects me, moves me, even. That's why I've studied Art history in my adult life. It's just that the insights that I've experienced in the past were never forced. They came to me spontaneously. The conditions were much different."

"Perhaps you need to be in a location that resonates with you more. Delos tomorrow should tell the tale." He checked his watch. "I must run. The lecture starts at 9 but I must prepare. Will you be able to join me for part of it?"

"The first bit, yes."

"Good luck with the search and I'll see you later." I watched as he strode away in his tux, scanning the faces in the dining room while I was at it. Definitely not a full house. Some passengers must be staying on Paros until 11:00 curfew. The only diners at this sitting appeared to be in the 40+ age range or those with children. The doctors from Milan sat holding hands across the table and another senior couple who I didn't recognize sat with what I assumed to be their granddaughter while two middle aged women toasted one another at the able across the way. Joining us in the dining room were the Jenkins, Wongs, and a handful of others I had yet to meet.

I hadn't quite finished my supper when Captain Adamos arrived to invite me to his table for cocktails. I graciously declined, explaining that I must get ready for my cabin mate's arrival. "She should be here any minute."

"We can alert you the moment she arrives," the captain assured me, looking magnificent in his white formal uniform. I doubted I'd have pulled off the same gravitas, uniform or not.

"Thank you, but not tonight. Tomorrow, perhaps?"

"Certainly." He smiled and sailed on to another table to invite the two women who I gathered from a furtive glance at the paper Nick provided were friends from London. My gaze brushed over the doctors from Milan. They had to be the best-dressed passengers on board, all couture and designer handbags. Nicolina would approve. Even I recognized a Birkin bag when I saw one. Don't ask me why I notice these things.

Minutes later, I escaped to my cabin where I bumped into Artino delivering fresh towels to my bathroom. He couldn't be much older than 25 and blessed with the kind of Adonis good looks that could break even a marble heart in two—longish curly black hair and a well-tended smile that contrasted nicely with his tan. Of course as a valet-cum-cabin-steward he had access to my room but, given the circumstances, I found that unsettling. I didn't see how or why he would be responsible for the tarot card, however—too obvious.

"Miss Baker, how lovely you look tonight. That dress captures the color of your eyes."

"Thanks, Artino. I bet you say that to all the women." Yes, it was a tired old refrain but then it went with an equally tired old line. He'd get the gist. I grinned, he grinned back, my smile communicating *That won't work on me, buddy*.

"Not all," he assured me. "Only two or three."

"Per every 5 cabins?" I laughed. "Anyway, my friend is due to arrive soon. Did you happen to add extra towels?"

"I did and set up fold down bed. See, I try to anticipate your every need." He was gazing deeply into my eyes and only a fool could miss the every need he hoped to anticipate. Yet, I sensed it was an automatic response sent to all females and meant nothing.

"My needs are pretty simple, actually: good service, a clean room, and plenty of amenities—no frills necessary." Actually, that wasn't true only I preferred my frills at my own discretion.

"Oh, of course." The deeply penetrating gaze retreated immediately but the smile beamed on. "I will return later to turn down your beds and introduce myself to Miss Williams. Until then."

I was about to tell him that I didn't need turndown service but he had already darted into the stateroom next to mine. Which was occupied by... In seconds I was inside my cabin pouring over Nick's sheets. I found what I was looking for immediately: the neighboring stateroom was occupied by a Mr. and Mrs. Rose from Glasgow. Okay then, good to know. I needed to meet them, too.

It turns out that Nicholas had approached his task with a historian's attention to detail. Every passenger was listed along with additional information including cabin numbers, their anticipated daily itinerary, and dinner reservation times. The same detail was provided for the crew including break times, shore leaves, and official tasks and responsibilities—ten sheets in total.

The 5 valets assigned to the cabins were also listed along with a schedule as to when they serviced cabins based on their guests dinner reservations, tour excursions, and breakfast times. It appeared as though the valets knew the whereabouts of their charges at all times and worked around their movements accordingly. With a schedule that tight, I couldn't see how Artino found time for canoodling. At the same time it brought home how a ship that size was run on the clock where every minute is carefully scripted.

I checked the passenger list again, noting that the late-bookers, the Tsaoussis guys, were part of the shore clubbing crowd. The doctors Bergognones, on the other hand hopefully would take in Nick's talk at 8:30. Those would be the first two cabins I'd check.

Using my phone camera, I photographed the lists and placed the pages into the safe. I was so absorbed in my task that by the time I looked up, it was already 8:10.

That done, I sat down to review my messages, sending a quick note to

Max and Serena that all was well. A message also awaited from Zann who requested my itinerary so she could alert me to must-see archaeological sites in the area. She went on to mention that she was unable to see her dad because of a Covid outbreak at his care home. He was fine, she assured me, but cloistered for his own safety. The inevitable wave of sympathy almost overwhelmed me but I held firm and refused to give her my whereabouts, just in case. I did attempt to console her about her dad, though, telling her that his quarantine was for the best.

When I next looked up, it was almost 8:25. Where was Peaches? She should have texted by now.

Checking her position on the group GPS, I saw that her dot was close to a nearby island called Naxos but did not appear to be moving. *Not moving.*

I shot her a quick text, counting the seconds waiting for her response. After 10 minutes and still no reply, I grabbed my bag and headed out the door. Damn it. Why hadn't I asked her for the ferry's name or number so I could at least check her progress?

I tracked down Leo Vitalis at the door of the theater where he stood greeting passengers as they drifted in for Nick's lecture.

"Good evening, Miss Baker. Will you be joining us tonight?" Smile, smile.

"No, unfortunately. I'm hoping you can help me. My friend hasn't yet arrived but she texted me from the ferry hours ago."

He nodded, still smiling. "No need for concern. These ferries are not regular this late in the season. Which one did she board?"

"I don't know."

"Ah, well. If she does not arrive soon, I will make calls. Some of these ferries will remain at port for 15 to 30 minutes so take longer than expected. Some cancel last minute or there are strikes, always strikes."

I'd heard about Greece's labor issues. After the economy collapsed pre-Covid, things had been bad enough but now the problems had multiplied. Transportation strikes were common and sometimes unexpected but nothing short of a ferry crew going on strike in the middle of a run would explain Peaches' floating off shore somewhere. My alarm mounted. Meanwhile, I couldn't disclose that I could track Peaches on her phone and knew she wasn't moving.

Slipping past him into the media room, a large home theater-style space designed with every possible multimedia enhancement, I tried to get Nick's attention. He was busy greeting the two women friends, in full charming host mode, and it took precious minutes before I could get his attention.

"I need to get to Naxos now," I whispered. "My GPS has Peaches floating somewhere offshore." I showed him my screen.

"Floating?"

"I hope not literally but she's not moving and not responding to my texts, either. Something's wrong."

Nick paled. "Do you think she's...?"

I didn't let him finish. "Just tell me where I can hire a boat. I'm a competent sailor and can follow a chart so can rent one onshore, if I have to."

"Naxos is 31 kilometers away, Phoebe, and it's dark. You'll never see anything. It's too dangerous! Tell the police."

Of course he didn't understand that for me danger was all a matter of degree and that the police are often ill-equipped to handle the kind of trouble I get into, at least initially. "Not yet. Besides, I just had an idea. I'll be in touch later."

And with that, I ran downstairs to the launch deck.

5

Giorgi answered his cell at once and after I explained the problem minus the details, he was happy to help for a modest 500 euro. I'd be willing to pay anything for his experience and the use of his speed boat. He even contacted the ship's tender's night shift guy to arranged for my shore passage where he'd pick me up. Luckily, Caspar, the onboard tender driver, spoke little English and seemed uninterested in why I suddenly had to go to shore an hour before curfew.

As promised, Giorgi was waiting for me at a little stone jetty where a few yachts and cabin cruisers were moored for the season. He'd brought the same ten-seater speed boat he'd used for his ship's contract which was a relief since it seemed seaworthy. From what I could see on the map, we needed to circumnavigate the top of Paros to reach Naxos. I brought him quickly up to date but there was no easy way to put it.

"She floats off Naxos?" His sharp eyes studied me from under his peaked cap.

"It's complicated but, yes. I have one of those new phones that can pinpoint the location of anyone who agrees to be tracked." Of course, that feature wasn't on the market but he didn't know that.

He took my phone and peered down, pinching the screen out so he could see more clearly. "She dead?"

I stifled my annoyance. "Of course she's not dead—her dot is still pulsing—but she could be if we don't get to her soon."

Giorgi passed back the phone, shook his head, and together we untied the ropes to push the boat away from the jetty.

"How long until we get there?"

"Maybe 40 minutes if lucky."

What the hell did that mean? "How do we get lucky?" I asked.

He grinned. "Go fast. How she get out there?"

"By ferry," I said. Actually, I could barely squeeze out the words. How *did* she get there?

"By ferry?" he asked incredulously. "What, she jump off a kilometer from shore?"

So Giorgi was a smart-ass, too. "I don't know, Giorgi. Could we just cut the chatter and find her before it's too late?"

He shoved a cigarette into the side of his mouth and manned the wheel, eyes fixed ahead. The boat zipped out of the harbor, past the *Sylvan Seas* and other ships, large and small. He kept the speed to a modest putter until we were farther offshore but afterwards, the boat's speed seemed grindingly slow even at full throttle. 40 minutes may as be an eternity.

If I expected a smooth ride around the island to Naxos, I was wrong. Yes, the seas were calm, the night clear, spangled with stars above, and the thumping rhythm of the speedboat hitting waves full-on hardly unexpected. It was all ship activity I didn't anticipate. Countless lights sprinkled the horizon, some heading towards us, others sailing away. Any notion I had of the Greek Isles being some calm backwater lost in time was quickly erased. This was like shipping lane central.

"What are all those ships?" I called.

"Ferries, cruise ships, containers," Giorgi shrugged. "Busy waters."

"Do ferries operate this late?"

"Car ferries, yes. Many cruise ships this route, too."

Well, hell, and somewhere Peaches was out there bobbing among them? After that, I kept quiet though more than once I wanted to rip the wheel from his hand and open the throttle further. But I knew better. A man knows his boat and his waters better than anyone. This was his territory and I needed to let him do the job.

Meanwhile, I kept trying to text Peaches with no success. For some reason I couldn't bear to think about, she was unable or unwilling to respond. The possible reasons were too devastating to take seriously. All I could do was hang on to my nerves.

Then Evan rang. "Phoebe, what's going on? Peaches' signal appears to be drifting off Naxos and she's not responding to my calls."

The alarm in his voice was deafening. "Since you're on our group map, you'll know that I'm heading towards her now. I'll call as soon as I know something."

"But I—"

"Sorry, got to go." A monster ship was barreling down at us on our righthand side. Where did that come from and why was it moving so fast? "Giorgi?"

"Athens/Crete ferry."

"But it's heading right for us!"

"We don't hit."

Tell me that land objects seem closer than they appear and I get it but at sea when a ship appears that close, it's probably that close. I clung to the dashboard and swallowed my yelp, doubling down when seconds later, a smaller catamaran came into view on track to intersect the ferry's path. Though it looked like a collision course, I knew that those captains probably had their routes timed to within minutes, maybe seconds which didn't explain why Giorgi seemed to be aiming right for them.

"What in hell are you doing?" I cried.

"Hold on!" he called.

We missed the ferry by meters while its wake slapped the side of our boat and sprayed sea into our faces. I held onto the dashboard while we were tossed and bucked around between the two wakes not bothering to stifle my curses. Giorgi laughed.

"That was deliberate!" I called over the ferry's throbbing engine.

"We do this when young," he called.

"Do what?"

"Chase ships!"

Chase ships? Then I got it: wake chasers were like stunt drivers back home—teenage boys burning testosterone along with rubber on the back roads. The boat version was equally dangerous and bonehead crazy. "But you're not a teenager!"

He laughed. "Sometimes I feel young!"

That single action gave me the clearest indication of Giorgi's character: an aging adrenalin junky. He loved danger and clearly wasn't getting enough of it in his present job. In other words, he was the right person for the task ahead, whatever the hell it involved.

After that, we left the strait between the islands and eased closer to shore. Giorgi cut back speed. Ahead, a cluster of lights marked the town of Naxos. On one side, what looked to be an airport since a small plane was coming in for a landing overhead.

"I'll give you directions," I said, opening my phone. Evan's super phone app worked the same as Google Maps only included the location signals for each member of the agency team. All I need do was press Peaches' green dot and up popped the coordinates with an option for oral directions which I engaged immediately. Evan's tech-generated voice spoke. "Proceed 37.1101 degrees North, 25.3724 degrees East." I hated the robotic version of Evan's deep timbered tones but right then, I'd take anything.

"That phone something else," Giorgi exclaimed. "I get one. How much?"

"It's a prototype. My friend's in the business so it's not on the market yet."

He muttered something in Greek and studied the lighted dials on his dashboard as he maneuvered along. Several minutes passed with him steering and me staring off at Naxos. We were cruising along the shoreline now, passing the occasional boat as we went.

"We go to Portara," Giorgi called, studying his instruments.

"Portara," I said, considering the word's possible root. "The doorway?"

"Door to Temple of Apollo," he said. "On small island. I have been many times."

Since he no longer needed coordinates, I tapped a text to Evan. *The door to the Temple of Apollo?*

He got back in less than a minute. Evan: *Built around 530 BC, believed to be dedicated to Apollo. Perhaps dedicated to Dionysus who was once worshipped on Naxos. Never finished. Only the doorway remains. Marble pieces were too large to be dismantled. What is happening, Phoebe?*

I glanced up. Now I could see two majestic spotlit marble pillars with a lintel across the top profiled on a low hill as we rounded a point of land. What the hell was happening? At least 26 feet high with four blocks of white marble possibly 16 feet or longer, I could see why those behemoth hunks were never pouched by ancient builders. Standing on a little island promontory facing the sea, it could be a portal to another world.

I typed *Must go* and switched back to the map app. The green dot that was Peaches was pulsing larger and appeared to be directly ahead...somewhere. "She's over there," I called.

Giorgi cut the engine and switched on a dash-mounted search light. Together we peered into the water. On one side a causeway, on the other the doorway on its rocky outcrop, and somewhere ahead, Peaches. And then the light caught the gleam of a small white boat drifting close to a scrabble beach. "There!"

Our boat coasted closer and as soon as I could, I plunged overboard to wade up to my waist towards the boat. There lay Peaches, splayed on her back in a dory, one long leg flung over each side, her head tipped back and her mouth open. Handfuls of long stemmed purple flowers and some kind of spiky fir branches that I didn't recognize had been scattered over her chest.

"Peaches!" When I tried shaking her, she didn't move. Grabbing the boat by the prow, I dragged it up to the beach. I took a couple of quick photos. In seconds, Giorgi was by my side and together we lifted her onto the pebbled sand where I knelt beside her and checked her pulse—strong —and did a preliminary check for wounds but found none.

"Peaches, what happened?" but she was clearly out cold.

Giorgi dumped her knapsack and her roller bag onto the shale beside her. "Not robbed. Roller lock not broken. Purse still inside duffle."

He was right. However she got there, her luggage and wallet came with her but those flowers were staged plus there were no oars in the boat. This felt wrong as if it were to be a funeral... or a sacrifice. I looked over at the door of Apollo bathed in the spotlights and shivered.

While Giorgi was studying the roller bag more closely, I plunged my hand under Peaches jacket to where she carried her phone in a specially made breast pocket under her shirt. Even through the thin material I could see the phone's red intruder light flashing. It recognized my fingerprints, of course, but had an attacker touched it, they'd lose a layer of skin, at the very least . Dropping the phone into my bag, I looked up at Giorgi. "Let's get her back to the ship."

"No doctor?"

"The ship's doctor can check her out if she doesn't rouse by then but her pulse is strong and it doesn't look like she's been hit or bludgeoned or shot..." just stop, Phoebe. "No blood," I finished.

Giorgi leaned over and sniffed. "Drunk!"

"No way," I protested. "Peaches can hold her liquor better than a Russian sailor and, besides, she never drinks on the...while traveling." I almost tripped up and said *on the job*.

"I smell ouzo. She is drunk."

So that's the licorice smell clogging my nostrils.

"Someone wanted her to look that way but it's a set-up."

He nodded. "So you in big trouble." He pointed towards the open water. "Someone put her in that boat to float. Thought she'd end up out at sea and hit by ship but did not know the tides bring her back. She lucky."

I nodded. "Help me get her aboard."

In minutes we had laid Peaches across stern's padded bench and were headed back the way we had come. I sat cradling her head on my lap trying to gently rouse her with water, anything I could think of. Nothing worked. A few texts back and forth to Evan along with the photo I took ended with me promising to phone him as soon as I got to the ship.

The way back was calm and free of traffic compared to ride over. About 15 minutes away from Paros, Giorgi phoned the ship's tender guy. A lively and querulous conversation followed in Greek. Giorgi hung up, still swearing. "Useless! He refuses to pick you up from shore. Says curfew over. I'll take you."

"Will they let me onboard?" It was almost 11:30.

"Leave to me."

Fifteen minutes later and we were cruising into the harbor, Peaches still unconscious.

"You need me," Giorgi said. "You hire me to help while on ship. I know these islands and crew. I help."

I looked across at him silhouetted against the harbor lights, his cigarette a glowing spark of red. "Help how? I can't very well bring you onboard as my assistant, can I?"

He grinned, the cigarette bobbing between his teeth. "They ask me to drive tender for them days ago. I refuse—pay poor—but you give me" he rubbed his fingers together "and I say yes. Then I stay on board to help you."

Given my circumstances, that sounded like an excellent deal, despite the obvious issues of logistics. "It's that easy, really?"

"I know crew. I report Castor now. He get fired. Not good worker—lazy. They want me. I am very good worker, understand?"

"How much?"

"100 euro per day, flat rate."

"That's robbery. You'll be being paid by the ship so anything I give you is just a bonus. Make it 25 euro a day extra."

"50 and we have deal."

"Fine but only if you can get us back on board and into my stateroom without a fuss. I don't want to draw attention. In the morning I'll just say that her ferry was late and you can explain away how we got through security to get back on board."

Peaches moaned from my lap. That would be her struggling to consciousness at the sound of me making a bad deal.

Giorgi rubbed his fingers together. "You got cash?"

Bribery made the world go round. "I have cash," I told him.

❧ 6 ❧

When we arrived at the ship, two crew members I didn't recognize were waiting to help get Peaches onboard. We took a back stairway to my stateroom, the guys carrying Peaches, Giorgi handling the luggage, no questions asked. I had them lay Peaches gently on my bed before sending everyone away, including Giorgi. I watched as he strode away whispering to the two helpers, passing wads of euros to each. Yes, that guy was worth the cost of admission.

Bolting the door behind me, I returned to the bed. Peaches was moaning as if struggling to waken. I checked her pulse again—still strong — and removed her boots and sodden jacket before wrapping her in a blanket. Though she wasn't otherwise soaked, her attackers had poured what must have been a bottle of ouzo over her shiny nylon biker jacket. Luckily the material repelled liquid so her shirt remained dry.

Dropping the reeking jacket into the shower stall, I gave my room the once-over to check for bugs with extra scrutiny applied to Peaches. All was clean. Whoever did this, did not expect her to live long enough to collect information from a surveillance device, unsettling in itself.

"Peaches," I whispered, gently shaking her shoulders.

She turned her head and moaned.

Should I call for the ship's doctor? If I did, I'd inevitably have to answer a myriad of questions that not only I couldn't answer but which would bring a police investigation down on my head.

Time to confer. I called Evan, set the phone on the live camera feature and propped it against the night table while I dashed around the cabin wetting towels and pouring water. "Evan, she's slowly rousing with no sign of trauma except that she's out cold. Did you get the pictures?"

"I did, and the manner in which she was laid out in that dory had elements of the ritualistic." He sounded so near and I wished like hell that was true.

"That's what I thought and she was found floating strewn with flowers near the door to the Temple of Apollo," I said, bathing her forehead. "No fever. No wounds. I'm debating whether to call a doctor."

"They wouldn't be able to diagnose anything without blood tests which would required a shore trip and no doubt involve the police. If she's slowly coming to, it's better to just leave doctors out of it."

I picked up the phone so I could see his face and those warm eyes better. He gave me a faint smile which kept me going.

"That's what I thought. Giorgi, my skipper, claimed she was drunk because she reeks of ouzo but that was just a cover. You know Peaches doesn't do drunk. Whoever did this wanted it to look like some bit of drunken foolery but why lay her out in that boat like a sacrifice?"

"Who did this, Phoebe?"

"Maybe somebody from the ancient civilization alternate history theorist group, or I think I got that right. Long story." So I gave him the short version.

"And do you trust Nick Pallas?"

"Yes and no," I said flatly, "I sense he's trustworthy but who knows who's involved in this network of speculative thinkers where he virtually hangs out? He has no idea who reads what in those group chats—nothing but fake names and avatars plus a lot of shady lurkers. He posted that I was coming to Athens to repatriate Athena's head and I gather I've been a topic of conversation ever since. Nick claims that everything I've done to date is rich in heady symbolism."

"As in a woman named Phoebe who returns the head of Athena to Athens?"

Of course, he knew his mythology, too. "More or less."

"I've always said that you are legendary, woman. According to the ancient Grecian belief system, those with high prophetic or intuitive abilities might become priestesses or even an oracle like a Pythia of Delphi, the most powerful woman in the ancient world at the time. She could tell fortunes, dispense advice, and generally divine the future. Men fell at her feet," he paused, "much like I fall at yours."

I smiled. "You don't appear to be falling anywhere near me at the moment."

"That can change."

"Anyway, Artemis was sister to Apollo so I see the Potara connection. By the way, I have no divination abilities other than to be a bloodhound who can sniff out lost objects."

"That you know of or are willing to admit. You've always undervalued your abilities. It was only a matter of time before you became widely known as one who can locate lost treasures against all odds."

"Great," I sighed, thinking that at that moment I'd like nothing better than to be known as the woman who knit weird wraps or, better yet, slip into the background in the boring and uninteresting department. Peaches moaned beside me. "That was Peaches, not me."

"Run the camera over her, please," Evan requested.

I did as he asked. "She has no wounds that I can see," I told him.

"Did you check her phone and scan for surveillance devices?"

"That's the first thing I did—nothing—and she wasn't robbed. But when I found her, her phone's intruder alert was activated. I'm betting somebody drugged her, tried to take her phone, and got the shock of his life—literally."

"She definitely appears to have been drugged," he said.

"Right. How else to you get a tall, strong woman who knows martial arts into a boat and float her out to sea? Evan, those waters are churning with ships. Somebody wanted her to get plowed under. This was attempted murder but how does she fit into this Artemis Key thing, if she does at all?"

"As a sacrifice."

"What?" Maybe at one level I'd reached the same conclusion but to hear it said aloud...

He may have murmured something about staying calm but needn't have bothered. I had reached that cool collected zone where I did what was necessary while keeping emotion in check. "Was Artemis associated with human sacrifice?"

"That I don't know but intend to find out. Phoebe, I'm going to give you instructions to unlock her phone and access what might have been recorded when the intruder app was activated. The phone captures fingerprints, videos and voices. Usually I can do it remotely but I'm not at my desk."

I pulled Peaches's phone out of my bag but since the battery was almost drained needed to plug it in first. That done, I followed his instructions to penetrate the phone's settings. We discovered that a fairly clear fingerprint had been captured the moment her attacker tried to nab the phone. Since the device had been shoved next to her bra, she must have already been out cold by then.

"Send that picture to me. Now we know that someone is running around with their thumb pad seared—bastard. He'll have more than that wrong with him by the time I'm finished." I loved it when he pulled all that manly stuff. "Now press the replay button and let's see what else the phone captured."

Seconds later a crackling voice could be heard muttering while another swore in English. "Jesus Christ! What the hell? That bloody thing burned my fingers!" British accent—male.

The the other swore vehemently—also British, also male.

"Two Englishmen," Evan remarked as if that fact startled him.

Since the phone never made it outside of Peaches's shirt, no pictures were recorded but other sounds followed—the ocean, faraway voices too distant to be understood, voices singing or chanting.

"That's it," I commented. I let the thing play out while I stroked Peaches forehead and Evan continued to listen.

"Send everything to me and, Phoebe," he said, "I'll be catching the next flight to Greece. I can't wait to see you, even if I can't envelope you into my arms the way I've been dreaming of for weeks and months. I'll book onto the ship disguised as an eccentric senior British gentleman of wealth and means."

"Modeled after Rupert?"

He smiled. "I've been his understudy for years, but in this case I may be unable to keep my hands off a certain redhead, and we know how Sir

Rupert maintains a level of propriety. Expect me to fall off script whenever possible. Stay safe in the meantime and tell no one but Peaches that I'm coming. See you soon." He ended the video.

I sat quietly for a moment, feeling unaccountably lonely with no idea how else to help my friend. It was late and I was exhausted.

After performing another room check and setting my phone's intruder alert, I headed for bed. That would be the fold down couch Artino had prepared since nothing but the main bed could accommodate Peaches long legs. Yet, that fold-down version was surprisingly comfy and I dropped off to sleep immediately, remaining deeply under right up until the screaming began.

"Get off me, you piece of shit!"

I fell out of bed, leapt to my feet, and sprung across the cabin, banging my shins on a table, ready to zap the intruder. The sun poured through the veranda windows, Peaches was sitting up in bed with the covers thrown off.

"Was that you screaming?" she demanded.

I laughed. "That was you but I'm glad you're awake, no matter how loudly you do it. I've been so worried." Dropping my phone on the bed, I gave her a monster hug.

She hugged me back briefly before setting me aside. "How'd I get here?"

"I'm hoping you can partly answer that."

"Oh," she rubbed her head. "I feel like I've been hit by a truck."

"Could have been a cruise ship."

"Pardon? I'm so damn thirsty." She grabbed the water on the nightstand and drank the bottle empty before falling back on the pillows. "And I feel like crap...helluva headache. Could you make me my detox tea? It's in my duffle, right-hand inside pocket." She bolted up again. "Have I been robbed?"

"No," I told her as I emptied one of her little travel packets into a mug and switched on the kettle. "Tell me what you remember. When you last texted me, you had just caught the ferry from Athens."

"Yes," she sighed, laying back and staring up at the ceiling. "The wrong ferry, as it turns out. There was this guy on the plane with me from London—Richard Longley from Birmingham. Said that he teaches engineering but was off for a holiday to the Greek isles. Spoke fluent Greek. Tall, with a six pack like you wouldn't believe. Sexy as hell."

"Sometimes sexy is hell," I muttered. This guy was pure Peaches bait. "And?"

"And like he was hitting on me and it had been awhile since I'd been with an interesting guy so I hit back—hard. The ferry seemed to be stopping at every port in the Aegean and I complained that at this rate, I'd never get to Paros so Richard suggested that we get off at Mykonos to hop a high speed catamaran. He was heading to Delos to study ancient engineering, he said, so it was no problem for him to go in the same direction. I don't remember much after that." She paused. "He must have drugged me, the bastard."

"That's what I'm guessing. Any idea where?"

"Had to have been on the ferry from Mykonos. They had this little bar where he bought me an ouzo and set fire to a little bean floating on the surface. I'm a sucker for that kind of thing. I remember laughing, him with his arm over my shoulder. That's where things get fuzzy and I started feeling sick."

"How many drinks did you have?"

"One. Not that fond of ouzo."

"Did he...?"

"Hell, no! Surely I'd remember that? or at least feel it waking up! I was definitely not raped or sexually assaulted. Besides, where could that even happen on a ferry? Wait, forget I said that—lots of places. Anyway, even if he didn't do something, doesn't mean he didn't drop flunitrazepam or gammahydroxybutyrate into my drink. I definitely detect some funky aftertaste going on."

"What are flunt—never mind. What are those?"

"Date rape drugs."

"Hell."

"Yeah, I'd better detox like mad to get these pollutants out of my system. And the bastard didn't take my stuff? Like, what's that all about? Imagine this happening to me? I'll kill him. How could I be such an idiot?"

"I suspect being human is to blame. You always say that to me when I do something less than brilliant. Anyway, your stuff's all here with the locks intact." I handed her the mug of tea. "We captured some data on your phone, including a fingerprint which I sent off to Evan."

"I'll get that bastard, I swear I will. No one fools around with me and gets away with it. How'd I get here?"

I had to break it to her sometime. I took a deep breath. "We tracked you to a little boat floating off the island of Naxos." Passing her my phone, I waited while she studied the image.

She swallowed hard. Setting the mug down on the table, she sprang to her feet, pacing the cabin while holding my phone in both hands. "Shit. Shit! What the hell is this? Flowers? I'm laid out like a sacrificial lamb of the bloody black sheep variety!" She swung to me. "Do you know what those flowers mean?"

"I have an inkling given the context. Juniper represents Artemis and poppy...death."

"So I was supposed to be like, what, a gift to a goddam goddess?"

"Maybe, but we really don't know—"

"And they put me in a boat and floated me to where, like across the river Styx?"

"More like the straight between Naxos and Paros. We found you near the Potara of Apollo which is the door-like ruins of an ancient temple."

"What century are we in, anyway?" she cried. "Or maybe I should ask what dimension?"

"Calm down. We'll sort this all out."

"I am calm! I can't believe this happened! What the hell is going on?"

Time for the next part of the story. "I'm going to order room service and invite a friend to join us for breakfast. In the meantime, let me fill you in on the backstory. Do you want a shower first? It would probably make you feel better."

She glared, slung her duffle over her shoulder, and strode to the bathroom. Minutes later when I turned after ordering breakfast and found her standing behind me holding up a card. "Found this in my inside my back pocket—the Hanged Man. Tell me this isn't happening. Tell me I can get off at the next port, the port of sane."

7

Nick, Peaches, and I sat around the little table on my balcony having a simple breakfast of fruit, bread, yogurt, and cheese. To my left the most amazing shade of turquoise danced in gentle swells as the ship sailed through the Cyclades towards the port of Delos—a very short distance, I was told. We were to drop anchor off one little island along the way for two hours of diving and snorkeling but otherwise, the Sylvan Seas retained its leisurely course to one of the most important archaeological sites of the ancient world.

But none of us were exactly rocking the holiday spirit that morning. Even the occasional dolphin sighting did nothing to improve our collective mood. In the center of the table propped against the bread basket, the Hangman card gave a stark reminder that the setting only looked like paradise but may actually be a few degrees north of deadly.

"So just so we're clear, that card was found on Peaches's person," Nicholas said.

"We already said that, Nick," Peaches told him as she spooned up more fruit cocktail. She had finally lost that haunted puffy-eyed look after liberal doses of her medicinal tea. Otherwise, she was taking to Nick with a degree of prickly skepticism which I was attempting to smooth over with doses of humor. "It was in my jacket pocket, I said."

"So, it's reasonable to assume that whoever put it there expected it to be found," he pointed out.

"After the fact," I commented while stirring my yogurt.

"Or found by Peaches herself when she came to," he said in that ever-hopeful tone I was beginning to recognize. "So it follows that he or she didn't mean the card to be anything other than a message." He spread his hands and smiled. "It could be that Peaches wasn't meant to die but to be found as part of this sequence of cryptic symbolic messages."

I put down my spoon while Peaches let hers clatter into her bowl. "Are you kidding me?" she said. "I was set to float unconscious into a shipping lane with hopes that something big would mow me down and feed me to the fishes. What is it about that doesn't look like someone wanted me dead?"

"Maybe not, is what I'm suggesting," he said, his eyes a warm melting brown. "True that it was a highly dangerous situation but other than being drugged, you were placed in that boat unharmed."

"Have you ever been drugged, as in laid out like a sacrifice and floated out to sea?" she asked.

"Ah, no, but—"

"Ah no but nothing. That's causing harm, get it? That's attempted murder."

"Ah, but what I'm suggesting is that maybe it was just another sign?" he asked hopefully.

"A sign that somebody tried to kill me."

"We need to look at this in a big picture view to distinguish patterns and messages," he offered.

I shook my head. "Nick, you're still not getting it. Didn't you study the picture? Her positioning had sacrificial quality. The only reason they didn't kill her outright was because they wanted her death to look like the accidental end to a drunken holiday night out."

"Did the ancient Greeks even make human sacrifices?" Peaches asked.

"Human sacrifices might have occurred in certain sects but we're not certain of the details. In the case of Artemis, sacrifices were usually of goats or bulls."

"That should count me out then, huh?" Peaches said. "Obviously these guys were taking creative liberties." She glowered down at her bowl.

"The only other incidents of human sacrifices were when the goddess believed her temple might be desecrated," Nick continued. "But I don't see how that factors in this case."

"Look," said I, "all we know is that someone tried to kill her and performed some kind of ritual in the process. Presumably, by the time she'd been hit by a ship or floated out to sea or capsized, most of the evidence would be gone. It was staged."

He stared. "But I don't understand why someone would do this." Picking up the Hanged Man card, he stared at it as if expecting it to speak. "This card denotes energy arrested or someone awaiting judgment. Isn't that like saying that we are to do nothing but wait for some grand design to play out?"

"What grand design?" Peaches and I said in unison.

"That we don't know but it is as if whoever is planting these cards wants us to take no action because he or she is saying that whatever will happen will occur regardless. At least, that's how I understand this card."

Peaches fixed him with her gaze. "My granny read Tarot cards, tea leaves, you name it, and that jumbo jumbo stuff always creeped me out. Still, I remember this card well enough. She'd pull one every day and lay it on the kitchen table saying that it was her message for the day. Anytime the Hanged Man was pulled, she'd say that it implied that only those who were wise, self-possessed, and have boat loads of patience would succeed in the given situation. That seems like a strange message to place in the pocket of a soon-to-be dead woman."

"Exactly my point," said Nick.

"And the surface symbolism of somebody hanged has other connotations." I shook my head.

"Somebody's playing a hand," Peaches said.

"Instead of reading the hand they've been played," I countered. "And they want me to know it but why?"

"It must have something to do with this Artemis Key. What is it, exactly?" Peaches asked, staring at Nick.

"We don't know exactly," Nick replied. "The Ancient Greeks believed that the Artemis Key could prophesy the future and lead supplicants to lost objects. This key supposedly lies hidden in one of the temples to Artemis."

"There were more than one?" Peaches asked.

"There were many different cults to Artemis in ancient Greece, each with different rituals and celebrations according to local customs. Some of these had mysterious rituals associated with them, possibly similar to the Elysian Mysteries."

"Where women dance around and perform weird rites?" Peaches asked.

"More or less," Nick acknowledged, "but in truth we know very little about them."

"So where does Phoebe fit in?"

"Nick is hoping I'll be able to locate the key and the temple using by lost art sniffer dog capabilities."

Nick cleared his throat. "Phoebe has highly honed intuitive skills combined with psychic abilities. We're hoping she may be able to use her gifts to locate the Artemis Key. The last Pythia at Delphi may have hidden it against invading forces."

Peaches turned to me. "So now you're an ancient Grecian lost sniffer dog'?"

"Diversify, they say." I shrugged.

"No," Nick countered, laying his hands flat in the table and pitching his voice to his most authoritative tone. "The bearer of the Artemis Key has multiple nuances of meaning and as the high priestesses in one of the many cults that permeated ancient Greece at the time, were doubtless powerful members of society. The high priestesses of goddesses such as Artemis or Athena were probably the most powerful women of the ancient world."

That struck me dumb for a second. "I always believed that women in ancient Greece were much like those in ancient Roman society—cloistered, muted, and hidden from public view."

"True enough." Nick said, "but the exceptions were the priestesses. It was considered a great honor to be named a high priestess or an oracle in ancient Greece, often one and the same. It was believed that the goddess spoke through her priestesses and thus supplicants brought gifts and made sacrifices to them on the goddesses's behalf."

Peaches looked at me and frowned. "Are you supposed to be a modern version of one of those? Forget it. I won't bow and scrape to you or anyone."

"Not necessary," I said with a nod, "and I can do without the sacrifice part, too, but if you want to give me that velvet scarf you bought in Venice last year, I'll accept it."

She stared at me with her most regal tilt of the chin. "Not happening but it looks as though somebody thought I'd make you a good sacrifice," she pointed out.

We gazed at one another, suddenly serious. Attempted murder is never funny. "God, I hope not," I whispered.

"We don't know as of yet what the intention was. However, if I may change the subject for a moment," Nick began. "What I'm having difficulty grappling with is that tarot cards are hardly the topic of alternate ancient civilization theorists, at least not directly, though we have been known to discuss secret knowledge as it relates to the ancients. The topic of spiritual archaeology has come up in the group but that was many months ago."

We turned towards him. "Spiritual archaeology?"

"That's the study of archaeology as it relates to sacred places, of which Greece has many," he explained. "Delos, for instance, was the ancient birthplace of a god and goddess and therefore considered a sacred place reportedly known for miracles in its day much like Mecca, Lourdes, or other holy power sites today."

"So what does a spiritual archaeologist do?" Peaches asked.

"The study is still based on traditional archaeology but goes beyond mere marble and physical remains to study what the ancients believed thousands of years ago. Religion is a truly human story, when you think about it, because in ancient Greek mythology—religion, I could say—the gods and goddesses often acted in very human ways, rife with all the passions and foibles we recognize in ourselves."

"So how does the tarot fit into this, if it does at all?" I asked. "Did you ever discuss them in your group?"

"Yes, but only as they relate to ancient symbolism."

"Because the symbolism in the cards is archetypal, even mythological, some of which may have originated in ancient Greece?" I asked.

"Far older, in fact. The tarot symbolism is believed to have originated in ancient Egypt which predates the Greeks by two millennia," he said. "The ancient Greek historian Ammianus wrote that there were secret hidden chambers beneath Egyptian temples carved with secret knowledge that some speculate may have contained elements of today's tarot. Many theorists believe that these symbols may be a legacy from ancient Egyptian priesthoods."

"Plus, Egyptian symbols can be found on some of the cards in the Rider-Waite deck such as the High Priestess," I added.

"And it is hypothesized that the Greek God Hermes was a derivative of the Egyptian god Thoth and the ancient Egyptian high priest Hermes Trismegistus," Nick said.

"Wait," Peaches interrupted. "These are all mythological figures, not religious ones, right?"

Nick shrugged. "You cannot separate the two. One religion will view the stories of another as myth. Christianity's stories of Jesus rising from the grave will sound like a myth to Buddhists or Muslims, for example, and likewise theirs will sound that way to us."

"It's an interesting dimension of religion to disbelieve another faith based on the fixation on the truth of our own." I acknowledged. "Stories of miracles are everywhere but it's the intent behind the rituals that celebrate them that is the key."

"So you're saying that we should respect the ancient Greek religion the way we'd respect any other?" Peaches asked.

"We should respect all religions as they represent humanity's quest to become their best selves. Long before the current world religions dominated," Nick continued, "other gods ruled."

"I agree with that in principle," I stated.

"And the tarot cards?" Peaches prompted.

"They are, many believe," Nick explained, "all that remains of the Egyptian god Thoth's 'Book of Secrets' which reportedly unlocked the mysteries of the universe handed down by the Egyptian gods. It would be the equivalent of the Bible to the Egyptians and the ancient Greeks may have been influenced by their beliefs."

"Only the illustrations we see on the Waite deck have been altered across the centuries. Their designer, Dr. Arthur Edward Waite, was a scholar of the Kabbalah and believed in the power of ancient symbolism.The modern version was most likely shaped in medieval Europe when the current pack were first discovered," I said.

"So where does this leave us?" Peaches asked.

"Right, let's bring this down to the here and now," I said, my brain cells gumming together by this discussion of religions and mythology before my third cup of coffee. "We need to find out who's doing this and why. Obviously, there's more than one person involved, which complicates matters. I'd hoped our search would be restricted to somebody on this ship but now it seems the reach is much broader."

"I have found something that may help." Nick reached inside the man bag he always carried. "So last night while all this excitement was going on, I scanned the group members list for my alternate ancient civilization theorists and studied the avatars and handles of all 132 of the members. You'll never guess what I found?" He removed the bread basket and dropped a printed copy onto the spot. "There's a member who calls himself "The Magician and used the Waite-Rider Magician tarot card of the same name as his avatar."

I snatched up the page and stared. "This Magician made 115 postings?"

"Over a six-month period, 56 of them after I announced that you were coming to Greece. Do you see how many comments and questions he asked? I was printing them off when Leo walked into the crew quarters where we keep the printer and computer. I'll get back on it after the tour of Delos. Are you ready for the start of our experiment today, Phoebe?"

"What experiment?" Peaches asked.

Busily reading, I didn't respond at first so Nick answered for me. "Phoebe agreed to put herself out there as a test case for my Artemis Key research today."

"Oh, right, and what does it mean 'to put herself out there'?" Peaches asked.

"I'm going ashore with Nick as part of the two Delos tours to see whether I have any sudden insights regarding the possible location of a lost temple...or something," I said without looking up.

Peaches sat back and crossed her arms. "That's crazy." I wasn't sure whether she meant the lost temple was the crazy part or me going ashore was nuts.

"She will be perfectly safe," Nick assured her. "I'll be at her side at all times and both tours are in broad daylight. This afternoon we remain primarily on the bus, which is a rare treat since vehicles are not usually permitted on the archaeological site. The ship received special permission in the interests of accessibility for our more senior passengers to use the museum's van. There are two tours: one this afternoon and a much longer walking tour tomorrow. Most passengers have signed up for the full-day excursion tomorrow."

"Is that suppose to comfort me?" Peaches demanded. "I'll be the one right by her side."

I looked up. "Peach, come today only. If most of the passengers will be on shore tomorrow, it's a prime opportunity for you to search for a pack of Tarot cards missing its High Priestess, that is, assuming that your Hanged Man belongs to another pack. Between the hours of 9 and 10:30, all the rooms are slated to be cleaned and Artino takes a break."

"I'm here as your bodyguard," she pointed out while not mentioning the fact that last night she could have used one herself, "so I plan to guard your body."

Nick looked across the table at her. "I'm sure Phoebe's body will be perfectly safe. I'll be right beside her the entire time." He paused to glance at his watch. "We have a staff meeting of the water crew in three minutes. Phoebe, are you going diving, too?"

"That's my plan," I began.

"Absolutely not!" Peaches erupted. "Do you think she's going to just ask for trouble?"

Nick glanced from Peaches to me and back again. "But nobody has attempted to harm her in any way. Why would they? She's incredibly important. In any case, I must run. Catch you later."

I watched him dash through my cabin and disappear through the door. When I turned, Peaches was staring at me. "What?"

"Is he for real?" she demanded.

I sighed. "I've come to realize that Nick is one of those rare souls who believes that the world is basically a good place populated predominantly by good people with a smattering of good people gone bad." She was staring. "That's a simplification, of course, but the point is that, yes, he's for real. He's highly intelligent, very knowledgeable in his area of study, and fascinated with the belief that Atlantis exists, miracles happen, and that someday an advanced alien species will descend to the earth and solve all the earth's problems. I just made that last part up but you get my drift."

"And he also believes that you'll just land on ancient soil and maybe sniff out a lost temple?" she asked.

"Something like that. I'm willing to go along with it in the hopes that I might learn something profound about my own sense of intuition and abilities. Don't scoff, Peach. I know that you're a concrete thinker who prefers empirical knowledge to anything esoteric but keep an open mind. There's so much about our own brains that we don't understand. Anyway, forget Nick for a moment. We have to find this Magician. He's a key to this, I'm sure of it." I indicated the printout in my hand. "Let's do some research."

But it was clear that Peaches had still not recovered enough to peer down at either text or screen.

"I don't like it, don't like any of it," she said as she lay back down on the bed with her arm shielding her eyes. "It's like we have to hunt down invisible foes hiding behind ancient symbols that hint at murderous intent. I'd rather have somebody shoot at me outright than have them creep around wearing a mask and pulling mumbo-jumbo stuff."

I agreed with her there. "If it's any consolation, the voices that your phone captured sounded like ordinary thugs."

"Yeah, so like that makes me feel better."

"But we could also detect chanting in the background."

"Mythic thugs, then," she said with a sigh.

"There," I said as I propped my legs on the coffee table and tapped SEND on my phone. "I just sent off the details about this Magician guy to Evan in hopes that he can set the Agency wheels in motion to investigate his true identity. Hopefully, we can get a few answers back before he arrives in Delos, which should be by tomorrow morning, at the very latest."

"He'll need to involve a hacker for that."

"We've got a few of those in our network and it's not as if these social media sites aren't impenetrable. At the very least, we could trace this guy's ip address and narrow in on his location to identify him that way. Scammers do it all the time. Listen to this. Here's the last thing the Magician posted before he went silent in the group. Interesting that it coincides with my arrival in Athens because after that, he makes no further postings."

I read from the printout: "*Imagine the significance of identifying a modern Artemis Key in the crucible of Ancient Greece? Imagine the power such an oracle could unlock? She is the one we seek.*"

"And what was the response from others in this group?"

"A smattering of enthusiastic agreements amid lamentations of the delay and the perils of Covid in general. One person suggests that I be invited as a guest speaker at a conference which was postponed due to Covid last year but later rebooked for next spring. Nick, in particular, was enthusiastic about that idea as it seems he's to be one of the guest speakers, too. Oh, backing up a bit, here's where Nick tells everyone that I'm coming to Athens: *I have just received word that the famed Phoebe McCabe, who is undoubtedly very gifted, will be arriving in Athens to repatriate the head of Athena to the Acropolis Museum.* He goes on to say that he plans to arrange a meeting."

"By pretending to be somebody he's not. How does that fit into your idea of his good boy status?"

I peered over the top of the page at her. "That just proves to me that he's willing to do the occasional unethical thing to follow his convictions. Otherwise, we can slot that one into the 'nobody's perfect' category."

She smiled at that but before we could discuss anything further, a knock at he door interrupted us. I checked the time. "That must be Artino, our cabin steward. We were supposed to take breakfast on deck so he can make up the room. Are you up for a stroll topside?"

"Sure." she said getting to her feet. "After all, we have monsters and magicians to track."

8

I opened the door to Artino's smiling face, his arms laden with fresh white towels and a cart full of amenities parked nearby. "At your service, my goddesses." And he proceeded to charm Peaches while attempting to prod her for information concerning her late arrival the night before, all of which she sidestepped with practiced dexterity. The goddess part she simply acknowledged as her due.

Just as we finally extracted ourselves and Artino had bolted into our cabin to begin room maintenance, the door of the neighboring state room opened and out came Mr. and Mrs. Rose from Glasgow. I recognized them as the senior couple I had seen lounging on deck the day before.

"Our neighbors!" the gentleman exclaimed with a delightful brogue. A tall lean man dressed in crisp white Bermuda shorts and coordinating short-sleeved shirt, he offered one hand for us to shake while leaning heavily with the other on what looked to be an antique carved walking stick. "Allow us to introduce ourselves: I am Peter Rose and this is my lovely wife, Heather, both hailing from Glasgow, Scotland. And you are?"

We introduced ourselves and shook hands accordingly. The lovely wife Heather squeezed a reluctant smile out through pursed lips and stood with her hands neatly clasped over the handbag she held pressed against her floral skirt. No handshaking happened there. "I am still not comfortable with the lessening of Covid restrictions in general," she explained. "I presume you have been vaccinated?"

"Of course. We all had to prove our vaccination status before boarding the ship." I tried to keep my smile going to bypass her aloofness. "Heather —may I call you Heather?" I asked, smiling over at her.

"You may. It is after all, the standard protocol these days among strangers, though I never did abide by it myself." The shrewd pale blue eyes studying me from over the top of her round clear-rimmed glasses held at least as much interest in me as I suspected mine did of her. Probably in her late sixties and younger than her husband who I took to be at least a decade or two older, she was almost as tall as he was and equally lean with clothes hanging on her lanky frame.

While Peaches chatted to Peter, enthusing over her first trip to Greece, I attempted to pump a little warmth into my relations with Heather Rose. "This is my longed-for vacation," I told her. "I have always dreamed of sailing through the Greek islands on a tall ship."

Another tight smile. "How wonderful for you to realize a dream. My husband and I are celebrating our 50th wedding anniversary, albeit the actual date was many months prior. Nevertheless, we have often taken vacations in Greece, it being one of our favorite holiday locales. Peter is a retired doctor, you know, with an intense interest in the ancients. And what is it that do you do, Phoebe?"

Since I was traveling under an assumed name but could still be recognized, I had my answer dovetailed neatly into my assumed identity. "I'm in art restoration. Are you attending the Delos tours?" I changed the topic quickly as we strolled towards the elevator.

"We are indeed. Peter refuses to miss a thing though we have attended many such excursions over the years. One always learns something new with each expert leader, I suppose. Indeed Peter is quite looking forward to hearing what Dr. Pallas has to say."

So Nick had achieved a level of fame among the touring crowd. "But not you?"

"I keep an open mind in hopes that I will hear something that I haven't heard countless times before," was her reply.

"Have you read Dr. Pallas's book?" I asked.

"And which book would that be?" she asked.

"*Unlocking Ancient Voices with your Mind,* I believe it's called."

"What nonsense," she said with a sniff. "I'm quite certain that Peter would not read such things, either. I prefer a good novel myself."

That ended that discussion. Peter rescued me by stepping up with a tidbit of information. "Did you realize that Delos is halfway between Athens and Asia Minor, Miss Phoebe?"

"Call me Phoebe, please. I did, yes. That's one of the reasons it became such an economic and spiritual powerhouse as well as the headquarters of the 5th century BC Delian League," I added. It's an unfortunate side of my personality that I sometimes feel the need to spout my knowledge. A shadow crossed Peter's pale blue eyes before I felt a twinge of shame. Really, I had to work towards becoming a better person.

The four of us piled into the lift since the Roses needed to take the elevator due to Peter's arthritis which we learned all about, including recent treatment options and the necessity of seeking out the best doctors in the UK. By the time we parted company on the upper deck, we knew more than we wanted to about Peter's medical problems and that the last-minute booking was due to his only recently feeling up to the journey.

"Scratch those two from the suspect list," Peaches remarked as left the Roses on the upper deck. "Peter appears to be losing his marbles. Repeated the same details about his bad knee at least twice. He used to be a pediatrician, by the way. They have two grown sons living in London."

"The Roses are still close enough to our cabin to slip a card under the door, providing Peter could even bend over," I said. "Poor guy is struggling. Let's agree to keep everyone on the list for now."

I had described George Baros to her earlier but had yet to see my Mykonos stalker again. He was still out there along with Peaches's attackers and of course, the card-slipping party, whoever they were. That was enough invisible enemies to keep us vigilant.

We couldn't wait for Evan to arrive for multiple reasons. He'd texted that morning to say that he expected to arrive by ferry by tomorrow and would meet up with us on Delos. I wondered if he knew how big an area Delos was but knowing him, he would have researched the place down to the last cubic inch.

Peaches and I stood side by side gazing up at the sails being lowered as we arrived at our diving locale, a tiny island encircled by a pristine reef.

Gone was any notion I may have had of sailors shimmying up the lines to lower the yards as in days of yore. It turned out that these uber modern tall ships handled many of those tasks electronically.

"Wow," Peaches said. "Impressive. Dizzying." She quickly lowered her gaze and leaned against the rails, fingers pressed to her temples.

"Maybe you should go back to the cabin and rest? Artino's probably finished by now," I suggested.

She straightened. "No way. I'm sticking to you like a second pair of underpants. Anywhere you go, I go."

Since I had originally planned to go diving but knew she wasn't yet up to anything so physical, that meant a few hours of lounging on deck researching on my tablet while the diving parties played with the fishes. It made for a relaxing late morning though not exactly what I had envisioned for my holiday. I wondered idly wether it would always be like this, whether I'd be targeted no matter what the circumstances and require a bodyguard constantly as if I were some royal personage. But unlike Queen Elizabeth, for instance, I didn't have a Balmoral retreat. The Lost Art Sniffer Dog oracle apparently needed a fortified doghouse for her escapes.

While Peaches stretched out on the sundeck in a bikini—she could really rock that thing while I kept my bountiful parts under wraps—I downloaded anything I could find on Artemis, Greek civilization, and Greek mythology in general. That did not make easy or concise reading, though I had always loved Greek mythology and had appreciated Greek art by inclination as well as by necessity. Luckily, my scanning capabilities had been honed from my student days so I could pull off information gathering with speed and accuracy despite the occasional detours. It always fascinated me which god or goddess did this or that to whom.

Occasionally, I'd look up from my tablet to survey the surroundings. The Sylvan Seas had turned the upper deck into a kind of cabana/lounging area so that those not snorkeling or diving could relax while sipping ice tea or their beverage of choice and gaze across at the turquoise water at the snorkelers bobbing in their gear. The sun was bright, the sky impossibly blue, and everything sparkled with intense color and light. Some practical side of me tried to estimate the UV index but gave up.

Farther to the left, the diving contingent were evident from the marker buoys and the guide boat. We had watched that group head out earlier, skippered by Giorgi and a woman who was listed among the crew as the diving master. Said master appeared to be an energetic young woman with spiky hair and a muscular physique who I'd glimpsed from a distance the day before. I couldn't help but feel envious of her job. Imagine herding the black-clad human fishes through glorious schools of the real thing in some underwater fantasy world? Meanwhile, Giorgi had only winked at me and tipped his hat as he sat in the boat waiting for the diving enthusiasts to pile in, which included most of the younger passengers. Interesting how he managed to pull off insinuating himself onto the staff just as he claimed he would. My euros apparently did the trick.

Nearby, a glass-bottomed boat maned by triple-duty Nick floated close to the ship for those unwilling or unable to get wet. I noted that the Roses were included in that group as well as another senior couple accompanied by their eight-year old granddaughter. The Dexters were British expats living in Spain, and I guessed they were probably in their late eighties and still fit. After checking their details, I saw that they had booked the trip months before the first Covid lockdown and, therefore, I had shifted them over to my mental Not Likely suspect list.

Stifling my water yearnings, I consoled myself with a stroll down the deck, leaving Peaches to doze under her huge sunhat. Over the side and below the hull, the water was so clear that I could see all the way to the bottom at the shapes of coral and brilliant darting fish. Nearby, in the glass-bottomed boat, Mrs. Dexter was tossing food into the water to attract the quarry while Heather Rose peered down at her feet with her lips forming a tight little O and Nick identified the sea life for them. But it was Peter Rose that caught my attention. He seemed to be stirring the water with his cane, occasionally poking at anything large that dared to surface.

Catching my gaze, he called up: "Phoebe, you should join us. Quite the variety of sea life here, I must say. We have just seen a darling little flotilla of baby squid which have the makings of a smashing lunch."

I only smiled, wondering if he meant "smashing" literally. The idea of him whacking baby squid with his cane to add to our noon buffet was a disturbing image. Turning away, I checked my phone for messages but other than a text from Max informing me that he had sold a Bornean Pua'kumba carpet, the airwaves remained silent. I did a quick check of the staff schedule I'd photographed onto my phone. As suspected, most of the crew were on duty somewhere leaving me with a few minutes to explore.

I bolted downstairs to the lowest level. This was no more than a scouting mission with snooping as the only agenda. The only staff member I encountered along the way was a steward delivering towels somewhere.

"Can I help you, miss?"

"Yes, thanks. I'm looking for the games room," I lied.

The guy smiled. "Sorry, wrong direction. The games room three decks up." He pointed up a few stairs towards a short hall to his right. "The elevator is there, Very busy right now but follow me, I take you to games room."

I smiled and pointed towards the elevator. "Sorry. I'm tired already—so many stairs. I'll wait for the lift, thanks."

He nodded and left me to pretend to wait for the lift before dashing down the steps to the bottom level. The crew quarters consisted of a corridor with every room marked by the occupant's name—Venari, Artino, etc.

The stewards appeared to occupy the cabins closest to the stairs while further down the hall, the doors held placards with other names I recognized from the crew list as chefs, cleaners, and deck hands. Near the very end, I found Nick and Giorgi's rooms among a handful of special employees like the dive crew. The captain, first mate, and Leo all occupied larger staterooms on other levels.

After checking over my shoulder at the deserted hall, I began trying doors. Most were unlocked and those that weren't soon became so with my delock app. A quick check of Artino's quarters revealed a simple narrow room tidily arranged with not a shoe out of line beneath the bed. A brief check of his two drawers disclosed no tarot cards and the only information I came away with there was that the guy favored black briefs plus a thong or two. He kept a wad of extra cash in his room safe.

Two doors further down, I poked my head into Giorgi's room, finding it sparse. The guy had two changes of clothes from what I could tell, a couple of t-shirts plus one jacket and one pair of spare shoes. I unlocked the safe and found it empty. Backing out, I tried Nick's, not surprised to find it also unlocked with nothing remarkable in sight but multiple books and a tablet which he didn't bother to lock away in the room safe provided.

Back in the hall, I opened a door labeled CREW and discovered a lounge area with a small mess hall, computers, and seating. A television on the wall played the BBC with Greek subtitles and I could hear voices around the corner out of site. A sudden vision of being caught down here sent me scurrying for the stairs. There was no time for me to do the job properly.

***

AFTER LUNCH, PEACHES AND I RETURNED TO OUR CABIN TO GET READY for Delos. The moment we strode into our quarters, Peaches began scanning every inch for listening devices while I changed into capris and a t-shirt before settling down on the couch to read.

"Artino moved our stuff," she said after a few minutes.

"He's our room steward; he's allowed to do things like that," I said without looking up.

"But in our business, we don't need that kind of tidying. He's even washed my jacket, hung up my clothes, and placed my undies in a drawer."

"So give him a good tip."

"But I don't like men handling my undies unless we have an understanding."

I looked up from where I had resumed studying the myths of Delos. So Peaches was not in a good mood. "Then you'll have to tell him that you only want him to clean, not tidy, our cabin, and to leave your undies alone." And then in an effort to distract her: "Did you know that Delos had no defensive capacity but remained a sacred site for thousands of years?" I stepped out to the balcony. "At one time it briefly became a kind of treasury but unlike many sacred sites in ancient Greece, it had no standing army and couldn't wage war."

"No, I didn't know that." From where I stood I could see her studying her three pairs of sandals and sneakers lined up at the bottom of our diminutive closet. "He put my shoes mixed in with yours. If he's such a tidy whiz, shouldn't our stuff be separate?"

Okay, so maybe she was a tad OCD at times. More distraction needed.

I stepped back into the cabin. "Listen to this. Here's how Delos was formed according to myth: apparently the Titan, Leto, daughter of Coeus and Phoebe—just thought I'd throw that in to remind you that I'm named after a Titan—got pregnant by Zeus but couldn't find refuge from Zeus's furious wife, Hera, to give birth to her twins."

"Why not go after her cheating husband?"

"Maybe because he was top god?" I offered.

"The age-old abuse of male power thing but go on."

"So she finally reached the barren island of Delos and there found the sanctuary to give birth to the twin gods, Apollo and Artemis, and it became sacred from that point on."

She gazed at me for a moment before turning away. "Huh," she said. "What a pile of jealous, brutal, and cruel gods these Greek deities were. They were all too human, from what I can see, and Nick says we should respect them as other people's deities?"

"Religion holds the mirror to the best we can become as human beings and in the case of the ancient Greeks, maybe the worst, too. That's what makes these stories so fascinating. We see a reflection of our own nature in them, good and bad."

"So I was named after Penelope, the woebegone heroine who waited for her absent husband while he took off to explore the world—another ancient tale I prefer to turn on its head."

"From Ulysses. I'm reading it now."

"This is what I'm reading now," and she held up a paperback with a man sporting bulging biceps on the cover, "and I won't be waiting for any man, ever. Damn, that Artino. He even threw away a half-filled packet of my detox tea. Can you believe that? I had it sitting there beside the kettle and now it's gone."

I waved my tablet before her eyes. "Look, here's a photo of the statue of Boreas, god of the north wind, carrying away the nymph Oreithyia. The original is in the museum at Delos, apparently. We'll see it today."

"Never heard of them." Scowling down at her empty suitcase, she wedged it back into the closet beside mine. "I should have left my bag locked. Once I unlocked it, it was like I issued an invitation for this guy to go through my stuff."

"Did you have anything in there you wouldn't want him to see besides your silky thongs and bras?"

"Of course not. Everything confidential is locked up inside my tablet tighter than a vestal virgin. You know how Ev sets up the Agency's devices so that even Poseidon couldn't get in there with a thunderbolt, not that I have any secret documents or anything."

"Trident."

"Pardon?"

"Poseidon, the god of the sea, used a trident, Zeus, top god, wielded a thunderbolt. Get your divine weapons straight, woman. Anyway, back to Boreas and Oreithyia: the story goes that Boreas was a purple-winged god of the north wind who fell madly in love with a beautiful maiden who he saw bathing in a spring. That—"

"So he saw a naked woman bathing and figured she was his to take? Got it."

"That's the way the wind blew back then. So her name was Oreithyia," I continued, "and he took her away to his home in the skies where they became lovers."

"It's probably more like he came, he saw, he conquered." Peaches snorted. "That's called rape and abduction where I come from. These myths glorify domination over women, right? Same old story. So what else is new?"

It was obvious that she was not in the mood for mythological tales of passion so I kept the rest of my reading to myself. By the time the ship was slipping through the waves for the short sail to Delos, I was more than ready for our shore excursion, admittedly also for a few moments alone with my thoughts. Peaches and I were compatible roomies when we each had our own space, but I wasn't certain how well this close cohabitation was going to work. Still, I reminded myself, this arrangement was about my protection and I always had my knitting for escape, if necessary.

Twenty minutes later, we stood by the railing on the upper deck, my gaze fixed on the approaching shore. I was eager to see if this amazing archaeological site of the Hellenistic world might induce some kind of intuitive moment in me. Peaches stood nearby outfitted in her version of walking clothes—a purple two piece short set enticing enough to throw Boreas off course. Nick had joined us by then, his gaze also fixed ahead.

"Looks arid," Peached remarked, staring at the rocky island scattered with broken columns that grew up from the stark landscape like a partially denuded marble forest.

"It is," Nick said. "The island itself may not look beautiful at first glance but once you set foot on its shores, don't be surprised to feel its power."

Peaches studied him out of the corner of her eye. "As in an electrical current? Will I get to recharge my phone?"

Nick ignored the sarcasm. "This is more subtle though no less powerful. Delos is on a ley line," he said. "Have you heard of those?"

"Of course. Apparently the great cathedrals of Europe were built on ley lines," she said, softening her tone. She had studied those during her engineering days, she had told me once, so I knew she was not a complete skeptic.

"As were the pyramids and holy sites of all beliefs including the Temple Mount in Jerusalem and Mecca," I added. "The ancients understood earth energy and built sites of worship where that power surged the strongest. They considered it a sacred energy."

"And Delos is one of those rare places where these energies are most powerful," Nick added, picking up the thread, "making human transformation possible as long as supplicants remain open to the possibilities. Delos, for instance, has more abatons than any other place in Greece."

"Abatons?" she asked.

"In ancient Greece, any place where a person experienced a miracle was walled off as a sacred spot called an abaton. Delos has hundreds of abatons scattered all over the island. An ancient Greek poet once wrote that 'gods from high above look down upon Delos that glows like a star in the dark sky that is earth'. It's that powerful. That's why I'm hoping Phoebe will experience something."

"Something like what again?" Peaches had turned fully towards him now, fixing him with a questioning gaze.

He spoke while still fixed on the approaching shore. "Every person will experience a miracle differently but since Phoebe has a rare gift, her insights might be very powerful."

Peaches side-glanced me to see how I was taking this proclamation but I kept my face serious. I did not take sacred places lightly. I knew they existed, could feel them in many of the ancient temples, cathedrals, or holy sites I'd entered across the globe. It didn't matter by what name we called God or how we framed our beliefs, universal energy existed and could be felt more acutely in certain locations. That said, I was prepared to see if I'd experience insight necessary to find a lost temple. I didn't realize that miracles were also part of the experiment. I wasn't sure i was up for one of those.

"Let's head down to the launch deck," Nick said, touching my arm. "We'll be taking a minibus around to the sites today—nothing too strenuous. The tour is only two hours long with an hour in the museum and is more like a mobile overview in preparation for tomorrow's walking excursion. Ready for an adventure?" He was beaming at me.

"Sure." I smiled back, thinking that if I truly had a gift, then Delos should theoretically activate something. After all, it was the mythological birthplace of the deities of the sun and mood respectively. For thousands of years it had drawn supplicants, revelers, worshippers and seekers of healing and wisdom to its shores with the promise of mystic awakening. Surely that would super-charge something inside me, at the very least clear my sinuses?

As we followed Nick to the central stairway, other passengers joined us along the way and while I greeted everybody, I tried to remain fixed on my upcoming possible psychic event. Maybe I needed to be alone to maximize the conditions necessary to prepare myself but I knew that wasn't going to happen.

Peaches was definitely not in the right state of mind for anything at a higher level of consciousness. "Maybe I'll see my bogus Richard Longley so I can beat the snot out of him," she whispered. Lifting her sunglasses, she surveyed the lower deck 350 degrees. "He's not on board, not that I expected him to be, but maybe he'll be slithering around Delos somewhere waiting for another sacrificial lamb to appear."

"Do you consider yourself a lamb?" I laughed.

"More like a kick-ass wolf in disguise. That's what makes me so dangerous."

I agreed with that in theory.

As we arrived at the launch deck, we saw that the crew had lowered a gangway which attached to a portable wharf from which the tender would ferry the 25 passengers to shore in two trips. Meanwhile, we could see a huge ferry arriving as smaller boats pulled up along a spit of land that must serve as a jetty.

"Busy place," I remarked to no-one in particular while looking out across the same harbor that served ancient Delos eons before. "Wonder what the locals think of all this congestion?"

"The locals, such as they are, live mostly from Mykonos," one of what I considered the arty women, Susan March from London, told me from her place nearby. I'd met her briefly at the lunch buffet earlier and identified her as my tribe. Attractive in a wildly individual way, she wore a long tunic over white capris with a silk scarf covering her curly blond hair. Her friend, Renata, standing on her other side, was short, bountiful and bodacious with a shape that filled her short, tight shift with back capri-length leggings worn beneath. They both looked fantastic with a style all their own. "No one inhabits the island except caretakers and the occasional archaeological party, but the place still sees plenty of tourists now that people are traveling again. I'm Susan, by the way. I've seen you around ship."

We chatted for a few moments where I learned that she and her part-ner, Renata, were on their dream cruise together.

"We've been trying to do this for years," Renata told me, leaning forward, "but it never worked out. Once we were both double-vaxed, we booked."

"I know the feeling," I enthused. "Escape to sunshine and ocean. Is this your first trip around the islands?"

"First trip by sailing ship," Susan said. "We were going somewhere every year before Covid struck but nothing quite this luxurious. We decided to treat ourselves. Anyway, the congestion should clear out once we enter the park. We're following the introductory route today."

Renata read from the brochure. "First the Sacred Way, past the sanctu-aries of Apollo, Artemis and Leto, beside the Sacred Lake, onto the Terrace of the Lions, and then we finish off at the museum."

"Sounds fantastic," I said.

"Tomorrow there will be time for everyone to amble about and sense the vibrations." Nick had appeared beside us. "Excuse us ladies" he said as he lead me away. "Phoebe, if you feel something significant today, raise your hand," he whispered. "I plan to make a quick stop on the way back to the harbor as a test." With that, he turned and dashed towards the passengers lining up for the tender. Giorgi passing me as he headed for the boat, tipped his hat, and winked.

Peaches, who followed close at my heels, leaned toward me. "Did I really just hear Nick say 'feel the vibrations'?"

Before I could respond, a crew member began calling for group A to take a lifejacket from the selection hanging on the rack provided, take a name tag, as many bottles of water as desired, and to board the boat. That group included us, the Roses, Renata and Susan, the Jenkins family, and Mr. and Mrs. Wong. Nick was with the second passenger group, leaving us with a crew member who introduced himself as Ari, short for Aristotle, he said, who ushered us to our seats while Giorgi manned the steering wheel and revved the engine. Once all safely settled, we puttered across the harbor towards the shore.

"Isn't this exciting?" Linda Jenkins enthused next to me. "I'm just so thrilled to see this place."

"Not much to see from what I can tell," son Luke grumbled. "Nothing but a bunch of old rocks."

"You like rock, Luke, remember? At least the hard kind," his sister Rebecca chided.

"Stop being such a pain," his mother told him. Open your mind to new experiences."

Twenty minutes later, we were standing on shore waiting for the second shuttle to arrive after leaving our lifejackets in the care of a crew member. I slathered myself with sunblock and remained safely under my sunglasses and hat. Greece like most of southern Europe had had a brutally hot summer and though autumn was cooler, the eye in the sky seemed no less intense to me as a pale, redheaded Londoner.

"Feel anything yet?" Peaches whispered.

I gazed down at the ground below my feet. "Hot." I took another sip of from my own water bottle while tucking away the one Ari had handed out. "Apollo definitely reigns here."

Peaches studied our surroundings. "The climate reminds me of home only dryer. I could use a bit of jungle right now. So, was this god of the sun a bad boy in Greek mythology, too? I just remember seeing paintings of him riding chariots across the sky. Always wanted one of those, preferably a twin-seater with a smoldering god of my own installed."

I stuttered mid-gulp. "All the gods and goddesses were both good and bad, like we said, but Apollo was probably one of the better ones, morally speaking. I had a crush on him as a kid after reading all about him in my parents' encyclopedias. Those sets were well-illustrated with Greek and Roman art, I can tell you, with lots of naked god statues to whip up the hormones. Anyway, it was only later that I realized that these hot gods would probably have made horrendous boyfriends, golden chariots not withstanding."

"Figures."

We watched as the second batch of Sylvan Seas passengers made their way towards us, their orange lifejackets brilliant against the blue backdrop. After our group had gathered complete, Nick and Ari led us past the line-ups snaking beside the ticket office and through the gates to our white minibus.

Despite my relief at having bypassed the queues, I was equally glad to climb under the shade of the bus's blue and white striped awning. We were introduced to the driver, Leander from Mykonos, while Peaches and I headed to the rear where we could better study the others.

"Apparently, we are the anointed ones to get this bus ride around. Usually vehicles are not permitted but the ship pulled strings," we heard one of the other passengers remark.

"That means we'll probably be blessed by dirty looks by the hot and bothered strolling around," another remarked.

Peaches and I watched the brothers Tsaoussis recently from Athens climb on. Both actually hailed from England, we'd learned, but were taking an extended vacation with family in Greece. Brent and Robert, in insurance and retail respectively, were both unemployed after having lost their jobs after Covid. They appeared comfortably well-off, nevertheless.

"Ready for the rock of ages, friends?" Brent, lean, fit, and thirtyish sporting a clean-shaven face in contrast to his older brother's bushy beard and chunkier build, called out as he took his seat beside his brother.

"Rifle through their stuff tomorrow when you search their cabin," I whispered to Peaches. "They were late bookers."

"Maybe their family bought them tickets to get them out of their hair," Peaches hissed back. "I'll rifle thoroughly."

Up front, Nick had manned the mic as the tour officially began. First, he launched into a summary of the island's history while the bus lurched into action. Delivered with passion and verve, Nick's lesson was anything but dry though the landscape around us seemed brutally so. I gazed out at the rocky landscape on an island only 5 kilometers long, parts of which looked positively desolate. No other buses kept us company on the road but plenty of foot traffic could be seen following the prescribed route either with guides or on their own.

"Do you think it's easy being an ancient citizen of such a wealthy and sacred city?" Nick was saying, "Not so. Your safety depended on who your allies were. Delos had no armies of her own so she relied on the protection of others, mostly powerful fortified cities. In the age of warring states and empires—"

"We're still an age of warring states and empires. Haven't you heard?" Brent countered. "Watch the news, dude."

"Dr. Dude, you mean," Nick said with a grin. He knew how to work the loudmouths while maintaining his professional dignity. "Right you are, Brent, and just like today, who you align with can determine your fate. At one point in its long history, Delos chose Rome as an ally for obvious reasons. Could one find a more powerful protector in the ancient world at the time? By 100 BC, the power of Athens had already eroded and become absorbed by Rome's imperial might. Delos had gone from being a revered sacred island to a thriving city of commerce and politics—always dangerous in the age of warring kings and empires. She was, as we say, a sitting duck."

"And the sitting duck got its feather's plucked, right?" Brent again. There's one in every group.

"She did. In 88 B.C., King Mithridates of Pontus sacked the city, slayed thousands of its inhabitants, took many more into slavery, and plundered the treasuries, leaving behind a ghost town vulnerable to looters for the next thousand years. Rome was too far away to respond, and what you see today is what's left of her picked-over bones."

As the bus rumbled over the dirt road towards first stop, all I could do was think of how fragile our civilizations were, no matter what the century, what the age. The physical structure of our imposing buildings only imparted an illusion of permanence. No physical structure withstands time, nothing is permanent. As the ancient Greek Heraclitus stated: *There is nothing permanent except change.*

But the past still lived in the imagination, in mine at least. I could dream of the marble buildings that had once covered the island in gleaming white majesty as I glimpsed the occasional sculpture rearing among the ruins. In my mind's eye, I saw what it must have looked like three thousand years ago as a bustling epicenter of the ancient world—people in tunics and togas bearing baskets of food and lugging carts, children running down the street, groups of robed citizens standing in the plaza discussing politics and commerce. But that was imagination playing through history, nothing more. What I could not imagine was having some kind of psychic event that would unlock the secrets of a hidden temple or a mysterious key. In the burning light of reality, that struck me as foolish.

We drove past the remains of temples as Nick continued with his "elevator" version of history—everything neatly packaged into a vivid spiel bout the rise and fall of this ancient city state with plenty of interruptions and questions by his audience along the way, mostly by the Tsaoussis brothers, both of whom knew enough history to let everybody know what they knew.

The bus stopped often so that we could disembark long enough to stand among the tumble of stone, look out towards the sea, and dream of the past. One stop landed us beside the temple of Leto and another along the Sacred Way where we could gaze at the lion sculptures lining the road and imagine the grand processions that must have once trod that path. Though those statues were replicas, we would see the real ones later in the museum.

We stopped by the Sacred Lake. "Here, according to the story of Artemis and Apollo, was where the twin gods were born and thus revered as a significant part of the Sacred Way," Nick told us as we gazed out at the round shape piled with rubble with a single palm growing from its center. "Water is sacred to the ancients, symbolic of the womb itself. Unfortunately, the water here was drained about a hundred years ago because the waters bred malaria that was making the excavators sick." Nick gazed mournfully towards the rubble-filled bowl as I stepped up beside him.

"I can imagine how beautiful Delos must have once been," I told him softly. "The pools, the buildings, the art, and the entire sense of a community gathering to celebrate spirit as well as for trade and worship,"

"It was all about celebrating beauty, art, and life," Peter Rose said huffing up beside us. "An old man like myself could partake of those waters, leave an offering to Artemis, and walk away feeling stronger and younger, if only in his mind."

I glanced up at him as he stared at the empty lake, his jaw clenched and one hand gripping his cane with whitened knuckles.

"We can still absorb the power of mind over body, can't we?" I said. "The power for this kind of miracle exists solely within ourselves. We only need something to unlock our inner flow, whether it be a sacred site, art, music—something." I hadn't meant to say that. It's not that I didn't believe it but I had never spoken those words aloud.

He gazed down at me and even with our sunglasses, I felt a brief connection. "Yes, indeed, Phoebe. We all have the power."

The exchange left me shaken but I wasn't sure why. Maybe the sun, not so much hot as intense. I reached for my water bottle, found it empty and opened one the ship provided.

"Where was the water source come from?" Renate asked, stepping between Nick and Peter.

"We believe it came from the same sacred spring that flows beneath the island, the very one that feeds the Minoan Fountain which you will see next," Nick replied. The spell broken, we returned to the bus and soon stopped beside the Minoan Fountain to stare at the rectangular-shaped foundation still bearing three broken columns with eleven steps leading down to a now sludgy pool.

"This is the first sacred spring and central to the life and existence of the people of Delos. It was once covered and guarded as the life-force for the people of Delos. Consider this: the fountain dates back deep into antiquity, perhaps as far back as 3,000 B.C.," Nick told us. "The foundation alone can be traced to the 6th century B.C. and its name connects it to the Minoans making this a Bronze Age site."

And I knew that Delos was once an active trading outpost for the Cretans, the links and connections among the ancients influencing the cultures. By now, I was feeling unaccountably weary, something I blamed on the sun.

Finding a bit of shade by a scrubby tree, I checked my phone for messages from Evan and found one from Zann, instead. Again, she asked where I was and though I didn't answer her directly, I did inquire if she knew of any archaeological digs in process on Delos. We'd be sailing off to the next stop before she could follow me here, should that her intention. I just needed information.

"Feel anything?" Peaches whispered, sidling up to me.

"Still nothing," I told her and took another swig of water, "And still hot. Besides, these jumble of personalities are distracting."

"Probably staring at a phone won't inspire the vibe or whatever."

She was right there even if mine was no ordinary phone. I tucked it away in my pocket.

Back in the bus, the tour continued like a film on slow motion with a discordant soundtrack rolling along in the background. This was not my idea of the ideal history tour but a common part of the packaged experience, none the less. That didn't mean that I wasn't learning something but I was beginning to feel unaccountably weary.

"Is that what I think it is?" Peaches was indicating the remains of a gigantic phallus perched on a square pediment ahead.

"In ancient Greece, the phallus was associated with Dionysus, god of fertility and wine," Nick was saying into the mic, "but the phallus was also the symbol of good fortune. Look around you, my friends," he continued, "try not to make assumptions about this culture based solely on our own. Eros, the God of love, hung out with Aphrodite, goddess of love, their passion being the fuel for humanity's continued existence. Our view of sexuality is still influenced by puritanical beliefs of procreation as being 'dirty' or 'sinful'. The ancients had no such notions of the human life-force. The Greeks saw love and lust as entwined sacred energies and worshipped it as fuel for rebirth."

"That explains the rape and abduction part," Peaches whispered. I only smiled and continued gazing out the window, thinking of Evan in ways that just made me hotter.

"Here is a culture so far beyond ours in certain areas that we realize that they have preceded us in their wisdom," Nick was saying.

"Consider this: music therapy was commonly practiced, as was art therapy."

At last the bus lurched to a stop beside the museum. Nick announced: "We'll have 45 minutes here and we are requested to turn off our phones to avoid the annoying rings that pester museum visitors."

Everyone muted their devices, after which we tumbled out of the bus glad to be able to stretch our legs. That is, all except Peter Rose who called for Ari to fetch him a wheelchair.

Inside, the museum was fascinating, the way I find all museums absorbing but this one especially so after the drive-through introduction. Here I saw the real statues of the replicas we viewed earlier plus other artifacts I could study for hours.

"What do you think, Phoebe?" Nick asked, sidling up to me as I stood admiring the statue of Boreas and Orythyia. .

I turned to face him. "Delos is amazing, but I didn't experience an 'event'. This isn't the way my gift works, Nick. Sorry."

"The conditions are probably all wrong—too much fractious energy with the tourists crawling everywhere, which is distracting. Before we head back to the boat, I've asked Leander to take a short detour up one of the dirt roads not accessible to the public to a stunning view point. It's strictly out of bounds since there's an active archaeological dig in process up that way but there is also a large abaton so I'm hoping that if you just stand inside for a few minutes, you may experience enlightenment."

And now I was to experience enlightenment along with a miracle. "Won't the others notice my absence?" I asked.

"I'll arrange a distraction while you climb into the enclosure."

"Climb into the enclosure?"

But Nick was already rushing over to help Peter Rose who was now waving at a mosaic with his cane while Peaches cautioned him to keep the stick to himself. Heather Rose stood, apparently entranced by a reconstructed amphora nearby, her back turned to her husband.

By now, I was weary, but more from my companions than the historical remains. I left the museum to stand outside, surprised to find that the wind had picked up and that the sun had sunk low in the sky, leaving me standing in the dying light of Delos while the breeze chilled my skin.

"Apparently the last ferry leaves in 15 minutes," Susan said joining me while her partner Renata took a seat on the steps, one hand holding down her hat.

"Pardon?" I asked.

"That's why everyone but us has gone."

For the first time I noticed that we were alone except for Leander and Ari standing by our bus. "That explains the sudden quiet."

She laughed. "Exactly. Nice, isn't it? Everybody's off to the harbor so they won't get stranded." She peered towards the water. "The wind has certainly picked up. Hope nobody gets seasick heading back to Mykonos in those smaller boats."

I followed her gaze. "It really is getting choppy."

"It's the time of year," Renata told me, still holding her hat. "In the fall the winds can get pretty intense. We vacationed in Mykonos this time of year once and on some days it was bloody unpleasant."

"We'd rather that than the heat," Susan said, nodding her partner. "On chilly days, we just hung out at the spa, remember, dear?"

Renata chuckled. "I had more massages in one week than I'd had all year."

I kept staring out towards the ferry making its way back to Mykonos, thinking of how Delos had once been a center of art in the ancient world with celebratory events, competitions, music, dance, and choral groups all gathering to fill the air with dance and song. I could almost hear the music of the ages. Now it was nothing but a tumble of remains baking in the sun.

"Oh, good. Here we go." Renata climbed to her feet and turned expectantly as our fellows wandered out of the museum. Closing time at last.

Ari began ushering us onboard the bus while passing out more bottles of water at the door. Nick dashed away to assist the entry process while Peaches apparently had been commandeered by Peter Rose to help him board. He seemed to be clinging to her arm now chatting away, which left me to sit in the empty seat beside Heather who stared into space sourly.

"Did you enjoy that?" I asked, trying to make conversation.

"About as much as I enjoyed the other three times we visited Delos, though Dr. Palos is a lively enough character."

I tried to draw her out about her past experiences but that was useless. Heather had sunk into some taciturn state while casting disapproving looks at Peaches and her husband in the seats across the aisle from ours.

Surely she didn't think Peaches had designs on her husband? By now, I just wanted to escape everybody.

The bus pulled away, abruptly leaving the marked road to bump its way upwards to the rocky hills. Several minutes later when we were up on one of the highest points of the island as the bus lurched to a stop.

"Here's one of the best vistas on the Delos that you'll see and you, my friends, will experience it a few hours before sunset, too," Nick announced, "Enjoy the view. Not everybody gets to be here this late in the day. I've talked my friend Leander here into letting you off long enough to take some photographs. Please be back on the bus in 15 minutes. They don't like us hanging around too much after closing."

If anyone noticed his rushed tone, they didn't let on. Everybody climbed out but Peter and Heather Rose. "I have had quite enough of old stone and bones for one day. I shall join my husband and rest," Heather muttered as I left to join the others.

I stepped up to Peaches. "Got commandeered, I see."

"Peter wouldn't leave me alone," she whispered. "Wherever I went, he went, and insisted that I help him at every opportunity. Don't trust him. I'm going through his cabin thoroughly tomorrow."

Ari soon began leading everyone to a viewing spot while Nick took my arm and lead me in the opposite direction, Peaches at our heels.

"It's just up this path here," he said. "The biggest abaton on the island, one said to have been the site of many miracles of stunning proportions and once attached to a small temple. Here, away from the others, I'm hoping you'll experience something."

I looked over my shoulder at the rest of the group standing with their backs to us, staring out to sea. Peaches caught my eye and shrugged. Nobody seemed to notice us leaving.

Turning back to the rocky path, I focused on keeping my footing as we trudged over broken pieces of marble and through tufts of brittle grass until we arrived beside a low wall. We stared.

"That's it?" Peaches asked.

Nick held up his hand. "Respect, please. Phoebe, allow me to help you inside and then we'll leave you for a few minutes of silence. We won't be far away."

"Leave her? No way. I'm not taking my eyes off her for one millisecond. I—" Peaches began.

"Peaches, please," I said, touching her arm. "I'll be right here. Look." He pointed to a spot not more than a few yards away.

While they watched, I tossed my bag in and climbed over the low wall and dropped into a grassy enclosure no wider than six by eight. The top of the wall reached my my nose, giving me a clear view of my companions gazing back. "Five minutes, tops." I held up one hand and wiggled my fingers. "All I'm going to do is stand here for a few moments and see if I can feel anything. Where's the danger in that? Now go wait with Nick, okay?" The sooner I got this over with, the better. I was so not into it by then.

Peaches scowled, turned on her heels, and strode off to stand behind a hunk of marble that must have once been a pediment for some massive structure. They were perhaps fifty feet away. "Can you hear me from here?" she called.

"Loud and clear," I called back.

"But you can't see me, right?" she asked.

"Nope."

"Nick, get your butt over here." Nick scrambled over to join her. "There." I heard her say. "Now start communing with the ancients or whatever you do and if you need us, we're right here."

I turned away to stare into the space now clotted with stark shadow that did not appear the least bit inspiring. It reminded me of my late father's garden back home—neglected, woebegone, and strangely depressing like the erosion of lost potential where a once-glorious bounty had gone to seed. Yet the lack of chattering people and Nick's voice going on and on was a welcome respite. Breathing deeply, I tried to get in touch with the ancients in some deep down part of myself. But they weren't talking and I was tired of trying to listen.

Wandering over the uneven ground, I mused over what miracles a long ago citizen may have experienced there. Did they find the cure for a rare disease, throw away their crutches to walk where previously they could not, or was this the kind of miracle that saw visions and witnessed the future?

When I reached the opposite wall, I reached out to touch the stone thinking that it had probably been stuccoed once, maybe even painted with vivid frescos. As much as I longed to experience the past, my flash insights remained locked away.

I stifled a yawn. Turning, I made my way towards another wall, tripped, and fell hard on the stony ground. Unhurt, I rolled over on my back to stare straight up towards the deep blue zenith.

The last thing I remembered was thinking that Boras probably flew up there looking for maidens to steal away with into the clouds...

9

"Phoebe, where the hell are you?" Peaches calling.

I sat up and stared straight head. Nothing but a dark mass surrounding me—shadows, no, *walls*. Above me a deep blue sky pricked by a single star but with still plenty of light in the sky. Where the hell was I?

"Phoebe McCabe?" I heard someone call.

"Phoebe!" Peaches again.

"Phoebe, where are you?" A frantic-sounding Nick.

"Over here!" I called.

"Over where?" They were getting closer.

I looked around. "I have no idea."

Suddenly, there were heads—Peaches, Nick, and two others whose faces were too deeply shadowed for me to recognize at first, all staring at me from over a wall, maybe. As my head began to clear, I realized that Peaches was climbing in followed by Brent Tsaoussis.

"She's here! We found her!" That was Brent. In seconds he was crouching beside me, Peaches beside him, nudging him away. "You alright?"

"Phoebe—are you okay?"

"Sure," I said. Why wouldn't I be?

"Get back, I said," Peaches told Brent. And then to me: "What happened?"

"Nothing" I said, puzzled. "Why all the excitement?"

Nick was ordering the others to stay out of the enclosure as even more faces crowded around. It felt as if I were in a cage.

"What the hell happened?" Peaches demanded again.

I stared up at her worried face, confused. "Nothing, I said." I struggled to get up but she held me back.

"What do you mean 'nothing'? You disappeared for like almost forty minutes. Don't you remember?"

"No," I whispered. "I must have fallen asleep."

"Let us through," a woman said with an Italian accent. "We are doctors."

I looked over to where the doctor from Milan was climbing over the wall to get to me, her physician husband following after. Brent and Peaches stepped back.

"Here," she said kneeling beside me. "Do you have headache, dizziness, confusion?" I welcomed her calm, professional tone next to everyone's hysteria and her hand on my forehead was gentle.

"Confusion," I decided. "I think I fell asleep."

"I hear no mumbling," her husband said from my other side. Nick was standing outside the enclosure still playing crowd control. "But best not to rule out a stroke," Dr. Bergoggones squeezed my hand. "We must get you to the ship. Can you follow my finger?" He was passing his digit before my eyes.

"Yes, of course." I fought the urge to slap his hand away. This was getting ridiculous.

"Do you feel well enough to stand?" the other Dr. Bergoggones asked.

"Let me try," I said. Struggling to stand even with the two of them propping me up on either side left me feeling unsteady.

They helped me to navigate the uneven ground until we reached the wall where Peaches elbowed Brent aside to help me climb over. "I can manage by myself," I griped, annoyed by all this attention. So what if I fell asleep? It happens.

Before I could utter another word, Peaches leapt over the wall and picked me up in her arms as if I were a toddler and proceeded to carry me downhill toward the bus, the others following.

"Stop this!" I protested. "I can walk."

"Doesn't look that way to me," she muttered. "Been out of my skin looking for you."

"Sorry," I said.

Nick was following close behind carrying my bag, the two doctors scurrying to keep up. "Phoebe, we looked all over for you but you were gone," he said in a frantic whisper.

"But I was just in the abaton where you left me," I reminded him.

"Not the same abaton," Peaches said between her teeth.

I looked over her shoulder back the way we had come, not recognizing the terrain. To the left, I could just see the edge of the enclosure I had climbed into earlier but that was not in the same direction. "But I...wasn't up there. I was over there. But you know that; you two were waiting for me not far away."

"That's what we thought, too." Peached voice was tight. "But that's not where we found you. Somehow you managed to get somewhere else."

As we descended the hill towards the bus, I realized how low the sun had sunk in the sky. Other passengers were standing outside the bus with many others coming from different directions, all part of some makeshift search party.

Bai Wong waved at me in delight while her husband scurried behind. Susan and Renate, the Jenkins, the two brothers, as well as the doctor spouses were at our heels while the other passengers now waited beside Leander with the bus. Judging from the looks of excitement and concern I read on everybody's faces, my absence certainly had livened up the tail end of the tour.

"Are you okay?" Susan asked, slipping up beside me.

"Fine," I said. "I just fell asleep."

"Oh, I get that. It's been an exhausting day, right? It's the sun." She was just being kind as if it was perfectly natural for a tour participant to crawl off into a sacred site for a bit of a nap. Now I just felt foolish.

As we approached the bus, I demanded that Peaches put me down, and something in my tone prompted her to do just that. That left me standing by the door of the bus facing Leander and Ari, both of whom stepped up to pat me on the back, asking if I was all right, while offering me more water.

"I'm fine, fine," I insisted.

"The ship waits for us. We must hurry," Leander said, looking agitated.

Meanwhile Ari passed his cell phone to Nick. "The captain," he said. Nick took the phone and turned away for a lively discussion in Greek.

I boarded the bus, passing the Dexters and the Roses as well as a few passengers who either decided not to join the search or had arrived back to the bus early. The faces greeting me ranged from concerned, relieved, to scowling in Heather Rose's case. I apologized profusely as I stumbled down the aisle.

"My dear Phoebe," Peter Rose said as I passed, "We were very worried. Apparently you had disappeared."

"Sorry to alarm you and hold up the bus but I'm fine," I assured him hurrying towards the back seat. "I just fell asleep." It may have been an unsatisfactory line but that was about the only thing that made sense to me at the moment.

The doctors tried to get me to lay down on the back seat but I wasn't having it. "Thank you very much, both of you. I appreciate your assistance but I'm fine," They sat nearby though Peaches claimed the closest spot.

"I'll just sit up. See? All good."

The physician duo exchanged glances. "We'll see when back on board," said Maria Bergoggones. "We will confer with the nurse."

We had a ship's nurse who I had seen from a distance but had yet to meet. Apparently in the event of a serious medical issue, the ship was instructed to dock at the closest port to seek medical attention for the ailing passenger. I flatly refused to fit into that category.

Meanwhile, remaining passengers and crew began piling on board. The last to board was Nick looking worried as he sat in the single seat behind the driver, picked up the mic, and announced: "All's well, folks. I apologize for the disruption but our missing passenger has been located safe and unharmed. Thank you to all who helped us in our search. Now, let's get back to the ship, shall we?"

There was a chorus of applause accompanied by a whistle, probably from young Luke who seemed to enjoy the excitement. Seconds later, the bus trundled down the hill and across the stark landscape towards the harbor where at the gates, staff were waiting. Obviously, they couldn't lock up until we were off the premises. The bus was to be parked somewhere on site, I realized, leaving the rest of us to walk too to catch the tender.

The wind had whipped the harbor into froth and chop as the sun skimmed the swells. I could see Giorgi waiting on the jetty. At the sight of us, he ground his cigarette under his shoe and turned to face us.

I escaped my caretakers to scramble ahead so I could reach him first. "Did you see anything?" I whispered when I arrived, Peaches right beside me.

"I wait for you here entire time. Must stay with boat. What happened?" he asked, his shrewd face studying me carefully.

"Quickly, before they come, what have you learned?" The two doctors were almost upon us but Peaches strode towards them to hold them off.

"Nightwatchman on ship says that on last trip to Delos, he see lights on island. At night when no lights should be there, see? I ask questions, I work for you."

"Good, so keep doing it. What kind of lights? How were they so odd?"

"Sailing around parts of island when no boat should be, Paolo thinks. Very strange. He tell captain but," he shrugged. "No interest. If you need boat, there is inflatable in hold. I could take you at night. You just ask." He was thumbing his chest.

Over my shoulder, Peaches was linking arms with the two doctors as Heather Rose marched past them.

"I'll call if I need you," I whispered and then turned away to stare at the Sylvan Seas which now struck me as a welcome refuge from all these personalities.

Heather Rose strode up beside me with a handful of others.

"I shall be seasick," she complained while staring morosely at the choppy water.

"I get you there fast," Giorgi assured her. "No problems."

"It's not far, anyway. Don't worry," Renate said, coming up on her other side trying to assure her. Meanwhile Mai Wong offered Heather a ginger chew which she accepted with a nod of thanks.

Despite my protests, I was awarded first shuttle again accompanied by a handful of others including Peaches, the two doctors, the Roses, the Dexters and their grandchild, the Jenkins, and the Wongs. Nick and Ari stayed behind with the remaining passengers as Giorgi maneuvered the swell to deliver us back to the Sylvan Seas. I kept my face turned towards the water pretending not to hear anybody's questions or well-meaning comments. By now all I wanted was to be alone.

Captain Adamos was waiting on the launch deck, Leo by his side. It was the first time I'd witnessed a scowl fused with a smile but the captain managed to pull off both simultaneously. Leo just nodded as if communicating that he was on my side, which I seriously doubted.

"Ms Baker, we have been most concerned when we heard that you were missing," the captain said.

"She fell asleep, okay?" Peaches told him. "Simple."

"But I must know the details for my report," Adamos insisted. "We take the disappearance of our passengers very seriously. Dr. Paulos informs me that he was conducting research."

"Not him, but me," I said. "Trust Dr. Paulos to be so gallant but it was I who insisted on crawling inside the abaton as an experiment. I wanted to see if I could witness a miracle and I did: I fell asleep finally after not sleeping well for days. Sorry for the bother. It won't happen again."

"But, of course. We are all relieved that you are safe," Leo intervened. Grin. Grin. "Perhaps after you rest, we can discuss further?"

"I'm sure that won't be necessary."

Despite the veiled pleasantries, I knew a thorough interrogation was planned but the doctors Bergoggones gave me a reprieve by insisting that I accompany them to Nurse Scala. That left the captain to request a moment to discuss my disappearance at a more opportune time.

A half an hour later, I was sitting in the sick bay while the two doctors and a lively grey-haired Nurse Scala discussed my vitals as if I weren't sitting right there. For a moment I sat studying my companions, thinking what an odd grouping we made: the two designer-clad physicians— diligent, eager to help for what I assumed were professional reasons even though they were on vacation, and the pragmatic, non-nonsense nurse.

"She has no fever," Scala said, a grey-haired woman in a white lab coat whose smiling face did nothing to detract from her authority. Her sickbay, her patient. There was no doubt who was in charge here. "Miss Baker's pulse is fine, her vitals excellent, so she will be released and I will check on her later. I see no need to hold her longer."

"A sudden collapse could be signs of other issues," Roberto Bergoggones stated. He had two tiny wings on his snazzy red sneakers—how fitting. Hermes, the herald of the gods, wore wings as his emblem, too.

"Possibly neurological," Maria offered. "We would be happy to take her onshore to visit a clinic."

How far does dedication go? Otherwise, they were, I decided, the most exquisitely dressed tourists, let alone doctors, I had ever witnessed—all understated elegance every inch of the way. Fashionable and competent. I might be able to pull off competent but forget the fashionable part.

"She did not collapse," the nurse said.

"I fell asleep," I said, not that anyone was listening.

"Nonetheless, I would advise transporting her to Athens for further tests," said the other Dr. Bergoggones, standing tall in his Emprorio Armani tee shirt and linen pants. Amazing what one focusses on in times of stress.

Then I finally clued into what he was saying. "No," I said, standing up. "Absolutely not. Thank you both for all your help, and Nurse Scala, I agree wholeheartedly: I'm fine."

And with that I strode from the room, past Peaches who had been leaning against the corridor wall, and headed straight for the elevator. Seeing it the floor light indicating it was two levels down and crawling, I veered for the stairs, instead.

Peaches strode up beside me. "What's the verdict?" she asked.

"Alive until further notice. I'm done and heading for our cabin."

Peaches took it upon herself to ride shotgun for me by smiling at everyone who approached along the way while keeping them at bay. She almost elbowed a couple of well-wishers aside.

"Nosy," she whispered to me.

"Curious," was my reply.

Once we reached the sanctuary of our cabin, I flopped on the couch and shielded my eyes with my arm.

"What really happened?" Peaches asked while scanning the room for bugs.

"The last thing I recall, I had tripped inside the abaton and just lay there for a moment taking a break, just musing. Obviously, I fell asleep."

"Obviously. And obviously you levitated in your dream-state 100 yards in the opposite direction to land in another abaton."

I sat up. "Is that really where I ended up?"

Peaches faced me. "That's why we couldn't find you at first. Nick and I waited a few minutes and then called for you with no response. I even rang your cell. Didn't your phone ring?"

Then I remembered. "I put it on Do Not Disturb at the museum and forgot to disengage it."

"Well, damn."

I pulled my phone from my pocket and switched it back to active.

"So twenty minutes later we found you on your back in another abaton maybe 100 yards further up the hill, your bag by your side."

"I have no memory of going anywhere but I must have been sleepwalking. The strong sunlight was getting to me."

"It was late afternoon. What does your phone say?"

"Nothing," I said, staring at it. "I guess the intruder alert doesn't activate when in airline mode. I doubt anybody touched it, anyway, though maybe they touched me."

"Are you saying someone might have moved you?" Peaches demanded.

"Well, if I didn't sleepwalk or levitate, somebody must have," I said.

"Around here, who knows? But how come you didn't wake up when this somebody relocated you?"

We stared at one another uncomprehendingly for a few seconds, at least until we heard a knock on the door.

Seconds later, a haggard-looking Nick entered and collapsed into one of the chairs. "I've just been dressed down by the captain for taking a detour. Thank you for saying it was your idea, Phoebe, but Adamos isn't buying it. He knows I do 'unconventional research'". He added air quotes. "I'm under advisement that further employment with this line may not be forthcoming should this occur again. What happened, Phoebe?"

I told my story once again.

"And you really have no memory of moving?"

"Not a thing," I assured him.

"Maybe you sleepwalked."

"Maybe, though I'm not prone to it."

He leaned forward, a touch of his innate positivity sparkling through. "A miracle! Don't you see?"

"No, I don't see. That was not my idea of a miracle," I said. "That was my idea of a mystery."

"What was the last thing you remember?" he asked.

"She was musing about the god of the north wind blowing across the sky plucking naked maidens from the glades. Are you going to suggest that Borax *blew* her to the other abaton?" Peaches demanded.

"Borax?" he asked, puzzled.

"She means Boreas," I clarified. I shot Peaches a warning look. "I did not experience a miracle, Nick. Maybe I did sleepwalk, though that sounds highly unlikely. Where were the others when you two realized I was missing?"

"I have no idea but we need to find out," Peaches replied. "We were looking around the hillside calling your name. The others could have been anywhere."

"I called Ari to alert him that you were missing," Nick said. "He asked for volunteers to start searching. He had to remain behind with the more infirm passengers and Leander was ordered to stay with the bus, too. Those are the rules, but I'll check with Ari to see if any of the others drifted away before then. He's supposed to know where everyone is at all times. So am I, by the way."

"How well do you know Ari?" Peaches asked.

"I've met him on a couple of cruise gigs before. He's been with the line for years but I wouldn't say that I know him and Leander was just contracted as a driver for the day. I've never met him before."

"I'm guessing that whoever moved me was not on that bus but hiding out somewhere on the island. Maybe they used chloroform, though I don't have a headache or any funky after effects. On the other hand, there's a chance I was drugged." I gazed at Nick. "Can you find out more about that archaeology dig working on Delos?"

"Of course, but it looks like they've recently stopped work for the season. I made a few inquiries," Nick replied.

"Closed up for the season?" Peaches repeated, "but this is Greece."

"It still gets cold here late October. Many teams stop work and return to their offices. Our idea of cold differs from yours in England," he pointed out.

"Obviously," she muttered, "And I thought we islanders complain about the cold."

"Anyway, when in season there's always at least one site being worked on the island at any one time as well as continued exploration of known excavations," he continued. "Teams are always attempting to recover structures all over Greece,"

"As in a hidden temple of Artemis?" I asked.

"Perhaps, but they would never openly state that was their quest. Rather, they would officially say that they are excavating a previously determined quadrant where typography had indicated a structure or structures existed. I'll add that a lost temple to a secret cult of Artemis has been in the archaeological mythos of Greece for a long time," he acknowledged. "I will make enquiries."

"You do that," Peaches said, now glowering at him.

"But you don't seriously think someone from an archaeological team moved you from one spot to another?" he asked.

"Why not? It makes about as much sense as someone on this ship doing it or the god of the north wind, for that matter. I'm not ruling anything out," I said.

"If it weren't for you, this group of speculative nutcases wouldn't even know she was here, would they?" Peaches said.

Nick caught her stormy gaze and climbed to his feet. "I'm sorry about that. I'd best get right on it then."

"Does that mean you're going back to Delos tonight?" I asked as he reached the door.

He turned. "Definitely not. No one's allowed on the island at night without special permission. The archaeological team camp there when a dig's in progress and the caretakers have cottages but that's it. See you at supper? I have another lecture at 9:00 PM."

"I'm going to order room service," I said. "After all the excitement today, I'm sure my absence won't surprise anybody."

After he had gone, I turned to Peaches. "Giorgi says that lights have been reported on Delos by the Sylvan's nightwatchman in the recent past —strange lights that shouldn't be there. He saw them last trip which would have been about a week ago. Something's going on, as if we don't know that already."

"Maybe we can catch something on video. I'll rig up a security camera using our phones. It'll mean propping one of them on the balcony and using WiFi and Bluetooth to capture the signal. Ev sent me instructions. That way if there are any interesting lights on Delos tonight, we'll get it on camera." She checked her watch. "I'd better get started. I said yes to an invitation from Susan and Renate to join them for supper tonight. They'd hoped you'd come, too, but I can let them know that we can't make it."

"Send my apologies. They'll understand after today. Besides, it makes no sense for you to stay behind with me. It's not like I need a babysitter."

"You do, actually."

"I promise to stay in my cabin and knit."

"Yeah, knitting protects you against everything," Peaches muttered. "It's especially useful for strangling attackers. Or maybe you could just stab them with your needles as per Agatha Christie."

At least somebody read the classics. "I always keep my phone nearby," I assured her, "and, in case you've forgotten, have self-defense training. Besides, you could use the opportunity to suss out more information from the others while dining. You should go." Let's face it, I craved privacy.

It took awhile but I finally convinced her that I was in no risk of being spirited across the waves in the arms of a god. Besides, the arms I was anticipating were winging their way to me at that moment. A text from Evan had popped up: he was overnighting in Athens and had booked the high-speed ferry for Mykonos the next morning and from there he'd take a boat to Delos. Once he had signed in onboard the Sylvan, he'd get a tender to Delos. He estimated his arrival for about noon and would keep me appraised of his progress. I was to wait for him onboard, he said, but I thought it more strategic if I go ashore with the others so as not to rouse suspicion. In the end, he agreed as long as I remained with the group at all times.

Afterwards, I settled down on my balcony with the view of Delos, Homer open on my tablet, waiting for supper to arrive, which it did 20 minutes later. Artino was hastily despatched without having any of his many questions answered. Meanwhile, may I just say that dining while the setting sun burns molten gold behind ancient hills was a dreamy experience and that the moussaka and salad that accompanied it were equally delectable. My dinner choice was the height of Greek comfort food.

I allowed the real world in only long enough to check my messages, thinking it odd that Zann had yet to get back to me with a response re: the Delos archaeological dig question. Unsettling, but then everything unsettled me by then. I put the tablet aside and closed my eyes.

For a time, I forgot all about the stress of the last few days, the press of irritable personalities, the mysteries that seemed to be thickening around me by the minute. When the air grew too breezy, the sky too dark, and the first stars pricked the horizon, I returned to the cabin for a shower and to plan what to bring ashore the next day. Before I entered my cabin, I cast one more look behind me, in time, in fact, to see a nearly full moon rising over the sacred island, exactly the same moon as the ancients had viewed eons before.

Only when I was reorganizing the tapestry backpack for the next morning did I find the card. I pulled out the Wheel of Fortune, stared, and then flung the thing on the floor, swearing. It was all I could do to keep from stomping on it. A few minutes later, I had calmed down long enough to place the card in a formation with the others on the table. I tried organizing them in the order in which they appeared: High Priestess, followed by The Fool, followed by the Wheel of Fortune. The Magician didn't belong in the hand per se but I felt him influencing all like an image hovering above the cards. What in hell was going on?

When Peaches returned later, she found me calmly studying the cards which I'd been moving around on the table in various formations while checking my phone for possible meanings.

"I've laid them out in the order which they appeared but if there's a message here, I'm missing it."

"Shit," she muttered as the door slammed behind her. "Where did you find that one?"

"In my bag next to my water bottle. I'm guessing that the perpetrator knew enough not to try to touch my phone but thought it safe enough to touch my bag and person. He's catching on and I think he drugged me while he was at it." I looked up at her scowling face.

"We're going to get this bastard."

"Bastards. Pretty certain we're dealing with the plural."

"Right: *bastards*."

"Did you learn anything from your dinner companions tonight?" I asked as I took a picture of the cards and proceeded to tuck them away.

"Yes and no. I caught up with Nick. He had managed to grill Ari who insisted that everybody but us three were on or around the bus right up until Nick called to say that you were missing. He also found out that the archaeologist team had packed up for the season a week ago. I guess that they really don't dig around here in late October or November."

"That's hard for a northerner to grasp," I said.

"Tell me about it. So this windy, cool weather is considered frigid in the Southern Mediterranean. Anything less than burning hot days and equally balmy nights is uninhabitable. I sort of get that coming from the Caribbean but I've had time to adjust. Anyways, the point is that the team has gone for the season, end of story."

I nodded.

"So Nick tried to put a call into the head archaeologist on the Delos dig on the mainland but no one answered," she continued. "Otherwise, there was a lot of chatter over dinner, plenty of questions about your health, and Renate and Susan duo were great."

"All sounds pretty ordinary so far. Anything else?"

"Um, the Roses showed up a bit late and I swear that Heather kept her lips pursed so tightly that she needed to suck her food down with a straw. Peter just flirted with me in passing which boggles me. I mean, what's that about?"

"Maybe he has a lust on for younger women who can look down their nose at him?"

"I'd bonk him on the nose if he tried anything."

"He won't—it's all for show. Any other interesting observations?"

"Yeah, so the Tsaoussis brothers sat with the Jenkins and the Jenkins sat with the Dexters. The two designer docs swept in wearing Gucci and ordered wine right off the bat. Hope that fortified them for when Peter Rose hobbled up to their table over desert to discuss his knee." She paused. "There. Think I covered all the bases. Now I've got to get to work rigging our phones. We'll use yours as an internal intruder alert and mine for the balcony."

"Sounds good."

"Just texted Ev who gave me a few refresher tips on how to make a recording security camera. He's arrived in Athens, by the way."

"I received the same message minus the security camera part. I can't wait to see him even if the version of him I see on Delos will look like he's aged by a few decades."

"Love burns eternal."

"Oh, stop." I'd long ago given up on denying my feelings for Evan to Peaches and, anyway, she'd known long before I had. I watched as she propped her phone against the ice bucket and stepped away. "Did he tell you that he planned to meet me on Delos tomorrow?"

"He did," she said without looking up. "I told him that I didn't like it. that I intended to stay by your side no matter what. He insisted that he'd be there soon and that as long as you remain with the group—no detours, no diversions—that I should stick with the plan to search the cabins. He believes that you need to be seen on Delos so he can keep his eyes peeled for unusual activity when he arrives."

"And as bait."

She stopped to face me. "That was your idea, I understand. I strongly protested but appeared to have be outvoted—again. Still, the only reason I agreed to let you go ashore without me tomorrow is on the condition that you promise to stick with the group. No drifting away to commune with wind gods or whatever."

I slapped one hand over my heart. "Promise. I will take no chances and, anyway, I don't find the wind god all that attractive—lacks substance, in my opinion. I'm more of a Poseidon kind of girl. Anyway, I will have my stun app ready and will stick to our group until the moment I see a tall, elderly gentlemen who desires my company. He said he'd text me."

"Right. Here, check your phone one more time before I put it into active security duty. Said gentleman sent a more detailed description." She passed my cell back to me and returned to her work.

I read the message from Evan saying to look out for a grey-haired mustachioed man wearing a wide-brimmed Tilley hat, cargo pants, sneakers, and a short-sleeved shirt with an expensive camera slung around his neck—the universal definition of sexy. I was not to approach him but to wait until he texted.

After rereading the description twice, I turned to make some remark but Peaches was already in the bathroom preparing for bed. Minutes later, she emerged to finish setting up my phone which I watched with only one eye open from under the covers. I must have fallen asleep before she finished because the next thing I remembered, the intruder alerts were ringing.

Peaches and I thudded into one another in a race to our phones. The cabin was dark, the blinds drawn, with the interior phone flashing red.

"It says 'Western perimeter alert! That's the balcony!" Peaches cried.

I banged my shins on that damn table again as I pulled back the curtains. The latch was secure, the door safely locked, but in seconds I was outside where I picked up the flashing phone. I didn't even look at it before I heard the distant sound of a motor zooming away.

"Look!" It was heading away from the Delos harbor towards the other side of the island.

Peaches arrived beside me and stared. "No damn pilot lights. They are definitely up to no good."

I checked the time: 2:12 A.M..

"Get dressed," I whispered while dialing Giorgi's cell. "We're going to Delos."

10

Giorgi instructed us to meet him on the launch deck but to be careful because the night watchman prowled at 30 minute intervals, at least in theory. He told me that he'd signal us once the guy had left the lower level because he wouldn't likely make another round for a couple hours. Apparently the security guard took a smoke break on the upper prow that lasted nearly 45 minutes every night. I didn't ask how Giorgi knew all this because I was too busy congratulating myself on my euros well spent. The skipper was worth every cent.

Peaches and I hastily donned our darkest clothes, which in my case consisted of black leggings and the rasher shirt I'd hope to use for diving. She went for nightshade purple stretch everything. Soon we were prowling down the hall towards the central stairs like a pair of bizarre action heroes until Peaches came to a sudden halt just before the stairs.

"Damn! I forgot the CCT cameras." She was pointing to a security camera positioned by the central stairs.

"Can't be helped." I gazed at the round glass eye that appeared to be motion activated while remaining safely out of its sightline. I took aim with my phone fully intending to zap the camera but she stayed my hand.

"Wait. That could set off the alarm," she whispered. "Instead, we'll navigate the blind spots." She snatched a handful of brochures sitting on a nearby table and threw them towards the stairs, causing the camera to swivel in that direction. "Follow me." Which I did, sliding along the wall until we reached the next level and could scuttle down towards the launch deck avoiding electronic scrutiny where necessary.

We arrived on the lower deck to find Giorgi bent over the railing. He had already jammed something between the camera and the wall to keep all surveillance focused on a life raft far to the right. Turning, he beckoned us towards him. "Help me get boat over the side." He pointed to a black four-seater inflatable leaning against another lifeboat and the three of us soon had the thing lowered to the water using the ropes provided.

I gazed down at the rocking boat.

"Okay, so how do we get down there?" I whispered.

Giorgi, who was busy dropping two sets of paddles into the boat, one by one, turned and grinned. "Rope ladder, see?"

No, I hadn't seen but once I had, I wasted no time getting up and over the railing to begin the ten-foot climb down to the boat. At the bottom, it took a few moments to secure the inflatable as it was tethered only by the rope and bucked in the swells like an obstinate horse but I soon had it steadied against the ladder. Once the other two had climbed in, Giorgi unhooked the tether, we picked up the paddles, and started paddling.

"No lights," I cautioned. "Head around the tip of the island away from the archaeological area. That's the direction we saw the boat heading," I told Giorgi.

Giorgi and Peaches provided the paddle power while I did lookout duty and studied the map on my phone. Meanwhile, all the nightwatchman had to do was make his rounds and see that ladder dangling from the side of the boat or notice that the inflatable was missing to sound the alarm. Where was he when somebody tried to board our balcony, anyway?

"Did this security dude even see the boat that just pulled up under our balcony awhile ago or was he too busy taking his extended break?" Peaches whispered as if catching my thoughts.

"A boat came that close?" Giorgi asked.

"Yes and we caught it on camera, or what we can see of it. Looks like the bastards were trying to climb onto our deck until our intruder alert went off—makes a buzzing sound," Peaches explained. "Couldn't make out any details, though. It looked like a speedboat but they must have cut the engine when they approach."

"You have intruder alert?" It was hard to see Giorgi's face in the dark but I heard unmistakable admiration.

"On our phones."

"You ladies have interesting phones."

"Yeah, tell me about it," Peaches said as she plowed the water. The surf was choppy enough to make the going strenuous. "So aren't watchmen supposed to look out for things like that?"

"Nobody worries," Giorgi said. "No pirates here. Too much sea traffic. Paulo he does the rounds, pokes head around corners, but not too worried. I join him for smoke some nights. Good man."

I resisted commenting on the good man who couldn't properly do his job. We had just rounded a point of land in the direction that our visitors had headed. The coastline made a stark outline under the moonlight, all shadow juxtaposed against a luminous sky with moon-limned earth. No signs of life. I expected to see at least something shining up in those hills, a flashlight, maybe.

"What happened to you on Delos yesterday?" Giorgi asked after a moment.

"I fell asleep," I said, determined not to disclose just how complicated the circumstances behind that incident really were. I was working on the need-to-know principle.

"The boat definitely went in this direction," Peaches said.

"According to the map there's nothing up this way. I'm checking the satellite image and it's barren except for a few roads crisscrossing the terrain." I was studying my screen while the inflatable rolled beneath me.

"Look for a cove. There has to be one around here," Peaches said. "Those bastards had to pull in somewhere unless they're heading back to Mykonos."

"Many coves," Giorgi remarked as he maneuvered the surf. "And not smart to go to Mykonos in small boat at night." No point in me mentioning that we had done something similar a few nights ago.

"Wait, I just saw a light up there!" Peaches exclaimed.

"Up where?" I asked. We could no longer see the Sylvan now that we were sheltered by the headland but we still couldn't use our own lights in case our quarry spited us.

"Up there."

We looked to where she was pointing but could see nothing but a back mass of low hills. I checked the map again. "Was it close or far?"

"Couldn't tell," she said.

We rowed closer to shore until we saw a small crescent of sand bleached white in the moonlight. "There!" I whispered. "I see tracks!"

In minutes we had plunged up to our waists in water to drag the inflatable up to the beach. Marks in the sand indicated that someone had done something similar not long before but there was no sign of a boat. Footprints and drag marks lead from the beach towards the hills.

"There's a path there. Looks like someone picked the boat up and carried it," Peaches remarked.

"Right, so let's put ours out of sight," I said.

Within seconds we had hidden the inflatable behind a mound of boulders, readily visible to anyone intent on looking but maybe not at first glance, and scrambled up the path lit only by moonlight. Everybody remained silent until Giorgi hissed for us to stop.

"Maybe not safe for you ladies. I go ahead," he whispered thumbing his chest.

Peaches turned to him. "Thanks, bud, but that's not happening. You stay behind us and we'll continue as planned."

"Besides, we need you to be our lookout, Giorgi," I added.

He clearly wasn't happy about this arrangement but followed us without another word. You have to love men who try to be gallant regardless of the circumstances.

We continued climbing the stony path for at least five more minutes before the ground leveled out and we could see the path weaving between two large rocks. A light glowed faintly beyond and to the right. We ducked behind the boulders and peered out.

Ahead, a flat open space, surrounded by a barbed-wire fence, abutted the side of a rocky hill glowing stark in the moonlight. A flashlight appeared to be moving at the far end beyond our range of vision. We watched silently for a minute or two.

"The place is guarded," Peaches whispered, "but only one light means only one guard."

"But what is this place?" I asked. And why guard a clearing with no visible structure? "Wait, there must be an entrance somewhere in that hillside."

"Footprints go through gate and disappear," Giorgi whispered.

We followed his finger to the gate ahead clearly outlined in the moonlight. A small sign posted in Greek hung on the wire fence.

"What does it say?" Peaches asked.

"Keep out," came Giorgi's reply.

"As if," she muttered. Turning to me, Peaches said: "What if you disarm the gate while I disarm the guard?"

"Go for it," I agreed. "He probably has a gun so be careful. Set the app to stun, remember."

While she crept along the shadow towards the light, I tugged Giorgi back behind the rock. "You stay here and watch our backs. If anyone comes or you see anything at all, you let us know, got it?"

I could feel his shadowed face studying me. "Who are you?"

It was only a matter of time before he asked. "Special agents," I told him truthfully.

"Like James Bond?"

Why did agents always have to be James Bond? There was more than one game in town.

"Sure," I lied, "Like Jane Bond. Now you stay here and keep your eyes peeled."

"I am your man!" he whispered. That wasn't true but appreciated the sentiment.

I stepped out into the moonlight, my phone set on the lock deactivation mode. Everything was still, only the sound of the wind and the waves beyond. In seconds, I had passed the phone over the gate and, as expected, a crackling sound followed along with a few sparks told me the electronic circuitry had been deactivated. The crackling was expected but the wailing accompanied by gun fire was not. Instinctively, I ducked.

"Watch out, he comes!" I heard Giorgi cry.

I swung towards the figure of a man running from the other direction at the same time that Giorgi scrambled out of the shadows waving his arms. I could see the gun in the man's hand, hear him calling something in Greek, see him aiming for Giorgi while Peaches ran behind him yelling for him to stop. I was switching my phone to the stun app when the guy fell to his knees before toppling face-first onto the ground.

"Bastard!" Peaches cried running up.

"Did you use stun?" I asked running up to the fallen man. Kneeling, I felt for the guy's pulse—strong, thankfully.

"That didn't even slow him down. He shot at me, missed and then took off," she panted. "This time I used a heavier charge." She swiped the gun out of his hand and shoved it into her jacket pocket while I turned the guy over.

"George Barros," I muttered, gazing at the face bathed in the moonlight. "I wondered when he'd turn up again."

"I know him," Giorgi said gazing down. "I see him hanging around dock. Always different hats and once a beard but same guy."

I had forgotten Giorgi was there. "Giorgi, next time don't come dashing out waving your arms around, okay? That's an invitation to get shot. He was aiming at you, see?"

"Luckily, the guy's a bad shot," Peaches added.

"Stay undercover and call us if you see anything," I continued without looking up. I was patting Baros down, looking for anything interesting in his pockets. "Well. look what I found." I plucked out his phone. "We'll leave it so if they track his signal, they'll think he's were he should be."

"Let's prop him against that rock over there and make it look like he fell asleep. Could buy us a couple of minutes if we need it," I suggested.

"Maybe he'll think he was dreaming," Peaches said with a grin. "I jumped out at him waving my arms and crying like an angry goddess and then shot him with my phone. Does that sound like a dream or what?"

"Inventive!" I grinned. "Maybe he'll wake up thinking he hit the ouzo too hard. Let's get back to work. The clock is ticking."

Giorgi and Peaches dragged Baros up against the rock where a propane cooker and a pile of blankets were stacked. I opened the gate and stepped into the enclosure, tracing footprints towards the hillside.

"What is this place?" Peaches asked, catching up with me minutes later.

"An archaeological dig, I think." I pointed to the tools propped in the shadows against the rocky hillside. "Somebody's camped here for an extended period of time, I'm guessing."

"But whatever they're digging for must be inside that hill," she said. "There's nothing out here."

We followed the prints around the left side of the hillside until we saw an opening covered in a thick blue plastic sheeting.

"Ta-dah," Peaches whispered. "Careful, they must be in there somewhere."

"Then why didn't they come running when the Baros bozo cried the alarm?" I asked. "If they are in there, they must be somewhere deep." Which was an unsettling thought.

"I'll go first," she said, tip-toeing towards the opening. "Me bodyguard, you priceless Phoebe."

I made a face but held back as she slowly pulled open a corner of the flap. After a few seconds of studying the darkness ahead with me hanging over her shoulder, we switched on our phone lights and stepped inside.

We were in a tunnel no more than six feet wide and six feet tall as if cut by man from living stone. It took a few seconds to grasp what we were seeing. Colorful figures jumped around us in every direction. On the right side wall, a procession of maidens danced along a path, laurel wreaths in their hair, joy on their faces, their saffron-colored robes vibrant in the sunlight. On the other side, donkeys hauled carts filled with more jubilant girls, each holding gifts and laughing as seabirds flew overhead and young men strode beside them playing musical instruments. Even the ceiling was painted in white clouds sailing against blue sky.

"Oh, my God," I whispered. "It's a procession for Artemis, goddess of young maidens. Look at them! They're all so joyful!" I leaned closer, hovering my fingers over the paint, obviously ancient yet still amazingly fresh. I could almost feel the brushstrokes. "Nobody discovered this until recently. It must have escaped the invasions, the wars, the disintegration of the eons! It's a miracle find!" I exclaimed.

"But who found it and how deep into the cave does it go?" Peaches asked, staring down the long tunnel. "A long way, by the looks of things. Can't see the end." She beamed her phone down the tunnel's throat, catching more color covering the same regularly-hewn walls as they disappeared downward.

We took a few tentative steps forwards, our feet scuffing on the sandy covering beneath our feet.

"What's on the floor?" I looked down.

"Plastic," she whispered.

In seconds, I was pulling back the covering expecting to see more frescos but finding only stone. It took a moment for Peaches and I to realize what we were looking at.

"Ancient wheel tracks grooved into the rock," she whispered.

"This is a real ancient processional road," I gasped. "This is incredible! These archaeologists have struck gold."

"Archaeologists? You mean the kind who shoot at you, try to board passenger ships, and then scuttle down a dig site to hide? No way!"

I straightened. She was right and I was letting my enthusiasm get the better of me. "But how can anybody hide something like this? The real archaeology team working on the island must know about it. You can't keep something like this a secret."

"Am I imagining things or is there a prick of light far down the tunnel?" she whispered. "Growing larger."

I stared. "Not imaging things. Let's go!"

I turned to leave but not before I took three quick photos of each side of the tunnel plus one of the ceiling. Then we scrambled out across the clearing, relieved to find Giorgi hovering by the gate looking as if a god had slapped him silly.

"Come on, Giorgi!" I cried. "Snap out of it: they're coming. Run!"

He was trying to tell us something but Peaches cut him off. "Just run!"

So we ran, all the way down the path, stumbling and recovering, and tripping again as we made our headlong rush back to the beach. When we got there, our inflatable was half in the water about to be washed away by the tide which made it easier to push it into the waves and climb onboard to paddle like mad. This time I took over rowing duty since Giorgi seemed to be in a weird state.

I dug my paddle into the water, occasionally glancing over my shoulder. A light was bobbing down the path in the hills. A shot fired into the night.

"If they hit the boat, we're toast," Peaches called. She was now propped up on one knee, war canoe style, and I joined on the opposite side thinking that looked like a good idea though a bit awkward. "Chanel the indigenous peoples and work that thing, McCabe!"

"Working it!" I cried.

We paddled like mad, one on each side, while the surf sprayed our faces and our adrenalin pulsed in overdrive.

After quick check over my shoulder, I could see three figures standing on the receding beach but no boat.

"Unless they plan to swim, we're good," I called. The next gunshots never came close and soon we were making our way around the point toward the Sylvan Seas which floated in the moonlight like the promised land. As we approached the ship, we were relieved to see no night-watchman and hear no signs of alarm, either.

"Giorgi, snap out of it!" I hissed. "We're approaching the Sylvan. What the hell's wrong with you?"

Giorgi seemed to rouse himself, snagging the tether floating on the surface and reaching for the robe ladder but all his movements seemed to be in slow motion as if on automatic, mind was elsewhere. When we had climbed to the launch deck and successfully used the pulley system to haul up the inflatable back on deck, I took the skipper by the shoulders and gave him a little shake. "Giorgi? What happened?"

"Saw body," he whispered. "Behind rocks. Dead."

✺ 11 ✺

So I dreamed again, this time of being lost in a dark tunnel where ghost-like frescoes of maidens leaped from the walls and attempted to guide me through the darkness with song and dance. But I was frightened. None of the dancers would speak to me, though I tried so desperately to communicate. Was it because I didn't know their language or because I was talking to ghosts? I remained trapped in this dark place right up until a crack of light sliced right into my eyeballs.

I bolted straight up in bed and looked around. Morning already. A cup of cold coffee sat on the table nearby and the curtains were partially open. I'd slept late, of course. Eight o'clock was late for me.

The tension drained from my shoulders when I realized that the tender to Delos wouldn't leave until ten. Plenty of time. Still, I had things to do.

Bounding out of bed, I was surprised to find the cabin empty, though a light breakfast awaited on the table along with a half-empty cereal bowl, a spoon and a partially eaten roll. I was almost dressed when Peaches burst into the room.

"Where were you?" I asked.

"Taking care of business," she replied, still wearing the same purple stretch outfit she'd been in the night before. "I stayed up after you went to bed in order to infiltrate the security feed that runs unattended in Vitalis's office. I noticed it when he was registering me yesterday. As I suspected, nobody monitors the thing. It just rewrites each night's activity the next morning. I managed to scroll through the feeds of all thirty cameras that supposedly protect this ship—nada."

"Nada as in?"

"Nada as in no strange activities around the ship's corridors after-hours were caught on camera. They picked up half of my leg in one frame, the monitor in the crew corridor caught Giorgi leaving and returning, and the launch deck recorded our voices. Don't worry, I erased everything. No exterior camera saw any boats coming or going, even the bridge cam registered nothing. Actually, I think that one's damaged judging from the crack in the glass."

"You broke into the bridge, too?"

"Of course—too easy—but the only thing I discovered there was that the security dude smokes in a corner out of view of the cameras and dozes after he completes a couple of rounds. Useless."

"Wow, I'm impressed. You said you were out twice?" I watched as she poured herself another coffee and topped off the granola in her bowl with the glass jar provided.

"Three times, really. First to check the feeds, second to nab breakfast, and third to get Nick out of bed."

"Did you even sleep last night?"

"Not much. I left that to you since I'll be swanning around the ship all day while you'll be on active duty on Delos. I'll nap after Evan arrives."

"We have to talk about the body Giorgi found," I said, taking a seat across from her, "and that incredible tunnel."

"I've been thinking about the body all morning but everything puts me right back to the problem of how we can alert the authorities without involving ourselves."

"An anonymous tip, maybe?" I suggested.

"Then everyone on board this ship who was anywhere on Delos yesterday will still be interrogated. We can't risk that, though it might happen, anyway."

"What, then? We have to do something because not only do we have George Baros waking up with some story but now those guys must know we were on-site last night."

"Yeah, trouble for sure, but they're already on to us."

A knock came at the door.

"That will be Nick," Peaches mumbled while stuffing a roll into her mouth. "Banged on his door this morning and told him to meet us here."

Nick stepped into the cabin right on cue, his face reading anxiety mixed with annoyance. "Something happened again, didn't it?" he said.

"Morning, Nick. Have a seat," I said. "Eat something. I can find another mug if you need caffeine."

"Yes, thank you." Nick sat down where I pointed and fixed Peaches with a wary eye. "I was told to come but I would have joined you without the royal command, I assure you. What happened this time?"

"Sorry to be so crabby with you earlier," Peaches explained while brushing crumbs off her stretch jacket.

"Crabby is not the term I would use. Imperious, overbearing, and unnecessarily hostile is more apt," he pointed out, sitting stiffly in a freshly ironed safari suit. I knew from his closet that he'd brought three, and I had to admit, he kept them pristine.

"Nice lexicon." She beamed. "It's just that when I told you to get your ass over here—very disrespectful and warranting another apology so consider it given—I thought you might be behind some of this stuff that's going on. Since then, I've reviewed the ship's security feed and discovered that you have not been prowling the corridors at night distributing tarot cards, moving Phoebe around, or anything else clandestine that I can see."

"You actually thought that I was behind those cards? And how could I have been involved in Phoebe's relocation yesterday when I was with you the whole time?"

I slid a mug of coffee under his nose and placed a plate nearby. "Would you like fruit? Yogurt, perhaps?"

"You could have had accomplices," Peaches pointed out before beaming one of her most charming grins, "but so far, I can find nothing to substantiate your involvement. I'm happy to announce that you've passed. As far as I can tell, you are who you seem, which is strange in itself. So, am I forgiven?"

"I have yet to hear the promised apology," he said.

"I'm sorry," she said.

"Forgive her," I added hastily, "because we have more to tell you, a whole lot more. We were on Delos last night—"

"You were on Delos last night!" he sputtered into his coffee. "What, you just swam over?"

"Don't be silly. Borax blew us across," Peaches said.

I shot her a quick glance. "We took a boat over with the help of Giorgi after someone tried to board the ship near our balcony. Forget that for a minute. It gets more interesting."

"Because we found an incredible archaeological dig in a tunnel covered in frescoes of a celebratory procession dedicated to Artemis, Phoebe thinks." Peaches was still grinning.

"What? Are you serious?" He turned to me, amazed.

I held up my phone, open on the pictures I'd taken. "Beautiful frescoes of young people in a procession leading down a tunnel, and the site's being excavated by somebody but not by any legitimate somebodies, or at least not at the moment."

"Show me! I'll arrange something with the custodians to take us there after the tour today. I can't believe my eyes! These are incredibly well-preserved, in such excellent condition. Do you know what this means?"

"Maybe, but listen, Nick, this is dangerous. The guy guarding the place was the same one stalking me on Mykonos, George Baros. By now he's come to—we zapped him—and he knows we've discovered the site. Who knows what problems that will unleash. Did you learn anything further about any active excavations in progress on Delos?"

But he was staring at the pictures, transfixed. I watched fascinated as his face flushed a warm cherub pink under his beard while he scrolled back and forth across the three frames. "My God, this is extraordinary! The dancers, the maidens—they look as fresh as the day they were painted! And the sky! And you say these were in a tunnel?"

"Yes, a tunnel in a hillside quite a distance away from any of the main sites, but, Nick—"

"The cave must be part of a hidden structure. There has long been rumor of a labyrinth of natural tunnels on these islands, possibly one of the inspirations for the labyrinth myths of Knossos. Could it be that this leads to an ancient ritualistic site? If so, it's extraordinary! Look how the maidens are wearing the saffron robes of the initiates of Artemis and it appears as though—"

"But they are Grecian not Cretan," Peaches pointed out.

"Yes, yes, but even three millennia ago the Mycenaeans absorbed the Cretans and then gave birth to Greece—long story."

"Okay, but, Nick," Peaches interrupted in her loudest voice. "Back to the present. We have problems."

"This could be the find of the century! I had no idea that they'd made such a discovery. Nothing's been leaked anywhere that I've heard and the archaeology circles in the islands are pretty tight," he enthused.

"Nick," I pressed. "About the archaeologists..." I leaned over and grabbed his wrist, which caused him to turn to me and stare unfocused. "I hear that you tried to contact the head archaeologist last night. Did you learn anything?"

He visibly pulled himself back into the present. "I couldn't get ahold of the director for the Delos excavations so I left a message on his cell. Dr. Angelopoulos was my instructor at university and a very well-respected archaeologist who landed a directorship of the Ephorate of Antiquities of Cyclades about six years ago. I idolized the guy as a young man. Anyway, since I also knew his office assistant, Eleni, I phoned her at home in Athens when I couldn't get in touch with him. That's how I learned that he'd disappeared just after they closed the dig for the season. She said he'd been on-site every day before then. Now he's—" Nick stopped, staring into space "—missing."

"When?" Peaches demanded.

"Six days ago. Surely you don't think he's behind all this? Paul Angelopoulos is an honorable man, a trait I've seen in action again and again. He would never agree to hiding a find of this significance. He values our historical legacy far too much. At a vulnerable time in my life, he was like a father to me."

Peaches and I exchanged glances.

"What?" he said, looking from one of us to the other.

"We don't think he hid anything," I said. "It's more likely that he became embroiled in a situation over which he had no control and somebody silenced him." I regretted those words the moment I spoke them.

"What do you mean 'silenced'? Surely you don't mean...?" The pink in his cheeks leeched to the pasty shade of coffee creamer.

"Giorgi saw a dead body last night—scared the bejesus out of him for all his bravado," Peaches said. "All he saw was a hand sticking out from under a pile of rocks several meters away from camp. Looks like an animal may have dug it up and dragged it out. Giorgi didn't investigate further, just took off like he'd seen a ghost. We're still trying to figure out how to alert the authorities without becoming involved."

I gazed pointedly at Peaches, hoping she'd catch the warning in my eyes, but she was on a roll. "We'd better come up with something soon. There may be other bodies. But why didn't they hide the body properly?" she asked. "It's like they were in a mad rush or something. Why not just drag it down inside the cave somewhere?"

Nick mumbled something. He was now sitting with his elbows propped on his knees, face buried in his hands. I felt like hell. We'd forgotten that this body was once a person and that this person had family, friends...

"Nick, are you all right? We have no idea if this person Giorgi saw was Dr. Angelopoulos. It could be anyone, maybe even another one of the site raiders or whoever they are. There could have been a disagreement among thieves. Let's not jump to conclusions."

He raised his stricken face. "But Dr. Angelopoulos is missing."

"Yes, but that's all we know," I said. "There may be no relation between the body Giorgi found and this man. Somebody hastily hid a body near that dig site; it could be one of their own after an argument, which is common enough among thieves."

"It's so ironic," he whispered, tears glistening in his eyes. "By the ancient laws, the dead were not allowed to be buried anywhere on Delos and desecrating a sacred site was considered the highest offense thereby calling forth the worst punishment by gods and men upon the heads of the defilers."

Peaches and I gazed at him in silence for a few seconds. "Nick, I doubt that these bastards care about gods or any law, ancient or otherwise. If they are murdering people to get at whatever lies at the end of that tunnel, they are ruled by greed alone. We need to stop them."

"Call the police," he whispered.

"Not yet," I warned. "In our business, it's not so simple. The local police are not equipped to deal with matters as complex as organized antiquities crime. By the time they figure out the enormity of what they are dealing with and call in the antiquities police or even Interpol, the site could be ruined and the perpetrators gone. No, we need to use more strategy than that."

"So we can't just go barreling up there in the daylight hours and risk chasing the bad guys away, either," Peaches added. "We're the ones in the best position to do the groundwork first, find out who's behind this, then call in the police."

"But we do need to contrive a way to get that body discovered at least," I said. "For that, including the local police will work nicely but only if we aren't implicated in the process. Imagine the mess we'd be in if it was ever discovered that we visited the island last night?"

Nick was holding my phone limply in one hand, his gaze fixed out the balcony window, staring toward the island. I leaned over and gently removed the device from his fingers as two texts had popped up onto the screen.

Turning away, I read the first one from Evan saying that he would be catching the nine a.m. high-speed ferry from Athens, which should put him on Delos around noon as anticipated.

The second came from Zann: *Took a flight from NY to Athens as soon as I got your message and then hopped over to Mykonos yesterday. Got lots to tell you. Been asking local archies I know. On the ferry to Delos now. Should be there by eleven-ish. Meet you there.*

Peaches caught my expression and removed the phone from my hands to read the message. Nick heard her swear under her breath and swung around. "What now?"

"Nothing," Peaches assured him. "Just catching up on agency business."

"Look, Nick," I said, linking my arm in his and leading him toward the door. "I'll be going over to Delos with you this morning as planned."

"But surely it's too dangerous, Phoebe," he said, his concern grooving his otherwise smooth forehead. "You need to stay here. I will hold myself accountable should anything happen to you. Please don't risk it. Had I known that my comments regarding your arrival in the alternate theorists group would cause so many problems—"

I patted his arm. "You are not responsible, at least not as far as what's going on on Delos is concerned. Whatever's happening there must have been in the works for days. And don't forget that this is the business we're in so I'm hardly unprepared."

His confusion was so visible, poor guy. We'd given him a lot to digest.

"Look," I said, "you probably need some time to collect your thoughts after we dropped all these bombs on you. I'll see you on the launch deck at 9:45, and try not to worry, okay? Remember, don't say a word to anyone in the meantime. We'll figure out how to get this matter settled. It's in our hands now."

He reluctantly left our company and strode away. "That's one sensitive guy," I remarked, shutting the door behind me. "I hope I didn't come off condescending or anything. I—"

"How in hell did Zann know we were on Delos?" She was holding up my phone.

"Because I sent her an email asking what she knows about the Delos digs yesterday. Who knew she was in Athens at the time? Looks like she caught the next ferry to Mykonos after she read my message and is on her way now."

"Shit. I'll throttle her."

"Think, Peach: besides being a pain in the neck, she's also an archaeologist with experience in Greece. Now that she's on her way, I see an opportunity waiting to happen."

"You've got to be kidding."

"An archaeologist can legitimately request to view the dig from a caretaker on Delos and maybe accidentally on purpose stumble upon the corpse. They won't allow her into the enclosure but that's not necessary and you can believe the bad guys will remain out of sight, no matter what happens. We'll make sure she's accompanied for her safety, but one way or the other, you've got to admit that she'll make the perfect foil for bringing in the local police to identify that body. That will give us at least twenty-four hours to get to the bottom of what's going on before the antiquities police arrive."

"But then the site becomes a crime scene," she pointed out.

"No matter; we can still get back over there tonight and penetrate that tunnel to the end, only this time we'll be ready and Evan will be with us."

She stared at me. "I don't like it."

"But you've got to admit that at least it's a workable plan. I'll go to Delos today and see if I can catch whoever's working against us among the passengers. I'll contact Zann, too. You search the cabins."

"What if the perps have already reburied the body?" she asked.

"That would confound everything but we still need to do something now. This is the best option. Besides, Evan's on his way."

"We do need reinforcements," she agreed.

"Right. I can't wait to see him." I hoisted up my backpack onto the bed and studied the contents, deciding to bring one of my multicolored knit scarves for a morale boost as much as anything else. "Dare I hope that this is all coming together? Soon we can find out what's going on."

I pulled up my empty water bottle, which I had bought at the Athens airport, one which sported stylized dolphins playing in curlicue waves reminiscent of Cretan frescoes. "Walking over Delos is thirsty work but I'm going to fill this baby with fizzy water from the minibar. I'm not taking chances."

12

I hadn't ruled out the possibility that I'd been drugged. Ari had passed everyone a bottle as we boarded the tender. Had mine been dosed with something? Just in case, I had filled my water bottle from the carbonated name brands in the minibar, listening with satisfaction to the sound of the screw top's seal cracking. As an added precaution, I also vowed to select my own bottle from the ship's offerings before going ashore that day.

Overall, I was feeling less anxious. Two friends were on the way to assist, and though I still needed to be careful, I could breathe easier.

With that in mind, I prepared for my day on Delos. The kitchen offered boxed lunches for participants but I stuffed my backpack with minibar finds plus a roll and cheese that I'd commandeered from breakfast. Besides assuring that my creature comforts and rehydrating needs were met, I resolved to keep my phone open on the stun app within ready reach and remain alert at all times.

But I was still filled with anticipation. Soon I'd see Evan again, which provoked a multitude of interesting physical reactions, including heart palpitations. Also, Delos had taken on an almost quest-like significance in my mind: there was something happening on that island and I was getting close to discovering what.

Nick had passed out a brochure the day before that I studied in detail, taking in our proposed path up through the House of the Trident, the House of Cleopatra, the House of Dionysus... How could I not be excited to view mosaics up close or to better understand the life of the people who once inhabited this island? Maybe they were the same people who had painted those incredible frescoes I'd glimpsed the night before, maybe the same dancers who had haunted my dreams so vividly.

I arrived at the launch deck fifteen minutes early to find Giorgi leaning over the balcony with his gaze fixed on Delos. A brisk wind blew in over the headland whipping up the surf while the sun remained shrouded behind a dark clot of cloud on the horizon. For a moment I could almost grasp why the locals considered late October wintery as I pulled my jacket more tightly around me.

Giorgi turned with a startled expression. Was that fear? Surely the deep grooves around his eyes hadn't been so prominent yesterday, but that could be due to lack of sleep—his and mine. He glanced behind him at the security camera now facing the right way around. I followed his gaze. Got it.

"You feel better from yesterday?" Giorgi asked.

The question was whether he felt better from last night. "Yes, much, thanks. It's amazing what a good night's sleep will do." As if I'd had one.

Other passengers began trickling down to the deck with Heather and Peter Rose leading the way, the latter leaning heavily on his cane and chatting amiably to Brent, who carried his foldable wheelchair. Beside him. Heather, dressed in a pair of linen trousers and a long beige sweater and sporting what looked to be brand-new running shoes, appeared more animated than I had yet to see and marched straight over to me.

"Chilly today, isn't it?" she said, fixing me with a scrutiny so intense that I had to keep myself from glancing down at my jeans in case I had something hanging out.

"It is. I was just thinking that I finally understand why the Greeks consider this to be wintery conditions," I said.

She actually laughed, if throwing her head back and hooting qualified. The sight struck me as so contrary to everything I thought I understood about the woman that it took me aback. "Winter for the Greeks is rain, which may occur today should those clouds ahead bear us ill-intent," she said. "For Peter and I, avoiding the heat is always key. I despise the heat with a vehemence. I'd rather be cold. Or wet. The summer here can be quite punishing. But we are ready for today, aren't we, Phoebe?"

I gazed up at her now sober face and felt a chill while pulling my jacket even tighter across my chest. Damn—I should have worn that extra sweater I had tucked away in my backpack. "Sure we are. We'll persevere," I laughed. Peter tapped his cane over to us, which offered a welcome respite from Heather's scrutiny.

"Will you be able to manage all right today, Mr. Rose?" I asked. I admired how he insisted on doing the activities he loved despite his challenges. Today, he had fastened his canvas hat firmly under his chin and had donned a flannel shirt.

"Do call me Peter, please. I despise formality." He fixed me with a long-toothed grin that illuminated his equally long face. "Indeed, I will manage very well. I have hired a young man on Delos—one of the custodian's sons —and Brent here has kindly offered to assist me to get settled, fine lad that he is."

Brent Tsaoussis standing nearby with a turtleneck under his jean jacket shot me an almost shy smile. So the loudmouth had turned into a fine lad. Obviously he had redeeming features.

"The boy onshore will assist me with the wheelchair in exchange for a small gratuity," Peter continued. "Of course, these ancient sites are not wheelchair accessible but I think it not unreasonable to expect more assistance be forthcoming given the ruinous terrain. The museum does a fine job, I'm happy to say, but the grounds require more ramps, and a few elevators would not be unreasonable."

And then Heather added: "I'm unable to assist him with the wheelchair due to a recent shoulder injury."

"And we can't have two of us incapacitated, can we, darling?" Peter said, leaning forward as if depositing his quote into the air among us. Unconsciously, I took a step back. "Thus, I may be slower moving along today compared to most," he remarked as if he'd been a speed demon yesterday, "but, indeed, I shall make progress. And what about you, Phoebe? Will you remain with our group or do you plan to explore the island on your own again today?"

Was that a barb? Heather was watching me as if truly interested in my answer while I observed the Jenkinses arrive minus Luke accompanied by Gerald Tsaoussis, the two doctors, and Susan and Renate.

"I'll remain with the group, of course. Excuse me for a moment," I said, turning away to greet Renate and Susan.

"Brrr...today feels almost frosty," Renate said, sliding up to me, her smile warm enough to chase away the chill. She had opted for a bright blue cotton scarf I had seen in the ship's gift shop worn over several layers of sweaters, one of which hung down to her knees. "We may even get some rain, I hear. I never expect rain in Greece," she grumbled, "not fair."

"But one of us is always prepared. Note the brolly," Renate laughed, indicating the umbrella fastened to the side of her backpack. "Sue said it never rains in Greece but that cloud says otherwise."

"Yes, dear, you are right as always." Susan leaned toward me and added sotto voce: "I always tell her she's right to help keep the peace."

"And because it happens to be true," Renate said with a nod.

"Don't be smug, dear." Susan nudged her partner

"With climate change, I guess we have to expect anything," I said. I really liked these two and desperately hoped that someday I'd have that kind of partnership with another. Evan would do nicely.

"Looks like there will be fewer of us today," Linda Jenkins said, stepping up to us. "The Dexters aren't coming and neither are the Wongs and many others have opted out of the walking tour in lieu of ship activities, including Luke, who complains that the island's cell service isn't up to his standards."

I turned to her. "It isn't?" I asked.

"Spotty, apparently," she told me. "He claims he can't keep in touch with his girlfriend, as if a few hours break would hurt him."

"I never noticed," I said. But then, I hadn't been constantly checking my phone yesterday, either. Today I would.

Her ten-year-old daughter, Andrea, piped up: "It goes in and out. If you stand near the café or gift shop you get the strongest signal."

"Or in the museum," her younger sister added. "I found a really good spot just inside the door."

Linda rolled her eyes.

Nick and Ari arrived to begin mustering the small group together.

"Are you ready for another thrilling day in ancient Greece?" Nick called as we all gathered around. "Today you will be able to explore the buildings in detail, journey deep into the center of the ancient lives that once populated Delos..."

But my attention had already drifted, being more interested now in studying my thirteen companions while attempting to force my intuitive skills to hone in on possible dark intentions, shifty demeanors, and otherwise noticeable ill-intent. What did ill-intent look like? Nothing obvious. Did I suspect the Tsaoussis brothers for being young, fit, and occasionally irksome? Possibly. Did I suspect the Roses, Jenkinses, Susan and Renate, the Drs. Bergognones? Yes, maybe, plus everybody and nobody at all. The whole situation baffled me. Then again, maybe I was losing my edge.

"How are you feeling today?" Dr. Maria asked as we lined up to board the tender. Today she had decked herself out in cream walking shorts, a cashmere (I brushed against it just to make sure) sweater, and an embossed gold Gucci logo baseball cap. How did she pull off such effortless style while I clomped around like a runaway hippie?

"Much better," I assured her. "Thank you both for all your help."

"We are happy to assist," Roberto assured me with a charming designer smile.

I donned the life jacket under Ari's watchful eye, took a name tag, refused a box lunch, shook my head at the offered water bottle, and climbed into the boat.

It was a choppy ride over despite the relative protection of the island's little harbor. Usually an energetic surf didn't bother me but today even I felt queasy. It was a relief to reach dry land where I soon learned that many of the smaller tour boats would not make the crossing from Mykonos that day. Now I wondered whether Zann would arrive, though I was confident Evan would since the larger ferry remained on schedule. Still, my unease increased. I checked my phone often, finding the signal flickering in and out.

"It's strongest in the gift shop," Andrea said, catching me glancing at my phone as we trailed behind Nick into the archeological park. Ahead, Brent and Peter were talking to a young man who was helping them with the wheelchair while Heather looked on. I scanned the perimeter, saw nothing to alarm me but a handful of determined day-trippers, and continued walking.

"Thanks. I may have to give that a try."

But not yet. We began in the square that had once been an open market and on to the House of Dionysus, so named because of its amazing mosaic that featured the god of wine. One of the rich private residences that had been uncovered during excavations, this structure gave us a glimpse of how a Delos citizen of wealth and means lived.

While absorbing Nick's every word, I kept my eye on who was nearby at all times, which wasn't difficult. The threat of rain kept our little group together like a flock of baby ducks filing behind our leader and I could sense a different mood in the group that day—quieter, more studious somehow. It was as if a pall had been cast over us. In my case, knowing that a body lay hastily buried near a stunning archaeological find was sobering enough.

We moved up through the House of Cleopatra, viewed another beautiful mosaic floor, saw the remains of its courtyard fountain, and gazed at the two headless statues at the entrance, the originals of which we had seen in the museum the day before.

"*Cleopatra, daughter of Adrastos from Myrrinous, erected this statue of her husband...for having offered the two silver delphic tripods to the Temple of Apollo on either side of the entrance...in Athens 138/137 BC,*" Nick translated from the base's inscription, adding: "We believe that this was a wealthy merchant family that must have done very well here in Delos to make such an expensive donation to Apollo."

We continued to the House of the Trident where a two-story partial restoration retained another beautiful mosaic that we admired from behind the ropes and plastic covering. Brilliant glass squares colored by metal oxides with a Greek key design framing an Aegean wave border. I took countless photos, noting the central design of an anchor and a trident, indicating Poseidon's protection. Despite the beauty of the design, it was the outer symbols that made me pause. Was there a connection between the Greek key symbol and the Key of Artemis?

Then my attention fixed on the mosaic itself. I knew that Delos had the largest collection of mosaics in the Grecian world, nearly three hundred and fifty pieces from all over the Mediterranean, created just after mosaics as an art form were beginning to come into their own. Before then, designs would be made from pebbles and colored stone but the discovery of glass opened up a whole new world to artists. The Romans and all the civilizations that followed could thank the ancient Greeks again for the development of one more art form.

Looking up, I was surprised to find myself suddenly alone inside a dark halogen-lit room. Startled, I turned and made a hasty retreat outside where I found Renate and Susan striding up to the tower entrance. "We noticed you weren't with us and came back to get you," Renate puffed. "Come on, woman. Dr. Nick is expounding on the glories of the Dionysus festival as we head toward the theater. Can't have you falling behind!"

Laughing, I fell into step with the two women as we wound our way up toward the site of the impressive marble theater that once hosted festivals to Apollo, the patron along with Dionysus, of theater arts, music, and dance. Once this theater had been the ancient equivalent of Hollywood for the performing arts and drew troupes all over the ancient Grecian world. To the Greeks, art and performance was so crucial to spiritual and religious life that its existence was considered indispensable to god and human alike.

I stood at the remains of the amphitheater similar at first glance to every Roman version I had visited before—not surprising since the Romans had absorbed the Greeks architectural prowess as well as their deities. But this theater celebrated art as opposed to violence and warfare. No gladiators killing animals and slaves here; no shows of brute strength with plenty of bloodletting, either, but instead music, dance, theater, song, and politics. The latter was at least as much about philosophy as governance as the voice of orators would have rung out in what must have been amazing acoustics.

"Aristotle—yes, that one, my friends," Nick was saying, "once visited here and was so impressed by the proceedings that he witnessed in this very theater that he went on to write *The Constitution of the Delians*. The people who once lived and breathed on this island may have been enacting the finest, most purist example of democracy that the world has ever known."

"Wish we could send our own politicians back a few thousand years to get a reboot," Linda Jenkins grumbled. "God knows they could use one."

Her husband, usually the silent partner, nodded. "And I would add that Aristotle be required reading for every politician just as it was for our political forebears," he added.

I gazed around, noting how every one of our diminutive group remained nearby, a rapt audience overlooking the ancient theater while the youngest members, Andrea and Suzanne in their ponytails and brightly patterned leggings, were less enthralled. They thumbed on their phones. The phones! Pulling sharply back to the present, I checked my own. One text each from Evan, Peaches, and Zann coming in on a strong signal.

Received, I turned away to read them.

Evan: *On the ferry now. On schedule to arrive on Delos for 1:45. I'll text you when I land. "There is the heat of Love, the pulsing rush of Loving, the lover's whisper, irresistible—magic to make the sanest man go mad."*

So my heart did something like a palpitation crossed with a tap-dance accompanied by an ancient chorus. Yes, I am susceptible to men quoting Homer, especially when delivered by the most heroic of men, my soon-to-be (maybe) lover. I couldn't wipe the smile off my face, looking up in time to see Heather staring. Turning, I took a few steps in the opposite direction to read my next message.

Peaches: *Found something interesting in my first batch of room searches. You won't believe it. I'll tell you in person. Ev's almost here!*

And the last one from Zann: *Just landed. Crazy bumpy ride over. Had to give the guy a hefty fee to take me over in a boat the size if a peapod. Where are you? We'll meet up.*

I texted her my location but told her to stay near the café and meet me in the washroom. We would soon be making our way down for lunch, according to the itinerary. I told her not to approach me but to wait for a sign. She sent back a thumbs-up.

"Look," I heard Susan say. She was pointing skyward where the last glowering cloud was rolling out to sea, revealing Apollo's orb blazing clear and brilliant overhead. "No rain now."

Nick caught up with me when we were halfway down the hill and heading for lunch. "Phoebe, I can't get those tunnels out of my head. I need to see it, you understand, don't you? I need to go with you tonight. Let me join you."

I leaned into him. "Nick, leave this to the professionals. Remember, there's a reason why the ancient Greeks warned us mortals not to tempt the fates."

❧ 13 ❦

The café, located next to the museum, had both indoor and outdoor seating but most of us sat indoors to escape the wind. I ordered a coffee with a spanakopita and then wedged myself in with Renate, Susan, and the two doctors around a little wooden table. We all chatted away while my companions picked away at their boxed lunches and drank their coffees.

"Why are you not eating the lunch provided?" Maria asked while carefully plucking a black olive from her salad with a plastic fork and delicately placing it into her mouth. I watched fascinated as she sucked on it, rolling it around in her mouth with a minimum of chewing.

"I wasn't all that hungry when we left," I told her while scanning the twenty or so diners that occupied the other tables. "I hate wasting food." Actually, I was almost always hungry and very little went to waste around me.

She flashed me a quick smile and slowly bisected a cube of feta. Her husband, on the other hand, sat half-turned away from us checking his phone. Just by happenstance, I glanced down and noticed again how his red sneakers had the little wing logo that heralded Hermes. "Fleet of foot, hey, Roberto?" He was too absorbed in his phone to hear me.

"This is pretty yummy," Susan said, forking up a tomato, "but your spanakopita looks delish, too."

"It is," I agreed, catching the eye of the lone woman by the window decked out in a red Philadelphia Phillies baseball cap with a red and white striped hoodie. She quickly lowered her eyes but I recognized Zann immediately. She knew how to blend. It wasn't until later when I picked up my backpack sitting between my legs and announced that I was off to find a washroom that I saw her stir.

"We'll keep an eye on your bag for you," Susan offered as I hoisted the thing over my shoulder.

"No problem," I said. "I need to change into my sweater, anyway. See you in a minute."

I was just rounding the corner toward the washrooms when Zann caught up.

"I'm not even going to ask why you followed me to Greece because I'm almost glad you're here," I whispered as we strode into the three-stalled facility. Luckily, it was empty but for a woman washing her hands who quickly left.

"You need me, I keep telling you that, and I can't do Dad any good right at the moment but I can help you. Besides, I found out stuff for you. One of my contacts on Mykonos says that the head archie for Delos, a Dr. Angelopoulos, is missing. The rumor is that he was close to finding the hidden temple of Artemis."

"I know," I told her. "We need you to perform a small service for us today but only in the safest manner."

"Safest manner?" she hissed. "What am I, a choir girl? Has anything I've been doing in the last decade been remotely safe? Tell me what you need and I'll do it and forget the safe part." She patted her crossbody bag. "Brought a gun."

"Like we want the sound of gunshots ringing over Delos." Still, that might come in handy before this game was done. "Though it's too complicated to get into now, something's going on here that involves me, the *Sylvan Seas* and this whole hidden temple business."

"I told you that Artemis was calling you."

"Well, it's coming in more like a yodel. So Peaches and I are working at identifying the perpetrators and Evan's on his way here with an ETA of

1:30." I checked my phone. "Thirty-five minutes away, if all goes well. We need you to nab a custodian to give you a tour of the excavation site and look for a dead body. As an archaeologist that should be doable. See if you can find something that fits that description, possibly the late Dr. Angelopoulos. Can you do that?"

"Find a dead body? Piece of cake. Might need some cash to grease the wheels."

"How much?"

"A hundred euros should do."

I passed her two fifties. "The remains were last seen about twenty meters away from the front gate buried under a pile of stones. You'll need to make an excuse to look around. Don't get us involved, though, or we'll be dragged into an investigation. You, however, only just arrived so—"

"I'm like the innocent bystander—got it. Why not call Interpol?"

"First we do the groundwork, then we bring in Interpol. We'll return to those tunnels tonight. If that place is guarded as well as I think it is, we'll need all hands on deck. We almost got caught last night. Are you with us?"

"I'm with you. I've always been with you, Phoebe. Just hoping that someday you'll recognize how valuable I am to the team."

"Repeat back to me what I just said."

"Don't you trust me?"

"Yes and no. What have I just asked you to do?"

"Find a custodian who will accompany me to the excavation site; look around for a dead body, if it's still visible. What am I, a kid passing a test or something? I told you I got it. Anything else?"

"You need a witness in case you find something and check out how they guard that place in the daytime."

"Got it. What about you?"

"I plan to catch whoever is targeting me today on Delos. He or she has to be part of this little group. Plenty of odd things are going on, too complicated to get into now. What do you know about a Dr. Nick Pallas?"

"Read his book—interesting stuff."

At that moment Linda Jenkins and her two daughters entered, sending Zann diving into a stall and me to a sink to make on like I was washing my face.

"You okay?" Linda asked.

"Fine," I said from under a scratchy paper towel, "just freshening up and changing." Which I proceeded to do while Linda and the girls used the toilet. When they emerged minutes later, I was wearing my sweater retrieved from the bottom of my backpack and was just pulling on my jacket.

"That should keep you warm," Linda remarked.

"Hope so. See you in a few minutes," I said, stepping into a stall. Only after I was sure that they had left, did I emerge.

Zann was waiting. "Well, that was fun."

"I've got to get back before someone else comes in to check my status. I guess I blacked out yesterday."

"Seriously?"

"I was probably drugged but I've yet to figure out how or even why."

"To throw you off your game, maybe, make you feel vulnerable?"

I hadn't thought of that. "Perhaps."

"Want to borrow my gun?"

"No thanks." I held up my phone. "I have something far more valuable."

"Yeah, you do," she said, removing her cap long enough to brush a hand through her inch of hair. "When this is done, get me one of those, will you?"

But I was already peering at my phone, relieved to find the signal strong here, too. Evan had arrived on Mykonos and was en route to Delos now. So far, everything was right on schedule. I looked up and smiled. "Good luck today. Got to run."

"I want to be in on the excavation site run tonight. Text me, okay?" she whispered after me.

On my way out of the washrooms, I wasn't surprised to find Dr. Maria striding around the corner toward me. "You were gone so long that we grew concerned," she said, her smooth bob still flawlessly tucked behind her ears beneath the chic little baseball cap. A home run for style.

"I'm fine, thanks. Just changing."

She carried on to the washroom while I returned to the café in time to find part of the group gathering for the second half of the tour while the rest bolted to the washroom, Nick among them.

"Everything okay?" he whispered in passing.

"Absolutely." I smiled at him.

While waiting for the group to reconvene, I texted Peaches with the information that I'd been in touch with Zann and so far, so good.

Minutes later, we resumed our trek to the temples of Apollo and Artemis. The sun poured down overhead, warming the air as we strode behind Nick into the temple complex.

What was left of the temples stood together among a tumble of stone. All I could do was gaze at the exposed foundations, blinking at the white gleam of broken marble. Very little remained structurally intact but for three slender marble pillars, the hips and torso of a colossal statue—too enormous for the ancient looters to remove, of course—and chunks of hewn stone lying around in heaps everywhere. And yet it was still immensely stunning. I could almost see how it must have looked thousands of years ago, understand how the ancients felt as they stepped into this sanctuary.

"The Temple of Artemis is possibly the oldest structure on Delos and preceded Apollo by millennia," Nick was saying. "Consider this, my friends: long before Apollo was worshipped as a god on this spot, a temple to the ancient mother goddess later known as Artemis stood here." He was pointing to the first strata of visible foundations below the others. "That has been dated as far back as 1200 BC."

"The Mycenaeans," said Peter, struggling to stand with his young employee's help. "In Delos, women were worshipped first and only later did the Greeks depict the goddess as running young, free, and virginal, the lady of the moon, mysterious and wild compared to the bright clear intellect of her male counterpart, Apollo," he intoned.

Nick, looking startled, nodded. "That is correct, but I ask you why was the Temple of Apollo, more recent by a few thousand years, built around the remains of what was to become his sister Artemis's temple? Was he to envelop the female and protect her?"

My lips moved despite myself. "Or perhaps to contain and control her —the male force taming and controlling the essence of the sacred feminine, the beginnings of what would eventually become global male domination." So much for keeping my mouth shut. "God was a woman first before the male force stamped her down." Crud, Phoebe, just shut up.

Peter caught my eye and smiled as did Heather beside him.

Gerald scratched his beard and added: "But the guys were put on earth to protect the weaker sex."

"Yeah, that's why we are taller and stronger," claimed his brother, flexing a puny bicep.

"Nonsense," Renate piped up. "Bet I could beat you at a game of chess any time, my boy. Brains not brawn rule the world."

"And I could probably whoop you at fencing," Susan added.

"Want to give it a try?" Gerald said with a grin, stepping forward. "I did a little fencing at school."

"Any time," Susan said more fiercely.

"I take kickboxing at school," Andrea piped up as she delivered an imaginary kick at an invisible opponent with moves that were anything but child's play. Wow. You go, girl.

What had I started?

"Wait," Nick said, holding up his hands. "Let's not turn this into male against female. Both energies are necessary for life and both were celebrated here on sacred Delos. The sexes are not meant to be enemies but partners necessary to balance the universal equation and to continue life. I was merely posing a question. Come, let me show you more wonders of the ancient world."

We continued traveling upward, heading along the path to more temples, more monuments. The sun seemed to become punishingly bright now, making the stones appear too sharp, the marble too hard. Behind us, even in his wheelchair, Peter seemed to be tiring. Digging around inside my backpack, I pulled out a water bottle and took a long refreshing swig.

"Isn't this sea air bracing?" Peter said, pausing beside me as his young employee popped open a soda.

"I love the sea air," I remarked, trying to recall a Homeric quote regarding the sea, surprised when nothing came to mind. Didn't I have those on automatic recall?

Nick was brilliant in his descriptions of all the sacred wonders we visited—the Tomb of the Hyperborean Maidens, the Minoan Fountain, the Temple of Aphrodite, and the House of Hermes, being only a few, each site rich with both history and myth, a powerful reminder of how the ancient Greeks lived and believed.

Truly, I thought as I trudged along, how modern life paled by comparison, how bare of magic and belief is the world in which we live. How could we go on existing this way? It's as if the modern world had been drained of its juices and left desiccated along the side of time like some poor beached jellyfish. And why in hell did I feel so dizzy?

Turning around, I gazed at my companions, straining to see beyond them at the people who lived long ago. I must have been standing a little too long at one point because Renate came up to me and linked her arm in mine to urge me along behind the others.

For some reason, I was lagging and I couldn't quite glom on to the facts I was hearing, either. Usually, I could easily dive into my mental databanks, layering in new information while retrieving dates and tasty information bits. Not that day. Everything had become a jumble of pieces sitting just out of reach at the bottom of a murky well.

"Are you all right?" Susan asked as we all sat together on a marble pediment during one of our breaks. Renate stood on one side, Susan on the other, Nick hovering nearby like an anxious parent, the doctors standing too close, shooting me concerned glances. This was getting claustrophobic.

"Fine," I lied, sounding forced even to myself. Why did Susan's brows seem permanently fused together when she looked at me? Oppressive. Maybe only concern. "I just find the sun so bright. Think I'll just stand over here in the shade for a moment."

The shade turned out to be no more than a cluster of broken columns fallen together in such a way that they carved out enough sharp angled shadow to provide relief from the sun.

Wedging myself into the deepest shade, I fumbled for my phone. Evan should be on the island by now; I would be seeing his tall figure striding up the path and hear his voice at any moment. His GPS would pinpoint my location.

I stared at the phone, my eyes going in and out of focus. No signal, seriously?

My heart was racing. My phone slipped from my fingers and fell to the ground. Damn. Picking it up turned out to be surprisingly difficult but I managed by bracing myself against a chunk of marble. Staring at the screen moments later was useless. Everything was gibberish. The phone slipped again. I bent to pick it up but this time the ground rose up to meet me.

It's a common truth that when your mind begins to go, you may be the last to know. But I did realize that I was in deep trouble, I just didn't know by how much or why. My limbs refused to move even to break my fall.

A scream followed by the crunch of pebbles underfoot. People were calling out. A gunshot far away. I felt a hand on my shoulder, someone trying to roll me over.

Susan saying: "Phoebe, speak to us!" A little shake. My eyes were open so I could see everything, hear everything, but my body refused to obey commands. God knows I tried.

A pair of black sneakers with a logo of white wings on the heel entered my line of vision. Hermes had arrived. "Phoebe, can you speak?" a man asked. I was rolled over onto my back.

I looked up at the man uncomprehendingly. My lips were stuck.

"She has had a stroke," he said. "She must be airlifted to Athens immediately! I will call the hospital now."

Stroke? I knew I hadn't had a stroke, though I couldn't remember exactly what a stroke was.

Something sharp pricked my arm before the blackness swallowed me whole.

14

The black-bodied satyr battled Achilles against the backdrop of a cracked sky. That sky may as well be my skull.

A jolt hit my temples as I turned my head on the pillow The rest of the room made no more sense—warm bright light flowing in from a tall window, a bureau with a single mounted amphora, two closed doors—one opposite me, the other in the corner. My whole body aching...

I struggled to sit up, groaning at the pain. I flexed every limb, one by one, under the smooth sheets. Nothing broken but where the hell was I? Not on the ship, that was for damn sure, but in a bedroom, a very luxe bedroom appointed with genuine antiquities. Maybe a ten-star hotel?

I needed a bathroom.

Swinging my legs out from under the covers, I was relieved to find myself still in my undies, though with no sign of my clothes anywhere. A white linen garment spread on the foot of the bed. I held it up, baffled. No sleeves, no buttons, no zippers—how was I supposed to wear that?

Clutching the fabric, I tried the door in the corner, relieved to find a modern, well-appointed bathroom on the other side. Flicking on the light, I stared in shock at the red-haired Medusa in the mirror. Curls twisting like crazed snakes in all directions, a bandage on her forehead, a bruise on her chin, one puffy eye...

I found the tiny bump on my upper biceps moments later. That had to be where the bastard pricked me with a needle. I remembered that sensation just before I went under.

After using the facilities, I did my best to clean myself up, taking advantage of the toiletries nearby. My efforts made little difference to the end result. I still looked a Gorgon.

And then I held up the garment provided, finally recognizing it as a chiton, an ancient Greek dress fashioned with a substantial amount of linen with an opening for the head that could be worn in multiple ways by either men or women. By draping and fastening the folds with broaches and sashes, various looks could be devised using the same fabric. Only I had no fasteners, though I found another length tucked within the other: a peblos, a shorter rectangle that also dropped over my head.

Seriously? I stared at myself in the mirror. There was a reason why the ancient artists only modeled lean women wearing these: the curvier ones may as well be wearing a hot-air balloon. At least I was fully clothed, though without a belt I'd probably trip over my own feet.

Minutes later, I found a long blue woven sash on the floor where I'd dropped it. If I wasn't mistaken, that and the fabric had been handwoven, making me appreciate the textile artistry if not the style sense. Now, I could hoist the linen up in folds around my waist and look presentable, at least according to the standards of a few thousand years ago.

Had I been kidnapped by ancient reenactment fanatics? Grecian dress in a modern house seemed like a big disconnect, but at least I had regained some measure of dignity. Don't ask me why I cared about that given the circumstances, but nothing makes one feel more vulnerable than being near-naked under the scrutiny of strangers. On the other hand, it's not like I could see a stranger around, or anyone else for that matter...

I padded over to the window, finding myself facing a stunning vista of wheeling gulls above foam-flecked blue sea with purple smudges of islands far in the distance. Not a single boat or another building in sight. I had to be high up on a cliff, on an island, maybe, with a straight drop to the rocks below.

Turning back to study the room, I took in the large Hellenistic black and sienna painted amphora propped in an iron stand on the bureau—definitely genuine, as was that framed fresco—and the otherwise bare walls, the bed in white linen, and fine cotton sheeting...

Where was my phone? I dove for the bed and felt around the sheets before scanning the top of the single marble nightstand, which contained only a glass of water. No phone, no clothes, no bag! My heart pounded. Without my technology, I may as well have had a limb amputated. To be alone, to be cut off *and* imprisoned!

It took every scrap of will and several deep breaths to force my panic back into its cage so my brain could take over. *Think, Phoebe.* The last thing I remembered was being dizzy on Delos. Then came the prick in my arm. I had been drugged, despite my precautions. It had to have been the doctors, but why? I rubbed my eyes. Couldn't figure it out and it didn't matter now, anyway. I was here, captive in somebody's gilded cage.

The outer door opened easily. Whoever brought me here had no fear that I could run away, which said plenty in itself. I peered down a long white marble corridor flooded with natural light from the floor-to-ceiling windows that formed a wall on one side. Stepping out, I gazed at the view, so high up that I felt as though I were wheeling with the gulls. The house had to be perched on a precipice. Sea in all directions, cliffs, pounding surf. How in hell would I escape this? Slowly, I walked down the hall, the marble cold on my bare feet.

To my right, more framed frescoes, some of them partials with the missing sections seamlessly blended in with fillers. Positioned halfway down the hall, a marble statue of Poseidon reared up among twisting octopi and sea creatures, some of which were missing fins and tentacles. The god himself had lost one arm. Hellenistic age, I guessed as I studied the piece. And probably not some Roman copy. Totally priceless. Totally hidden away from the rest of the world.

Where the hell was I? Somebody had amassed a fortune in ancient Greek art for his or her personal pleasure? To hell with sharing with the rest of us plebes through galleries and museums. I strode down the hall, determined to confront my art-raping host and to hell with the consequences. My head was pounding, my anger surging, but all I cared about was voicing my mounting outrage.

After a few minutes of striding around the hall seeing nothing but more marble halls, more statues, more busts, and more mounted priceless

Grecian pottery bathed in natural light, I was baffled. Maybe I was alone inside some amazing museum, some feat of modern architectural engineering designed to anoint antiquity in the purest of light. Ancient Beauty and the Beast, only judging from the mirror, those roles could be easily reversed.

Doors opened onto spacious light-filled rooms, some lined with books, always with art. One door led into a large lounge furnished in white leather couches positioned to gaze out through the expansive windows at the waves beyond, another onto a library with walls of books including scrolls locked in climate-controlled chambers, everywhere ancient art tucked into lit niches, some mounted on thousand year old cornices and pedestals. The place seemed to go on forever and be surrounded by water. Twice I doubled back on myself, all without having seen another human being.

By now, I was growing weary, hungry, and thirsty. My stomach felt woozy. I estimated it to be midmorning, which meant that I had been here —wherever here was—for at least eighteen hours or more. My team would know I was missing. There would be people looking for me with search teams, maybe Interpol, definitely Evan and Peaches. Kidnapping was serious business and yet there seemed to have been no urgency on the part of my captors, which could mean that they weren't worried that I'd be found.

How desperately I craved my phone. Like any modern citizen, my devices had become part of my life, if not my actual person. Not once had I seen a piece of electronic equipment, a phone or computer. Electricity and plumbing were the only nod to the modern world.

I seemed to be going in circles. After several passes around the top level, I turned a corner and found a spiral staircase that opened out onto a three-story-high atrium-style marble foyer. A single statue stood on a circular mosaic below. As I descended, my robe bunched in my hand, I studied the mosaic—Medusa's head centered in concentric borders of laurel leaves and waves fashioned from chips of bronze, white marble, and onyx. The piece was exquisite. Ancient. Hidden. When I arrived at the bottom, I gently brushed one foot over the surface before meeting the marble eyes of Aphrodite. Frozen in loveliness, apparently. Maybe that was how ancient Greece preferred their women.

Swaying slightly, I had to grab on to the goddess's broken arm to keep from toppling. Cautiously, I took another step. Obviously, I had not yet recovered from whatever drug with which I'd been injected.

Several groupings of white leather sectional couches had been gathered into little conversation nooks about the atrium, each with its own glorious view. I could just see what looked to be the edge of a garden beyond the window far to the right but saw no way to access it from where I stood.

Overwhelmed and exhausted, I collapsed onto a deep poofy chair and waited. Perhaps if I stayed there long enough, someone would come find me...or I'd turn to stone. Otherwise, what was the point?

Maybe I sat for five minutes, maybe longer, but it seemed that soon enough I saw a figure gliding down the hall above me. A woman in a long white robe draped over one shoulder with a blue silk sash at her waist, curly dark hair artfully draped high on her head, and carrying a tray. She was so graceful that her feet barely seemed to touch the tiles. Either I was hallucinating or I truly had landed in some kind of ancient costume event.

Only one way to find out. I bounded to my feet and took the steps two at a time up the spiral staircase, tripped once, regained my balance, hoisted my robe farther over one arm, and chased her down.

Though she had disappeared by the time I reached the floor, she couldn't have gone far. The hall ended with another tall window framing yet another sea view but I now glimpsed a smaller tributary between two potted palm trees. Must have missed that earlier. I stepped between the foliage down the hall, my bare feet silent, following the sounds of voices, a man and a woman speaking Greek.

Stealth wasn't my objective. I arrived at the door of a bright, cedar-paneled office backed by more sea vistas where the robe-clad woman stood speaking to a man seated at a desk.

I didn't recognize, either. The man glanced up. Fiftyish, bearded, well-built, completely bald, and very tanned, his lean form garbed in what looked to be a white toga with a purple sash over one shoulder. Sitting at a modern desk. In a toga. I was in a chiton so why not?

"Did I get kidnapped by an elaborate costume party?" I demanded.

"Phoebe!" he exclaimed, getting to his feet. "How delightful that you are up and around." Only a touch of a Greek accent. "I thought to let you rest but here you are, already up. Forgive me for not being available to greet you. You must be hungry and thirsty both."

"Why am I here and where are my clothes and phone?"

He addressed the woman in Greek, who nodded before quickly exiting. "We will bring you food and drink, but please, do have some juice while you wait and take a seat while I answer your questions." He indicated a chair at the desk and began pouring deep red liquid into a glass to pass toward me. "Pomegranate—" he smiled "—from trees grown in my very own orchards."

So he would ply me with fruit juice and possibly answer my questions— a start. Though I didn't touch the juice, I sat in the seat indicated because I'd have toppled over otherwise. "Who are you and why am I here?" I repeated.

"Drink. It is neither poisoned nor drugged. You are here as my guest, so no harm will befall you. The phone was left on Delos where you dropped it."

"Do you always kidnap and drug your guests?"

He smiled a bright, sunny smile like a father greeting his child after a long separation. It was disarming and unsettling. "Only on rare occasions when their extraction from the modern world must be abrupt and abso- lute. I have it on good authority that you would not have agreed to come otherwise."

"It's true that nearly killing my friend would have made me disinclined to listen to anything you had to say." He had blue eyes, too. Why did that surprise me? The man was an enigma.

"Ah, yes, the Peaches incident."

"Not just the 'Peaches incident.' There is the matter of a dead man buried somewhere on Delos beside an ancient processional path that may be being plundered as we speak. Of course, perhaps you are doing the plundering."

He swung around to stare out the window, his frown knitting his brows. "No damage will be done to that site. The unfortunate death of the archae- ologist was an affront to the sacred island of Delos but completely unavoidable. I blame the lack of time but I will not tolerate such sloppi- ness in the future. I wanted no deaths on my hands but others claim it is unavoidable. Perhaps they are right."

Was he speaking to himself or to me? "So Peaches is safe?" And Evan?

And Zann? Maybe he didn't know about their arrival. He wouldn't hear it from me.

"Your friends are fine, Phoebe," he said, turning to face me, "including your Mr. Barrows and Zann Masters, neither of whom particularly interest me. Mr. Barrows could be very useful to my mission but I know that he will neither be bought nor convinced."

"And you think I will?"

But he continued without responding. "And Zann Masters is too unstable for the work I do. Otherwise, as long as they both remain out of my orbit, they will survive."

"So why was I drugged and moved to another location on Delos?"

The dismissive hand again. "Another parlor trick by amateurs."

"Do you hire amateurs?"

"I do not but those I am associated with do, unfortunately."

"Speaking of amateurs, my agency employs a different breed. You know that they will find me," I said.

"They are actively searching for you now but they will not be successful."

"Don't be so sure."

That sunny smile again. "I am sure of many things, Phoebe, and that is one. You are secure in a place that few know exists and even fewer can access—my sanctuary, my escape from the modern world, albeit with a few conveniences installed." He shrugged.

"And are you the Magician in the tarot cards that have been appearing as if by magic around me lately?"

A shadow crossed his face. "No. That is not my doing. Do not allow those to distract you. As I said earlier, some team members have their own ideas and practices, which I tolerate in the interests of collaboration. I attempt to work in a democratic fashion wherever feasible."

Yes, and kidnapping is so democratic. But the key information was that there were renegade team members running around on the *Sylvan Seas* and Delos planting tarot cards and playing tricks. That could explain the voices heard on my recording the night Peaches ended up in that boat. "Did you find out about my arrival in Greece from an ancient civilization theorists group?" I wanted to eek as much information out of this guy as I could.

"Partly." He nodded. "I have been an active part of that group since the beginning as has my colleague, and my son unknowingly keeps me informed."

"Your son?"

"My son is Nickolas. I believe you know him." My expression must have registered shock. "Yes, that Nickolas. He took his mother's name after we parted ways."

"Nickolas Pallas?" I gaped.

"Don't concern yourself, Phoebe," he said as if reading my mind. "Nick would never knowingly do you harm. My son was born with an unrealistic notion of right and wrong, which makes him totally unprepared to live in either this world or the one he prefers to inhabit—anywhere populated by humans, in fact. Once we were as close as father and son could be but we have not spoken for years. Very sad but one must move on."

Nick. Why hadn't I asked him more about his background? "He doesn't know about this place?"

"He may suspect it exists but that is all," he acknowledged. "My dear boy doesn't know half as much as he thinks he does."

"Not even about your ancient Greek art collection?" I spread my hands.

"Ah—" he flashed a little smile "—that was the point of our divergence. He disagrees with what he considers to be my practices, making it necessary to keep the extent of my collection and this sanctuary a secret from him."

"Your sanctuary or your vault? You're hiding a fortune of looted ancient art here." At that moment, I was distracted by a wall-mounted mosaic of a single eye composed of hundreds of brown, tan, and white pebbles. A pot light beamed down on the exquisite detailing of this rare piece I estimated to date before the third century BC.

"It's beautiful, isn't it?" He followed my gaze. "That was rescued from the ruins of an ancient private residence on Halkidiki."

"Rescued or stolen?" I snapped.

"Rescued," he assured me. "Most of the art you see in here would not exist if it were not for my efforts to retrieve and preserve them. The world complains about the private collectors without acknowledging that we have done more to preserve art during war, violence, and economic decline than any other group."

"An excuse by any other name."

"A reality. My country works valiantly to preserve the antiquities that lay beneath our feet before time inflicts its inevitable destruction. Already we have lost so much but there are not enough resources to preserve what remains. Climate change—many important sites were lost this summer in the fires that ravaged Greece alone—war, changes of fortune, and politics. Let's be frank, Phoebe: my country is broke. Though I donate millions to museums and antiquities groups, as do many other countries and universities, so much falls through the cracks of bureaucracy and human failure. If I didn't take matters into my own hands and launch my own rescue missions, we would have very little left for the next generation to enjoy."

I knew the truth of his words but that didn't make it sit better. "And yet your rescued art isn't in a museum."

"Not yet, but someday my collection will end up in the hands of my people, once I am assured that they are ready to welcome and protect them as necessary. At this moment, thar is not the case. There are not enough resources, perhaps not even enough will, given that so many have lost much either due to the pandemic or to the economic collapse that preceded it. Now, my task is to keep these treasures safe for the generations to follow."

I stared at him, turning his words over in my mind and reluctantly—painfully—seeing his point. I knew resources were lacking but that didn't justify his actions, did it? "To me, when someone steals art, they are an art thief, period." My thoughts landed on one art thief in particular. "There are no good art thieves. Your son and I are on the same page." But I remembered too well a time when I believed otherwise.

And as if catching my thoughts a second time, he said: "But that wasn't always the case, was it?"

My eyes met his. He couldn't possibly be talking about Noel. There was that smile again. "Look around you, Phoebe." He spread his hands. "Here is where you can escape to the golden age of my ancestors, to a time when thinking alone was considered a worthy occupation, when beauty existed as a testament to a divine presence of gods, and when humanity embraced art with all of their hearts and souls."

"It was also a time of war, famine, and political unrest," I said.

"As is today." He smiled. So, I fell into that one.

"Granted, the ancient Greeks approached art in extraordinary ways."

"Exactly. Art is key to defining ancient Greece. It was a brief glorious moment in civilization, one of humanity's finest. We had no technological distractions nor no need of them. Our communication came either from the written or spoken word, or through art. Entertainment was physical activity, theater, dance, and song, the way it should be, the way we humans were designed. Our physical love for one another was fluid and not considered a sin."

"For men, yes, but women, as always, were kept secluded and not permitted to walk the streets unaccompanied unless as sex workers."

"Men had to protect their seed and ensure that their children were their own. That was the way," he pointed out.

Why was I engaging in this discussion? It was pointless to argue women's rights with a man who believed life three millennia ago to be vastly superior to our own. In many ways that was true, in others not so much. Perhaps he needed to lecture me on the glories of ancient Greece as a justification for what he had done or had yet to do. Or maybe he was trying to distract me. Either way, I was done.

"So you found out about me through the theorist group—nice. And how do I fit into all this?" The room had begun to spin. I rubbed my temples to make it stop.

He was up and striding around the room now, his sandals slapping softly on the marble, his well-muscled legs bare below his toga, while my head pounded with a brutal thud.

I don't even know why I asked the next question since he hadn't answered my first. "Why the togas and the chitons? Isn't that going too far?"

"Are they not more comfortable, more graceful, and more pleasant to see and wear?" he asked. "No bindings, no restrictions on legs or arms, and should one desire, there are short tunics to provide a full range of motion, though the nude body is still the most beautiful garb of all, is it not? Tonight, you will be one of my honored guests at dinner and will dress accordingly. You will have the full use of this house, in the meantime. No part is restricted to you."

"Because you're convinced that I can't escape." I leaned back against the chair and closed my eyes.

"Because I *know* that you can't escape. To try would expend energy best reserved for another purpose."

"Which brings me to why I'm here." I opened my eyes and tried to fix on his face but couldn't focus.

At that moment the door opened and the woman returned bearing a tray heaped with bowls of fruit, bread, cheese, juice, and a carafe of coffee. She set the tray down on a table by the window, dipped her head to her master, and quickly retreated, leaving a whiff of jasmine in the air behind her.

"Your servant or your slave?" I asked after she'd gone.

He actually laughed, a full-throated guffaw. "She is paid very well for her services, Phoebe, believe me. Though I adhere to the path of my ancestors in many ways, I abhor slavery. As long as they follow my rules, remain loyal and trustworthy, my employees are paid well, treated even better, and guaranteed to retire as wealthy men and women."

"And if they don't?"

"Come sit and share breakfast with me. I have answered enough of your questions for now, all in the attempt to form a bridge of trust between us. You are very important to me, Phoebe."

"I can tell. Drugged and kidnapped makes me feel oh so special." Could Nick know more about his father's location than Dad suspected? Might he have a search team after me now?

He chuckled, or tried to. It sounded lame to me. "One has only to look at your face to recognize a desperate need of sustenance. Food, blessed food, the best my country has to offer, is yours for the taking. I shall pour you coffee and a glass of pure spring water to begin. Come, eat and drink!"

I followed him over to the low table beside the window and sank into the cushions while trying to adjust the folds of my robe demurely over my legs. Failing that, I left them bunched in my lap and drank deeply from the water provided before filling my mosaic patterned plate with cheese, bread, honey, figs, and fresh fruit. There was no point in him poisoning or drugging me at this point. He had me where he wanted me, so I ate with gusto while trying to retain a semblance of decorum as I stuffed the hole that apparently yawned inside me. No conversation followed until I felt restored enough to finally filter all the information thrown at me in the last few hours.

"Where is this place?" I asked as if expecting him to answer.

"On a little-known island in the Aegean."

"Fine. You answer all my questions except the ones I want to know most," I said while sipping my coffee. "Who are you and why have you brought me here, Mr. Pallas?"

He was gazing at me as one would a beloved friend. "As I said, my last name is not the same as my son's. Are you fishing? You may call me Sebastian. That is all you need to know about me except to say that I have made my fortune from shipping, as have many of my countrymen and my ancestors before me. My sole goal in life has been to preserve the glories of my ancestors and, more recently, to locate a sacred object of great spiritual value that has thus far eluded my grasp. To that end, I have brought you here. You will assist us, Phoebe."

"Why would I do that?"

"Because if you don't, the world as you know it will end, as will yourself and every person you love."

There it was. What took him so long? "Sounds simple enough."

He spread his hands. "You, Phoebe, may be the only one on earth able to locate this key with your uncanny ability to retrieve lost and hidden objects. Either reach down the dusty throat of time and retrieve the Artemis Key or you will die a slow and painful death and take the world down with you."

15

Dry, dusty throat of time be damned. "I love those kinds of stories as much as the next person but seriously?" Not the most articulate of responses but I might be forgiven under the circumstances.

"I am discussing the destruction of the world, Phoebe, which can take many forms and may not always be the result of a single cataclysmic event. Some would argue that it is already in progress. Either way, humanity's continued existence may lay in locating a powerful sign, the same one that drew the ancient Greeks, even the Romans, to Delphi three thousand years ago to hear the oracle speak the truth. That is until the Byzantines intervened. The Christian emperor Theodosius outlawed all supposed pagan practices and silenced the prophetic voice forever more. The last Pythia of Delphi reportedly escaped with the Artemis Key to Delos where she hid it deep within a labyrinth. There it lies still."

A labyrinth...the tunnels in the hillside that reportedly linked to other underground passages. What in hell had I fallen into? "And you think that I can locate this key and become a modern Delphi oracle spitting out wisdom like a twenty-first century Nostradamus?" I tried to keep my tone free from judgment or derision but failed. Actually, I honored soothsayers, just not me in that role.

JANE THORNLEY

Until then I hadn't believed him crazy but now I wasn't so sure.

His eyes sparkled. "Yes, because the Artemis Key is a powerful sacred symbol believed to have been passed from the Egyptian priests to generations of Pythias. Think of it as the ancient Greek version of the Holy Chalice of Christendom or the Ark of the Covenant. Very few of the ancient historians actually saw this priceless object with their own eyes except possibly Herodotus, who claimed it was a gold, jewel-encrusted ankh that had been a gift from an Egyptian high priest. Imagine yourself holding this sacred ancient symbol and speaking truth to a world so broken that it is finally ready to listen?"

I stared at him, feeling sick. It took a few seconds before I could speak. "But this isn't the same world as a millennia ago. Many people say the truth today but still no one listens , at least not in sufficient numbers to change things. We've become too big, too diverse. There's too much noise and distraction for a single voice to be heard in the wilderness."

As if to prove my point, he wasn't listening. "Think of it this way, Phoebe. The Artemis Key, once in the hands of the ancient priests and priestesses, may have led the Egyptians to build the pyramids and the Greeks to herald forth democracy, leading humanity out of the darkness. The key was the light that once illuminated entire civilizations, one that we desperately need today."

"Based on what research?" I'd hoped to add a little balance to the scales because everything he said struck me as totally off-kilter.

"Our civilization is crumbling. Perhaps had we obtained the key two years earlier, the devastating catastrophes that have beset us in recent times would have been avoided. The ability to prevent disaster depends on our knowledge of what is to come, which, in turn, fortifies our will to avert the destruction."

I leaned forward. "And I would argue that humanity still barrels on the same destructive path regardless of the warnings. For instance, how many times must we hear of the perils of climate change before we have the global will to avert it? Industry and profit are the only gods our world listens to today. Power is money. We're too big, too crowded, to hear ourselves speak."

"Unless we hear the right voice."

"And how do I know that you don't want this Artemis Key to add to your collection or use it to find more priceless art to decorate your house? It is, as you say, priceless, the perfect keystone to your incredible collection."

He leaned forward, our knees almost touching, his hands clasped before him. "I am the person who must protect it and you have been chosen to locate it. We humans are beginning to see the light, don't you feel it? All we need is one powerful symbol of change to lead people to a global revolution, one symbol that rises above a single religion, political group, or ideology, something that predates all religions—the Artemis Key! And if we do not find it soon, another, more devastating catastrophe may beset us all. Or, what's worse, the key may become the property of those who will wield it for their own dark purposes. It is priceless beyond billions but there are those who only measure worth by monetary terms alone. Consider the destruction that would follow. There is great urgency here, Phoebe."

It is nearly impossible to talk to those deranged by fervor. I'd almost rather battle someone driven by the collector's lust alone. Those demons I stand a chance to counter.

At that moment a young man dressed in a loincloth and very little else appeared. He rattled off something in Greek that pitched Sebastian to his feet and sent him bolting out the door. "We will talk more over supper tonight, Phoebe," he said over his shoulder. "Until then, make yourself at home and forgive me for abandoning you. Something requires my attention."

I watched him disappear. Turning back to the window, I stared out at the sea, attempting to regain my equilibrium. Here I was in the hands of a powerful man, not a villain exactly but one driven by some kind of misplaced messiah syndrome. Surely he didn't believe that I was a modern oracle who could locate an ancient symbol and lead the world from darkness. Me. Some days I couldn't find my shoes.

Yes, I had a gift. Everyone had a gift. Mine just happened to be locating lost and stolen art, but mostly by using a combination of tools and always with others, never just by conjuring locations up out of my head.

Burying my head in my hands, I tried to think but my thoughts skittered across my brain like marbles on glass. I knew only one thing for certain: I had to get out of here and fast.

I began searching the room for clues. This was an office; there had to be notes, forms, communication systems—something—but Sebastian's desk, though not bare exactly, held nothing but sketches and longhand jottings scripted on paper with a fountain pen, everything in Greek. I tried the drawers and found them unaccountably bare except for lists that appeared to be of art objects, though even those seemed to be sparse. How could a shipping magnate run his empire by paper and pen alone?

There had to be a communication center here somewhere, too. Business empires didn't operate on vibes and that messenger didn't run all the way from Athens or wherever over water. And what about transportation? I needed both now.

I was still scanning the room when I heard footsteps behind me.

"Hello, Phoebe."

Swinging around, I faced a young woman dressed in a white calf-length woolen tunic with a length of red silk over one shoulder sashed at her waist —beautiful woven fabric, naturally dyed. She dangled a pair of leather sandals by the laces.

"And you are?"

"Thalia. I have brought you sandals for your comfort. I will be your assistant while you are here. Anything you need, just ask."

"Thank you." I took the shoes and tied them on. "How about a phone?"

She flashed a brilliant smile. "There are no phones in the oikos."

The oikos meaning house. Did I believe there were no phones in this grand oikos? No way, but I thought it best to try to play the game. Only I couldn't quite keep myself in check. "Do you run this establishment on thought waves alone? How about transportation?"

Her sweet smile tightened slightly. "We have no need of transportation on the island."

"No need of food and supplies, either? Everything is blown in on the wind?"

Thalia stiffened. "We have no need of transportation," she clarified, "because those of us who live here go nowhere and have no wish to leave." Which sidestepped my question. "I will give you a tour and you may assess these things for yourself."

I followed behind her wondering what Sebastian did to bind her and his other employees to this island. No phone, no YouTube, no TikTok, or

Netflicks for the most connected generation in human history. Was she paid heaps of money?

She couldn't be older than her early twenties, gorgeous, and well-practiced in the art of tour guiding as if she had filled this role many times to many others before me. Retracing my steps around the complex, floor by floor, she provided the background for every piece of art encountered, including where it came from, what techniques were used to rescue it from its original location, and how it fit into the timeline of ancient Greek civilization. At every opportunity, I sought an outside exit, but except for a veranda suspended high over the cliffs, none appeared.

She led me up a narrow set of stairs to a circular glassed-in observation deck approximately twenty feet in diameter decorated by potted olive trees, marble benches, a fountain, and a statue of Hermes in his signature winged helmet and twined snake staff, looking as though he was about to spring for the sky.

"Well, this is lovely," I said, strolling around the perimeter trying to peer down at the topography below. All I could see from that angle were the edges of walkways, patios, and something that could be a pool.

"Sebastian loves to come here to gaze out across the sea," she told me. "This is where he comes to think and dream."

"He loves his views, doesn't he? I suppose Hermes there is authentic?" I said, turning toward the bronze statue.

She smiled. "Of course. Everything here is authentic."

"Except maybe the century."

Turning abruptly on her sandaled feet, she beckoned me on. "I will show you the lower floors next."

We descended to the middle level, pausing before a glass case filled with ancient Greek jewelry, the sight so gleaming and magnificent that I couldn't speak at first.

"These pieces have been collected over many years," she told me, "and represent the most brilliant craftsmanship of the Hellenistic jeweler's art. Regard the delicate nature of the leaves of the headdresses."

I gazed up at the ten gilded laurel wreaths. At one time, every hero or honored guest wore a laurel wreath in ceremony or during parties. These specimens were exquisite. Sir Rupert, known to have a collection of his own, would have wept at the sight. Or maybe he'd just complain because he didn't possess them himself. Smiling to myself, I realized how much I missed him, missed everybody, in fact.

"This way."

Swinging around, I followed her down the corridor to the atrium stairs, which we descended quickly, me trying to keep up, until she had led me down a hallway beside a bank of glass walls to a little foyer.

"Here you see a bronze figure of an athlete by the sculptor Polykletos in the contrapposto pose," Thalia said, pausing by the statue. "Ahead you see our gymnasium and bath areas."

Busy peering past the statue toward the pool beyond with my thoughts fixed on escape, I suddenly swerved my attention back to the statue. A life-sized bronze of a standing male positioned on one foot with the other gracefully bent behind him, it was a style that had influenced centuries of sculpture to follow.

"But it can't be an original Polykleitos," I protested. "No Grecian originals have survived. We only know of Roman copies."

"This is authentic," she said with authority, "rescued from Hercula-neum nearly three years ago. We believe the owner of the villa had amassed a collection of Greek art."

"But how? How could Sebastian remove a priceless sculpture from an archaeological site in Italy and smuggle it to Greece?" I was allowing myself to get excited again, jeopardizing my best intentions.

I sensed the steel beneath her smile. "It is not so difficult when you have the means. A shipping company and powerful friends can be very useful in the Mediterranean. Please follow me. There is much more to see."

I followed her into the exercise area while trying to imagine a priceless bronze statue being hefted up from the ash-covered remains of a great Roman town right under the noses of the Italian authorities. Sebastian must have an entire ground team of skilled operatives ready and able to do his bidding throughout the Mediterranean.

Thalia brought us to a halt inside the gymnasium where two nude men were wrestling. So absorbed in the ancient art of unarmed combat, the men appeared not to notice our presence until the younger one caught Thalia's eye and smiled before being slammed to the floor.

"The human body is the most beautiful of natural forms," she whispered as we watched the men struggling for dominance, their muscles slick with what I suspected was olive oil in keeping with the ancient tradition. "It is beauty in motion."

Another ancient Grecian concept vividly portrayed in their art. Thalia's gaze remained fixed on the young combatant with a quickened interest I suspected went beyond mere aesthetics while my thoughts strayed briefly to Evan. That man could hold his own anywhere.

Tearing her gaze away, my guide led me into the richly tiled bath area where heated and frigid pools awaited the gymnasts post-workout but I was more interested in what I saw through the door beyond—another terrace, another pool, what looked to be steps beyond and...an open door.

I sprung for freedom, out the door, past the pool where several nude people splashed, and bounded up a set of rock-hewn steps climbing through the wooded cliff. It was a desperate move but I needed to shake this alternate universe and just *breathe*. Thalia called after me but I ignored her. Maybe if I gained a scope of this place, I could find my escape hatch.

The path led through small groves of cedar trees clinging to the rock with gnarly roots, the sea visible through the branches far below. I bounded past benches, small naturalized fountains, winding wooded stretches that felt ancient and lost in time. Statues of the Greek gods lined the path, but halfway along, dizziness struck with such intensity that it left me gasping. Surely I could find one clear spot, a lookout, maybe, where I could gain the lay of the land? But after four more flights of uneven stairs, I lost steam and collapsed on a bench. Damn, I had to be still recovering from whatever they had injected in my veins.

It took mere minutes for Thalia and four nude people now accompanying her to catch up. They were following at a leisurely pace chatting away as if aware that their quarry couldn't get far—four people as naked as the day they were born, including the two wrestlers plus two others, a man and a woman, all fit and healthy-looking.

Doubled over on the bench trying to catch my breath, I watched as the naked people arrived with Thalia, all of them gazing at me with mild curiosity, me gazing back.

"I feel overdressed," I remarked.

One of the older men smiled—maybe in his fifties, his body that of a much younger man. "Please join us, remove your clothes, and celebrate the glory of the human form at home in nature." Nice voice, nice everything. I couldn't help looking, considering what was in my line of vision.

"Some other time, perhaps, maybe when I haven't just been kidnapped and forced to pretend that I've fallen into another time," I said.

"We have much to learn from the ancestors, Phoebe," the other woman offered. "We live like this because we feel wholly human, a state of mind we can never achieve in the world we left behind. Here we are free."

"But I am not," I pointed out, thinking how bizarre it was to be speaking to naked people while sitting in a glade dressed in a chiton. "Maybe one of you could help. I'm looking for transportation or possibly one of those useful but slavish trappings of modern life, the phone." Just making a point.

The older man shook his head. "We have no need of transportation or phones here."

"You might not but I do." I got up and strode past them to continue climbing, the whole crew accompanying me, the older guy even offering me an arm to hold as we climbed up and around. They were all so congenial as if accompanying me on a stroll around a park. When I finally reached the hoped-for lookout, a flat promontory rimmed by a low wall, all I saw was another stunning view of the Aegean with tiny ships so far in the distance I may as well be in another galaxy. On the other hand, if I could just get back up here after dark and signal a passing ship somehow...

"What is the name of this island?" I asked.

"The name does not matter," one of my companions replied.

"How did you arrive?" was my next question.

"The same way you did," came the response.

This frustrating feint and parry was driving me nuts. I couldn't see a single jetty or any other way to launch a boat, though one had to exist. These guys were not going to help me, guaranteed.

Without another word, I sank onto another marble bench and wrapped my robe closer around my arms. A chill stirred in the sunny breeze that sent my teeth chattering. I admit to taking a perverse satisfaction in seeing my naked companions' goose bumps.

"You are exhausted as well as cold," Thalia remarked. Removing her robe, she tossed it around my shoulders. Great, now everyone was naked but me yet I was still the only one shivering. "Perhaps you would like to return to your room and rest?" she asked.

Under the circumstances, that seemed an excellent idea. We were halfway down the narrow steps when the beat of a helicopter roared overhead.

Shielding, my eyes, I looked up. Got it.

☙ 16 ❧

Not that I could fly a helicopter. Boats were another story and there had to be one of those around here somewhere. Meanwhile, I slept, which, under the circumstances, seemed sensible considering that I needed to power up for my escape later.

But I didn't expect to sleep so long or so deeply. I awoke to Thalia standing over me accompanied by two other young women. "We have come to dress you for dinner," she said.

"Dinner already?" I shot to sitting and looked around the room. Darkness gathering beyond the window, torches burning in sconces in the hall... "No electric lights?"

"We prefer to use the light of my ancestors when darkness falls," Thalia said.

The light of her ancestors—how poetic, but it made absolutely no sense. "Thanks, anyway, but I can dress myself," I pointed out. "Actually, I've been doing it for years."

Thalia smiled. "But tonight you will need assistance. Please follow us."

Dropping my by-then seriously wrinkled linen robes back over my head, I followed the three women down the hall to a room that I had poked my head into earlier—a bathroom, only I soon realized as I stepped inside, a bathroom like no other, at least not in this century. Designed in the ancient Grecian style, a sunken pool with floating flower petals featured in a tiny courtyard open to the sky by an oculus high above. Braziers emitting some floral fragrance I couldn't define—frankincense, maybe—lit the space while rows of small containers lined shelves around the room.

The three women obviously expected me to disrobe and climb in to bathe under their watchful eyes. I hesitated but figured, why not? Let the twenty-year-olds see the almost forty-year-old in the flesh—slightly less perky in places but still holding her own. I tossed off the robe and waded into the warm scented water, still in my undies. The moment I sunk up to my neck, they tossed off their robes and joined me, giggling like we were in a hot tub on a girls' night out.

Women in ancient Greece lived cloistered lives but the physical flow had been far more relaxed than in modern times, at least until recently. There was artistic evidence that sex among all genders was common, that prostitution had been state-run, and that citizens, males in particular, enjoyed a wide range of sexual experiences with no sense of shame. I, on the other hand, remained very old-school in some quarters.

"Wait a minute!" I protested as they ganged up on me to pull off my underwear and toss off my bra, laughing away. Then came the splash play with the three of them flicking water in one another's faces while periodically holding me down to wash my hair. Any attempt to be more intimate provoked a well-aimed kick on my part so they soon stopped that line of fun. "It's just not my inclination," I explained. "No judgment."

They laughed and accepted my wishes.

"You have a handsome lover waiting for you," Thalia said.

I took it as a question. "Yes, and I miss him terribly." Thoughts of Evan and I alone in this watery bower was enough to send my imagination elsewhere.

"But he may be with you tonight," she added.

Wouldn't that be grand, but I was too distracted to reply. One woman began massaging scented oil into my scalp, and after a few blissful minutes, I was so relaxed my limbs turned al dente and floated to the surface while Thalia's cradled me in her arms. Then I was dried off and rubbed down with soft linen towels followed by a massage with more scented oil.

By the time I sat wrapped in a soft winding robe like a huge linen-cased sausage, the women were working on my hair. I refused the offered wine but accepted the fruit-flavored water instead. They were tugging at my curls, piling my hair up on my head, and wrapping tendrils around a metal rod they had heating on top of one of the braziers. For a moment I feared I was being trussed up in ringlets.

That done, the linen cloth was wound off my body and I was helped into strophic, the Greek version of a bandeau bra, with a perizoma or unisex loincloth to wear under everything—the underwear of the ancients.

The first robe dropped over my head and following that was pleated silk the color of bronze green, and so much like Mariano Fortuny's Delphi column dress that it brought tears to my eyes. "Who made the cloth?" I asked.

"We have all been taught but the silk is my mother's work," one woman said. So, there had to be many generations living here.

Earrings were fastened on, a necklace placed around my throat, and a final single length of marigold silk fastened over one shoulder and cinched at my waist with a golden braided rope. My dressing complete, Thalia held a mirror up for me to witness the transformation.

Medusa had been banished, replaced by some creature from another world, lovely, dignified, beautiful...yes, actually beautiful, or maybe it was only the light enhancing the overall effect of silk, jewels, glossy curls, and diaphanous robes. Perhaps a woman who believes herself beautiful is beautiful, and at that moment, I believed I could launch a thousand ships, or maybe a rescue mission, at the very least. So transfixed by the image was I that I barely noticed one of the women tying leather sandals on my feet.

When Thalia beckoned for me to follow, I went without comment, in a strange, almost subdued state of mind. I stood a little straighter, walked a little more gracefully, even attempted to glide across the marble floor instead of doing my usual shuffle.

Women of the modern age understood the power of female beauty, too, considering how our vision of loveliness has been corrupted by the youth-pushing media. But at nearly forty, any moment of perceived beauty had a heady effect on my sense of self, not because I felt young but because youth suddenly didn't matter.

But I was struggling to regain my sense of self, trying not to be seduced. I reminded myself that all this ritual was not of my doing. I was being groomed, prepared for some kind of sacrificial purpose.

The two companions drifted away, leaving me to trail behind Thalia through the museum-like fortress that had now taken on an otherworldly sense of aborted time. We passed statues gleaming in the flickering brazier light, mosaics, frescoes, every one of them mesmerizing. I glanced up to meet the marble eyes of Artemis and sent a silent prayer for my escape. If she was the spirit of female freedom, I needed a little help about now.

Descending the central stairway to the atrium, I realized that the space now brimmed with people gathering around chatting and sipping wine like a cocktail party for antiquity. A hush descended the crowd as I attempted to walk down the stairs without tripping. Somehow I managed to hold up my robes without falling flat on my face.

"Lovely," I heard someone whisper in English.

My cheeks burned. I felt like a prized cow, Best in Show. Some of the faces I recognized from earlier and one of the previously nude wrestlers lifted a glass and toasted me in Greek. The others joined in the toast, repeating the words, smiling, and cheering.

"They say, 'Drink! And live among the good,'" Thalia translated as we crossed the atrium.

"Homer again," I muttered. The ancient poet seemed to be stalking me, weaving Ariadne's thread between my world and his. But I reminded myself, this was not ancient Greece, despite evidence to the contrary. I was captive in an elaborate dress-up party and by now the novelty was wearing thin.

We proceeded down a long corridor to a wall of friezes depicting diners lounging while servants filled their cups with wine. Third century BC, I guessed. The wall slid open to reveal another scene from ancient times, this one in 3D Surround Sound: an ancient Greek courtyard with a central square pool open to the sky, columns in all four corners behind which opened a large central interior room. Braziers and torches flickering everywhere accompanied by the sound of flutes and lyres. I turned to comment but Thalia had disappeared.

This was all very enchanting but enough of this time machine. I strode across the tiles toward the open room, not surprised when Sebastian stepped out to greet me.

"Phoebe, you look like Aphrodite herself, a vision of loveliness."

I refused to be gracious. "Sebastian, let's get on with this charade. Explain exactly how you expect me to find this Artemis Key so I can get on with my life." As if I intended to play along.

The planes of his face danced in light and shadow, his eyes dark and hard. The silence seemed to freeze the air around us.

"You don't expect me to ever return to my old life," I said after a moment.

"I am hoping that you will never want to. What does your old life offer you that ancient Greece cannot?"

"Freedom."

"Freedom can be defined in many ways and I would argue that in this world you are more liberated than can ever be possible compared to your former life. Phoebe, I am speaking of your destiny."

Shit. Never trust a man who says he knows a woman's destiny. "I find my own," I said.

"That is not how it works. Come, let us converse further over dinner." He stepped aside so I could preceed him into the banquet area. Tables laden with aromatic bread fresh from the oven, plates of roasted fowl and fish, heaps of glistening fruit, tureens of something fragrant with herbs, and other bowls and dishes I could not identify, all sitting on long tables with servants standing nearby.

At least twenty dining couches awaited guests, the dining couch being like a daybed piled with pillows next to a low table for placing wineglasses and plates. The ancients ate propped on one elbow. God help you if you had a stiff back.

"Who's joining us?" I asked.

"Once we have had time to converse in private, I shall invite my friends and our other guest of honor to share our celebration."

"Another guest of honor?" Another trussed-up captive?

"Please, take a seat." He indicated a satin-cushioned couch where I was expected to recline. Only I wasn't in the reclining mood.

"What celebration?" I asked. "I'm hardly feeling celebratory."

"Perhaps you will be when you learn of how we will honor you."

"Honor the kidnapped guest? That's a new one. Will we be joined by the toga- and robe-clad ancient Greek revivalists I saw in the atrium?"

He was smiling but it wasn't pleasure I saw in his eyes. "Of course," he said, accepting a kylix, a Greek wine cup, from a servant and offering me another. I took the proffered cup, which I couldn't help notice appeared to be genuine. Who drinks from a priceless ancient cup? I took the kylix with no intention of using it.

I sat down on the edge of a cushioned bench while he reclined nearby, Greek style, and snapped his fingers. One servant rushed to fill our cups while another delivered a plate of sliced fruit arranged in a wave formation around the plate. Too beautiful to eat, I plucked a few melon pieces from the outside ring onto the plate provided and tried to catch the young man's eye. He kept his gaze averted in slavish deference, reminding me that democracy was for citizens alone and that servants need not apply.

"Let's get this over with, Sebastian," I said. "You want me to find this Artemis Key, correct?"

"Ah," he said, sipping his wine, "if only it were that easy, Phoebe. You cannot locate the Artemis Key without being fully immersed in the civilization that hid it in the first place. You must live and feel as did the Pythia millennia ago."

"And you expect me to do that by dressing up in a chiton?"

"If it were so easy, it would have been discovered by now. People have been seeking the Artemis Key for millennia, Phoebe, the archaeologists, historians, and adventurers digging, digging, digging. I brought you here to immerse you in the age that birthed this symbol and to attempt a different method to seek the truth."

Oh, my God, that meant the pantomime had just begun. I nibbled on the fruit. "So consider me immersed. Can we just get on with it?"

He laughed. "Soon enough, Phoebe, soon enough. Now relax and enjoy. This feast is in your honor."

The Last Supper by any other name. Was I like an ancient warrior banqueting before plunging into battle fully expecting to either conquer or die? The melon rolled around and around in my mouth. I may as well be mixing cement.

Any moment might be our last, Homer reminded me. Thanks for that, bud.

While I continued to sit upright, more food began to circulate while other guests arrived. Those I had met earlier plus unfamiliar faces took their places at the reclining couches, each of them toasting me as they passed.

Had I my phone, I'd stage a zap attack, launch a strategy that would incapacitate a maximum number of these robed actors; I'd call my team and turbo-thrust myself out of this century. As it was, all I could do was sit in my silken robes imagining the endgame, feeling totally unprepared. Could my armed combat skills take on all these muscled athletes? Very unlikely.

"Phoebe, we honor you!" Sebastian cried. "Come stand with me."

Oh, please. I gazed up to see Sebastian standing before me, one arm extended. Slowly, I got to my feet and stood by his side.

"To you, we give thanks this night and celebrate your bravery, your vision, your beauty!" he cried, raising his cup.

"Everything is more beautiful because we are doomed," I said, unable to keep Homer at bay now.

The others cheered, each raising a kylix while I scanned their faces wondering where all the women had gone. So much for equality. Women never joined these kinds of dinners in ancient Greece unless they were slaves or courtesans. So where did I fit in? There was an energy in the room I couldn't define, something edgy, heated, like pressure rising as a pot simmering to a boil.

I turned to Sebastian. "I'm out of here."

And I pushed past the men with their smiling faces, their crazy commitment to a life left far behind, and bolted for the door.

The braziers illuminated the courtyard pool, the stars sparkled overhead, and I was seriously considering making a jump right over the edge into the Aegean, if I had to. Take my chances with the sea, swim like hell, find a damn boat.

Dodging a pair of startled servants, my robe bunched in my hand, I ran in the direction of the false wall and was halfway there when it slid back to reveal a tall, lean figure standing in the smoky shadows.

"Get out of my way!" I demanded. The figure remained, backlit by the flaming braziers that flanked him.

"Ah, Phoebe, my warrior goddess," he said, stepping into the light. "You haven't changed a bit. Still trying to escape your destiny. You look lovely by the way."

❧ 17 ❧

Shock hit me in countless ways. I almost couldn't breathe. Noel!
Thinner than I remembered, the skin sucked deep under the high cheekbones, the dark eyes drilled into the sockets, and that sensual mouth still quirking like all the world was his private joke.

"Why in hell are *you even* here?" I whispered.

"To see you, my love—" he lifted his hands and took another step "—and because my friend, Sebastian, has graciously permitted me to recuperate in this ancient Grecian resort and spa after you broke my heart, literally and figuratively. You've got to admit, it's perfect—sunshine, fresh food, lovely maidens tending to my every need, clothing optional. Slowly, my poor heart mends."

"You should be dead!" I practically spat out the words. My ability to find fitting words around this man was notorious.

He pulled aside the top half of his robe, revealing the phone-sized reddened scar over his heart. "And if you wanted to kill me, dead I would be, my love. I had a gun, remember? You could have taken that and shot me. Instead, you tasered me with that little gizmo your boy toy devised. But you didn't mean it. You never meant to kill me."

"Damn you all to hell. If the charge had been stronger, it would have stopped that black ticker of yours forever."

185

He took another step forward. "Seriously, Phoebe? Think I don't know you better than that? You could never kill me; you could never kill anything —such a bleeding heart. Besides, you love me. You and I are bound together forever, true soul mates. I just pissed you off in Morocco, which activated that cute little red-haired temper of yours."

Why was I crying? How much humiliation could I bear?

"But," he lifted his hands, "I'm willing to forgive and forget and pack everything into the 'shit happens' category. Granted, my health may never be the same but I'm willing to rise above that in the name of love. Besides, you keep helping me along—even killed Baldi for me. How can I hold a grudge?"

"Zann killed Baldi with a little help. Do you remember her, another woman you screwed?"

I took a step back as he continued moving forward. "When a girl throws herself at a man, what can he do?"

I backed right into one of Sebastian's cronies, who gripped me by the shoulders and held me tight. If I had struggled, it would have only provided entertainment for the men so I froze myself to the spot.

Sebastian stepped between Noel and me.

"And what's your role in this charade?" I asked him.

"As Noel says, he and I are friends, Phoebe. He's like a son, since my own has forsaken me."

"A son—him?" I tried to laugh but couldn't pull it off. "He has a real father, do you know? And he's forsaken him by being such a cut-throat, double-barreled, shit-faced bastard."

"Forgive her," Noel said with a grin. "She has a terrible track record with adjectives."

"Sebastian," I cried. "You're being suckered! Noel is the evil, money-grubbing villain you fear the most. You've put him right at the heart of your collection, at the source of every bloody piece of priceless art he could have ever dreamed of. You're being played!" I was close to losing it.

"When working for Baldi, Noel provided me many services and helped deliver much of the priceless art you see around you. Furthermore, he remains committed to doing more of the same. Now he will help me to locate the Artemis Key through you."

"He won't. He'll steal everything for himself. It's all about using me as his sniffer hound. I get it," I said. Taking a deep breath, I struggled for calm. Shouting never works. "And the fact that he deals with an arms cartel doesn't sully your noble cause?" I asked more calmly. "A rich bit of Grecian theater, isn't it?"

That seemed to wound him. "I do not judge my equals; I merely ensure that their goals align with mine. Through Noel and indirectly Nick, I first learned of your abilities to find lost art. You will help us locate the Artemis Key, Phoebe. It is the greatest honor bestowed upon any mortal woman."

"Oh, please. And if I don't or can't?"

Noel stood watching this exchange with a pained expression, probably feigned. "If you don't, Phoebe, I may be unable to save you this time."

I nearly choked on that one. "Save me this time?" I sputtered, losing it again. "I always save myself, remember? All you ever did was put me in danger, bastard." Actually, I used several, much stronger words.

"Whatever. The point is that the quest for the Artemis Key is far bigger than all of us combined and not fully in our control," Noel added.

Oh, my God, not this destiny shit again.

"We will engage in a ritual that will unlock your abilities," Sebastian explained with solemnity, "a very ancient, very sacred, ceremony designed to tap into the hidden depths of your subconscious mind. My ancestors performed similar ceremonies at the Panhellenic Sanctuary as a part of the cult of Demeter and Persephone and throughout the Greek world in various cults devoted to Artemis and her initiates."

"Do you mean something like the Eleusinian Mysteries?But nobody knows what went on in those ceremonies, which is why they were considered *mysteries*."

"Indeed," Sebastian said, "but pottery and other evidence preserved in art plus the ancient historians themselves indicate that women played a central role as they concerned rebirth and the sacred feminine. It is believed that a similar ritual preceded the anointing of the Pythia of Delphi, ensuring that she would emerge from the darkness to awaken her inner sight, reborn in by the hand of the gods as a goddess in her own right."

Emerge from the darkness. "The descent, the search, and the ascent," I whispered, the age-old hero's journey that echoed all through humanity's storied past. I wanted to spit. "So what, a group of men are going to invent a phony ritual to fulfill their own devious plan now?"

"Phoebe—" Noel spoke softly as if he were my lover instead of my bastard nemesis "—we do have scholarly theory on our side, not to mention the assistance of those practiced in the art of the world's occult studies. And you. You are the key to this entire search because you are special and will emerge from the darkness victorious with the Artemis Key in hand, a goddess among women. We already know the area where the Pythia hid the key. That's where we'll begin."

"I thought I zapped you in the heart, not the head. Maybe I got it wrong. You're all nuts if you think you're going to make me play some kind of ancient game of fetch." I kicked out behind me, taking my captor by surprise. He fell backward as I lunged past Noel and Sebastian, heading for the open wall ahead.

Maybe I wouldn't get far, maybe I didn't care, but I was still going to run like hell.

"You won't get away, Phoebe," Noel called. "There's no place to go!"

Luckily, the atrium had emptied as I scrambled across the Medusa mosaic toward a corner where Thalia had led me earlier. The gymnasium and outside doors lay in that direction. If I could just find a way to the other side of the house, then maybe I could find the wharf, the communication station...

The torches were lit along the walkways, pools and patios. I ran toward the lookout path with plans to diverge. Behind me the beat of footfalls and men shouting in two languages grew closer, though I doubted they were exerting themselves much after all that wine. But they were probably still practiced sprinters and I was not. Maybe I couldn't outrun them but I had a chance to outthink them.

I bolted up the stone path, untying my sash and yanking my robe over my head as I went. The wind had picked up, blowing a chill gusty breath down the glade while, to my right, a full moon sailed high over the Aegean. Weren't all these ancient rites held by the light of the full moon? Scripted in advance, then. Once again, everyone had played into Noel's hands. Well, damned if I was going to let him keep me there.

I had reached the first marble bench. Bundling the clothing under one arm, I dove off the path into the woods and ducked there counting the seconds as footsteps pounded past.

"She's heading for the top!" I heard one say. "Thinks she's trying to see where we keep the boats."

Thanks for the info, bozo. Once they'd passed, I plunged through the woods, which began as a thick copse of cedar, sycamore, and pines opening onto stony outcrops amid clusters of skinny trees. Now in my loincloth and bandeau, at least I could climb but I needed to hang on to the bundle of silk, too. That meant crawling over the rocks with the silk wrapped around my waist, secured by the golden cord.

With the moon silvering the landscape and the shadows between the rocks as deep as Hades, I could easily skid to a wicked end at any time. At one point, I hid behind the rocks hearing voices calling from somewhere, whether from left or right, I couldn't tell. Maybe to my right towards the lookout—no, wait, to the left. Both directions at once.

Leaving my boulder, I crept across the stones over the crest of the knoll until I reached a thin fringe of trees that was the only barrier between me and the lights below—electric lights, not torches. Keeping behind the cover of branches, I gazed down, trying to pick out the details. A paved area that could be a helipad with an open garage nearby. Lights around the pavement's perimeter, steps leading down to the sea... Bingo— I'd reached the business end of the property.

But how to get down? It was a straight 30ft drop from my perch to the pavement with no handholds worth grasping. I began unwinding the silk from around my waist. Tearing the fabric with my teeth, I ripped it into two, long pieces. Tying the two pieces together, I wrapped one end to a gnarly cedar, the other triple-wrapped around my hands, and dropped over the edge, rappelling down the cliff face while slowly releasing lengths of it as I dropped.

Good thing it wasn't far because what works in theory doesn't always in practice. The slippery silk frayed against every jagged outcrop and turned out to be too short, besides. I ended up jumping the last five feet which jarred every bone in my body.

Nothing sprained, I recovered and dashed for cover behind a bronze Zeus while scanning the interior of the open door. Definitely a garage with a single interior door at one end—green. Don't ask me why I notice these things. A man in white coveralls was busy working over some piece of equipment, his back to me.

I scuttled across the pavement keeping low and ducking behind whatever I could find until I was deep inside the building. Within moments I had reached the green door. Slipping out from behind a barrel, I yanked the spring-loaded thing open and dashed inside, careful to ease the door closed behind me.

It took grinding seconds for my heart to settle. A long hallway with doors opening on each side stretched ahead. Men's voices somewhere. The scent of diesel and the hum of something mechanical. Unconsciously, I felt for my phone but my hand came away empty. I was on my own. Leaving the door, I crept down the hall, ducking behind a door at the sound of voices crossing the corridor. Once they'd gone, I continued.

Two doors down, I paused at the entrance of a large empty room with meters blinking on the wall. A boiler or engine room? Here lay the beating heart of Sebastian's alternate universe and I might not recognize half those machines but a phone I definitely would. Seeing nothing that looked like a communication device, I crept onto the next. Computers lined this space, one every foot or two on tables against three of the four walls, each featuring a screensaver with a Poseidon-esque logo. Okay then, computers I understood, too.

Easing around the corner into the empty room, I tapped the keyboard of the closest machine. Password-free, it flipped open onto an active home screen with plenty of apps to choose from. All I needed was a browser with a mail feature, which I found in seconds—a Google mail account, everything in Greek. Activating the message app, I typed in Evan's address plus Peaches's and wrote: *HELP! Kidnapped to an island by Nick's father. Noel's here! Phoebe.* I hit Send. Relief washed over me in seconds. Done.

"The message will go nowhere" a man said in English. "Everything is monitored."

I swung around to see the coveralled man standing there and hurled a rolling chair in his direction. He was calling out in Greek, men were shouting back, and I barreled past him to another door on a headlong run to what looked to be a side exit.

The moment I opened the door, an alarm pealed. I was halfway down a set of steel stairs heading for the jetty before I realized that other alarms were sounding all over the island. Boots were pounding on the steel behind me, the dark sea was churning below.

Shit, shit, shit! I reached the bottom and dashed across the cement jetty. Flooded with lights, I could see a cabin cruiser moored ahead plus a speedboat nearby. I was going to make it!

The speedboat might be my best option but the cruiser was closer. I couldn't risk sprinting that ten additional yards without them catching up. Springing on board the cruiser, I began untying the ropes, thinking that I'd get the engine going and fight my attackers off somehow. Suddenly there were lights. Someone tackled me from behind. I kicked back, but hitting a shin with my sandals made little impact. Another man grabbed me from the other side while someone else pulled a foul-smelling bag over my head, tying it fast around my torso until I was encased. I was pushed back against the rear seat still kicking.

More men's voices. Sebastian calling out instructions from the jetty. Two men held me down while someone else gripped my legs and another bound my ankles. Thrown over somebody's shoulder, I was then tossed onto the jetty and into another man's arms. Seconds later, I lay facedown on the cement bucking like a tuna.

"Phoebe, Phoebe...it is never wise to fight your destiny," Sebastian said overhead.

"Go to hell, you crazy bastard!" I mumbled, but speaking was challenging since my head wasn't alone in that bag. Slimy, finny, fishy-smelling things kept me company, some still moving. Something slippery wrapped around my neck. I was briefly distracted by the sound of wheels rolling across the cement. The moment they stopped, I heard Noel's voice.

"Phoebe, still taking the hard way home, are you? Some things never change."

"We will need to subdue her," Sebastian said. "Hold still, my goddess. We will deliver you to your destiny now."

"No!" Something slithered against my lips, but before I could form another word, the needle sucked me back down into a blackened world.

❧ 18 ❧

I fell in and out of consciousness, the darkness seeming absolute. I heard men shouting over some loud mechanical beating sound before being dragged back under. Next, I came to while clinging to aware- ness, my body vibrating as if I lay on top of some quivering beast. Halfway between this world and the next I remained, aware that I was now being carried somewhere. I heard the sea surging nearby and voices, so many voices. But my limbs refused to move. All I could do was lay waiting for my life to return, that is until the darkness sucked me back down.

I awoke inside a small room, the blindfold gone. A figure leaned over me and shadows hovered nearby. I blinked. So much yellow—yellow walls, yellow ceiling. A fire burning in the corner.

"She awakens," the woman said. I knew that voice. "Come tend her."

Another woman arrived, placing a cool cloth on my forehead. Now I was being helped to sitting, though I seemed unable to move my head and could only gaze down at my bare legs.

"What's wrong with her?" one asked.

"The drug," said the Italian accent. "It will soon wear off."

"Better happen pronto because we can't bring her out like this."

"Give it time," the Italian said. "I have given her something to bring her around sooner."

"She smells of fish."

"We must wash her."

A scented cloth wiped down my arms, neck, and shoulders, jasmine, maybe.

They were trying to dress me now, moving my limbs around like I was a doll, dropping something silken over my head, poking my arms through holes. Still I couldn't lift my head. Blue-green fabric gleamed in my range of vision.

"She's lost one earring."

"Bring the other one"

"Can she stand?"

"Let us try."

Holding me by each arm, they lifted me to my feet where I stood swaying. I finally managed to raise my head. Painted walls of figures bearing gifts to a throned woman, a swirl of birds and vines in the sky. They were bringing her a goat. Old, very old...

"Where...am I?" I whispered.

"She rouses."

I slowly turned to the voice, gazing befuddled at a woman I did not recognize dressed in a white gown with a golden laurel wreath on her head. She smiled.

"Quickly, get the water," the one on the opposite side ordered.

I turned to stare at her. Maria Bergognone. "You've got to be kidding," I whispered. Someone handed me a cup of water, which I shoved away. "Are you seriously part of this...costume event?"

"Do not resist," Maria said, standing in her yellow robe with the laurel tiara. "Be honored this night."

"Be honored to be kidnapped...and drugged over and over again?"

"The drugs will help you on your journey. The ancients took them to reach higher consciousness, as must you. Come, we must hurry. The others await. Drink the water; it will fortify you. It is has not been tampered with."

"Did you douse my water on Delos?" I asked. She didn't respond but I knew the answer. Of course she did. I drank the water, anyway, sensing that this time it was clean and I needed all the nourishment I could get.

"We must bind her hands," the younger woman said. "She will try to escape again."

"Yes, but not so tight," Maria ordered. "Use the silk."

I didn't struggle, couldn't, in fact—still too weak—as the woman bound my hands in the wrappings.

"Where is this place?" I asked again.

"You are in the sacred temple of Artemis," Maria said.

"The secret one, the hidden one?" I gazed around at a room that reminded me of the partial houses of Pompeii only much older and strangely intact. "When did you find it? It's incredible..."

"Others will answer your questions," Maria said.

Two young girls arrived, no older than twelve, giggling and excited in their brilliant saffron tunics. Each of them tossed flowers at my feet before stepping behind me.

"You brought children into... this mess?"

"They are honored," Maria said. "Cover her eyes!"

In a silken blindfold with my hands bound, I was guided forward, a hand on each arm. I could see nothing ahead but a faint glow through the fabric bindings—torches or braziers burning something fragrant, maybe frankincense and myrrh. Beneath my sandaled feet, the ground felt smooth as if paved in marble with petals scattered over the surface. Far in the distance, I could hear music playing—reeds and stringed instruments.

"This is crazy!" I whispered.

"Ritual is not crazy," Maria said solemnly, "though it may seem so to those who look in from the outside. All ritual binds humanity together in the darkness."

"Only this human happens to be bound physically. Doesn't that strike you as just a little ironic?" No answer. Didn't expect one. I continued to shuffle down what I sensed to be a long, long corridor. "Are we underground?"

"We are," Maria acknowledged, "far underground. No one will ever find us. This place has been hidden for millennia."

My heard was throbbing. *Oh, my God, they had found the secret temple of Artemis, but how, when?* I shuddered. "Why are you playing this game? Don't you know that men are pulling the strings for greed alone and that all this is just an elaborate charade?"

"Be quiet," Maria ordered. "You will understand soon enough."

Soon enough came only after musicians joined our procession. The lyres played and the reed pipes blew an ancient melody while the beating drums caught the rhythm of my heart.

Now I felt the space opening around us as others joined the procession, the sound of singing in a language I couldn't understand— beautiful, haunting, both joyful and poignant all at once.

I was guided across a large area where braziers burned all around, the light turning my blindfold an orangey-red. Hands guided me up one step, two steps, and at the third, I was turned and gently urged to sit on something that felt like hard, smooth stone. Then the blindfold was whipped off from over my eyes.

For a moment, all I could do was stare. A large painted cavernous room opened around me in the center of which stood a golden statue of Artemis running with a stag and hound, her quiver of arrows flung over one shoulder and a bow in her hands, authentic and ancient like the rest of this incredible place. Various cups and gold objects lay at her feet along with jeweled boxes and wreaths of flowers. Figures on the wall danced and plucked instruments while the living players they represented stood around in a huge circle, clapping, playing, still singing. Everywhere huge tripods held burning cauldrons bubbling with some noxious scent. Then abruptly the music stopped.

"No," I whispered.

"Yes," I heard a voice say.

I turned, shocked to discover that I was not alone on that dais. A long-faced man sat throned on my left, garbed in a brilliant red robe and wearing a golden headdress. One hand grasped something that looked for all the world to be a shaft of gilded wheat.

Peter Rose was the last person I expected. "This is a joke—you as the Hierophant! I knew those tarot cards would make an appearance sometime but not as characters in this...costume party. Should I expect the Fool next?" As if I could joke my way out of this.

He did not see the humor, anyway. "The Hierophant represents traditional knowledge, the high priest of the known world, but always he is balanced by his mate, the High Priestess, the keeper of the secret knowledge."

For a terrible moment I thought he meant me but a female spoke on my right.

"You will replace us."

I turned, not surprised to see Heather Rose yet shocked to my core. She sat garbed in blue robes with a silvered horned headdress featuring a moonstone orb caught like a huge pearl between antlers perched on her head. I wanted to laugh but couldn't. "Aren't you two mangling your symbolisms? What do the tarot images have to do with ancient Greece and the Temple of Artemis?" I knew the answer but damned if I was going to make this easy for anyone.

"The Greeks were greatly influenced by Egyptians and by the civilizations before and after. All symbolisms interconnect in sacred images that speak through time directly to the human heart, images embedded into the tarot cards. Listen to the ancient wisdom, Phoebe," Peter began. "From darkness comes light, from death rebirth. Those are the oldest truths known to mankind."

From the circle of robed spectators, one figure stepped forward—Sebastian. I had been expecting him. "Phoebe, you know full well how religious and ritual symbolisms morph across the centuries. How Christian Easter accommodates the eggs and rabbits of ancient fertility rites being only one such example. Why does this surprise you? We bring together all the secret symbols into this sanctuary in order to enact the sacred rites."

I had to keep him talking. At that moment, he seemed like the only link to sanity, albeit a thin one. "Where is this place?"

"Farther away than you can imagine but not as far away as you'd expect," he said. "We are in a system of underground caves and tunnels used for sacred worship for millennia, lost in time but then rediscovered, the site of the secret temple of Artemis. You are before her now."

My gaze swerved over his head to where the golden goddess raced with her stag and hounds—the priceless cella. Would he add that to his collection?

"So the archaeologists discovered this place and you killed them for it," I said. "That tunnel Peaches and I saw leads here."

"Yes and no," Peter said beside me. "It was necessary to silence them before they penetrated the full length of the Processional Way and discovered the temple. Painful yet unavoidable. We could not allow this to become exposed to the gaze of thousands. The nature of its sacredness lies in secrecy."

"And who gets to decide who sees it and who doesn't—you?" I asked, unable to mask my contempt.

"Yes, us," Heather said. "We revere and honor the ancients, therefore we accept the burden of protecting them."

I stared at her. She actually believed this stuff.

"However," Sebastian added, "the Processional Way you glimpsed would only lead them partway. Before the journey continues, there must be a blood sacrifice to the ancients. The true entrance to the temple lies elsewhere, hidden by a clever trick our ancestors deployed to protect their sanctuary. None of the uninitiated will ever find the way. To you, Phoebe, we bestow a great honor. You will bring us the lost key of Artemis."

Here we go. So, we were not on Delos? "You really expect me to be your sacred bloodhound and sniff out this lost key, seriously? How do you know it's even here?"

"It is here," he said, stepping right up to the dais and resting one sandaled foot on the first marble stair. "Look around you, Phoebe. Twelve passages connect to this cavern."

He said something in Greek and the robed and tunic-clad standers-by stepped away from entrances, some of which were lit but most not. "Here is a veritable maze of tunnels and chambers that are the original source of the labyrinth myth. The Cretans were frequent visitors in the past. The Pythia of Delphi escaped here, bringing the Artemis Key, which she reportedly hid in a labyrinth, this labyrinth. The *labyrinth*."

"And you expect me to enter this labyrinth to find something that has been lost for thousands of years?"

"And so you shall," Heather announced. "I had hoped it would be me but I have not your gifts. Though I have followed the ancient path in ritual and ceremony for many years, still no insight befalls me. Now the time has come to pass on the torch," she said. "You will retrieve the Artemis Key and return to this temple victorious where we will celebrate you as you deserve."

"Then you and your mate will take your seats upon these thrones, release us from our work, and usher in the dawn of a new day," Peter said.

"My mate? What in hell does that mean?" I didn't want to know the answer and yet a sick certainty knotted in my gut.

Four men entered the circle carrying a litter on which sat a man on a gilded chair. It took a moment to recognize the thin man seated there as Noel Halloran.

"I'll freeze in hell before I ever become a mate of yours," I said, half standing. A hand behind my seat pushed me down.

"That can be arranged, my sweet." He remained sitting on his chair before me, that little smile twisting his lips. "But let us not go through this again, Phoebe. You know we are meant to be together."

Decked out in a white robe with a red cloak thrown over his shoulders and what looked to be an infinity symbol balanced like a crown on his head, I just gaped. "The Magician—*you?*"

He grinned. "Yes, I am the Magician. I thought you would have figured that out by now. Didn't you read the hand I played? You are the High Priestess, I am the Magician. I don't much like the Hierophant—not sexy enough, in my opinion—but if you follow the Wheel of Fortune, it brings the two of us together again and again for I am your ultimate destiny. The Hanged Man was just a warning. Oh, and I had one other card to play but didn't get the chance last night—the Lovers. That's you and me, my sweet."

I wrestled all my curses to the ground. "Oh, please. Still playing without a full deck, I see. Since when did you concern yourself with occult or spirituality of any kind?" I demanded.

"Since you ruined my health, Phoebe. Such personal catastrophes cause a man to ponder the bigger issues of life and death while seeking meaning in existence. I am a changed man—enlightened, ready for the next stage." He placed one hand over his scarred heart and grinned.

Sebastian, who had been watching the exchange in silence, turned and caught Noel's eye.

"But no matter, my goddess," Noel hastened to say, "my friend reminds me that the time has come to enact your quest." He flicked his hand and two men stepped toward me to lift me up by the arms and drag me down the steps to stand before him. "You will go into the labyrinth and return with the Artemis Key, after which you will be crowned the High Priestess at my side."

"You crazy rat-shit bastard! What you really want is to screw these poor gamers here and run away with the goods! Don't believe anything he says! This is your real monster..." But the words died on my lips. Two women stepped from the watching circle bearing what looked to be gilded cup and a large ball of string. I watched in horror as they approached, dipped me a bow, and held their offerings with outstretched arms. "What the hell is this?" I whispered.

"You will be prepared for your quest in the manner of the ancient heroes—a drink to quench your thirst and a ball of twine to help find your way back through the labyrinth," Sebastian intoned. "A sacrifice in your honor has already been performed."

I stared at him in disbelief. "What sacrifice?"

"It is enough to know that the blood shed in your name will inspire the goddess to lead you through the darkness to find the key."

Every smart-assed retort died on my lips. Evan, Peaches, Zann? "Did you kill...?"

He raised a hand to silence me. "Enough. The moon rises high and time cannot be wasted. You must begin your journey now." Standing aside, he indicated a tunnel ahead, blissfully lit with torches. Relief washed over me at the thought that they would not send me down some dark hole without a light. Someone draped a thick wool cloak over my shoulders.

"The torches burn for but a short time and then you will be in darkness. Most of your journey must be without light, which is the ancient way. The goddess will guide you."

"And if she doesn't?" I had to keep panic at bay. Panic would not serve me. Panic would only drag me under.

"If she does not, it means that you are unworthy. The unworthy can never return." That was Heather speaking. "Use the thread to lead you back to this chamber only if you are successful and bring us the key. If you return empty-handed, you will be killed."

"It is so ordained," Peter said, sitting on his throne like some trumped-up bogeyman, "but we have faith that you are the One and so we send you forth with much love in our hearts. Let us begin!"

"I believe in you, Phoebe!" Noel called. "Come back to take your seat beside me according to your destiny."

And then the circus around me began to surge forward. I was half dragged toward the tunnel entrance while the musicians played, others sang and danced, children tossed flowers into my path, and Peter and Heather Rose chanted some unintelligible verse.s

How could I survive this pantomime, this fancy-dress ball of the ancient ritual revivalists? Their fervor was as real as any enacted in any church, synagogue, mosque, or place of worship the world over. Faith cannot be argued with, its rituals fused into the soul of its believers with a power outsiders can never counter. Noel was another beast altogether. He just played the game.

As much as my rational mind struggled to maintain dominance, a deep panic took hold because, unlike the ancients, I didn't believe that Artemis would help me survive this journey. I didn't believe in those gods and goddesses, period. Hell, I didn't even believe that the Artemis Key existed, let alone that I had a hope in hell of finding it. Where did that leave me once the lights went out?

My captors brought me to a standstill before the tunnel mouth. Beyond the doorway, the torches illuminated figures similar to those I'd seen inside the Processional Way. Did this tunnel link with that one? Was that the way out? "Has anyone mapped these tunnels using subsurface mapping equipment?" I asked in admittedly a small voice.

Sebastian, standing nearby, laughed. "Nobody knows these tunnels exist. To the rest of the world they are rumored only. This is the original labyrinth, Phoebe. Only you can find your way through and deliver the answers."

I shot a quick glance over my shoulder, estimating how many people I could engage in hand-to-hand combat or maybe startle enough to escape... but escape to where? There were tunnels all around. I had no idea what path my captors had taken to deliver me here, but at least a labyrinth supposedly offered a way out. My heart thumped relentlessly.

When I turned back towards the crowd, Maria stood before me holding the chalice. "Drink."

I gazed from the cup to her glassy eyes. "What is it?"

"Wine mixed with opium. It will help keep you calm and open your mind to the voice of the goddess."

"At least that's an honest answer. Are you even a doctor?"

"I am a doctor, yes."

"So when did you swap your Hippocratic Oath for the hypocritical kind?"

No response. She continued to gaze at me without blinking.

"No." I pushed the cup away. "I've had enough drugs for now."

"Then I will leave the chalice inside the door. Should you make your way back without the key, you may wish to drink of it to ease your death."

Holy hell. I watched in disbelief as she set the cup on a small table in the tunnel's mouth.

"Take the string."

I turned to my right to see Roberto Bergognone holding a ball of gold-colored twine. "This will be your way back to this chamber should you be successful."

"And what if I die inside those tunnels, Doc?" I asked.

"Then we will follow the string to see if you have acquired the key before you expired. If you have been successful, we will carry you back here and honor you with a hero's feast."

"Some consolation to poor little dead me. And if I don't have the key?"

"Then we will leave your body to rot in the tunnel unsung without honor."

I gazed into his strangely unfocused eyes, realizing that his pupils were dilated. Were all these wannabe ancients on drugs? I whipped the ball of string from his hands and strode to the tunnel; turning to face the crowd, I waved. "Let the show begin!" If the labyrinth was my only way to freedom, then I'd take it and run.

Don't ask what I expected next—more song and dance, maybe, cries of encouragement, anything but the earth-grinding screech of a huge boulder being hefted into place over the opening. I watched, stunned, as the stone blocked me in. A few thousand pounds of solid rock now lay between me and humanity, maybe forever more.

❧ 19 ❧

T took a few moments before I mustered the nerve to turn
around.

Ahead, the tunnel stretched down into a darkness lit inter-
mittently by torches illuminating the white and saffron tunic-clad walkers
on the walls. They would keep me company along the path. I was not the
first to take this journey. Who knew how many other women had gone
before me, sent down the throat of the labyrinth with the quest to bring
back what didn't exist? I studied the celebrants on the walls but they gave
no sign.

After tying the end of the string to the stone table leg, I took my first
step forward, unwinding the string as I went. Ariadne, the daughter of
Pasiphae and the Cretan king Minos, had gifted a jeweled thread to her
lover, Theseus, to help him find his way from the labyrinth. That is, after
he'd bested the Minotaur, or so the story went. I'd always thought the
Minotaur was symbolic of the fears that lurk in our unconscious minds,
our dark imaginings, the monsters hidden deep within.

I shivered at the thought. My handmaidens had draped me with a warm
woolen cloak that should chase away the worst of the tunnel's chill but
nothing could warm the fear that chilled me. My Minotaur breathed down

my neck with every step. Would I die alone in here, one of humanity's oldest fears being to enter and journey the dark alone?

I kept my gaze fixed on my one-dimensional companions on either side hoping for a little moral support. Painted in the archaic style with black snaking curls, lyres held upright, and expressions far more serious than those in the processional tunnel, they only increased my sense of loneliness. And they looked for all the world to be Minoan. That old. At least they had the decency not to dance and sing while they led me on. I longed to make contact with them, to feel their presence somehow, but the ancients were mute.

The deep dark ahead seemed absolute. How far did the tunnel go, how deep? Stay focused, I reminded myself. Don't let the monsters get you. I would get out of here, I *had* to get out of here. Labyrinths didn't exist with no way out. That would be cheating, but then, this wasn't any old labyrinth. This was *the old* labyrinth, maybe the original one upon which the myths were based. I truly hoped that the only monsters I'd encounter were those I left on the other side of that door.

After several feet, yards which may as well be miles, the wall art stopped just below the last torch. I stared at the junction of three tunnels branching off into darkness, each as black as the next, gazing down each, one by one. Which way? I looked up at my processional companions, hoping for a sign, but found none.

But one thing struck me at once: a single female figure dressed in blue robes and a cloak like mine stood staring straight ahead holding a candle high over her head. What was she saying? Hard to tell since most of her head had been blackened by the soot of many torches, but I felt she held a message.

"Did you ever come back?" I whispered. No response.

I needed to find my own light. I reached up and lifted the reed and resin-doused torch from its bracket and carried that in one hand with the ball of string in the other and took my first step into the tunnel straight ahead. But it felt wrong almost at once. I stared down the tunnel throat, an entrance without decoration or even signs of human intervention, more like a natural opening.

Backing out I tried the one on the left. Same thing. Next, I stepped into the right tunnel. Equally bare of decoration or signs of human handwork, the dark here seemed thicker and yet I could breathe easier. Why was that? Why did the other two tunnels smell stale and stuffy while this one slightly fresher? Holding the torch aloft, I strode down this tunnel as if I knew exactly where I was going, which was sickeningly far from the truth.

All I could think of was the cruelty we humans inflict upon one another in the name of our faith, how we used our religions to twist the words of our holy ones to excuse the abuse of power and domination over others. History is a wreckage of holy wars that crushed contrary voices while humanity continually endorses domination of one sex, one race, one rule, over another. When would it end?

And here I was shoved into a dark tunnel to seek a mythic object that probably did not exist, one more life playing into the hands of a cult—no other definition applied—led by men. Anger burned deep in my core tempered by compassion for all those who went before and all those world-wide who suffered still. And the children, always the most helpless of all victims.

Who was I, really? Nobody special. Just one lone woman walking in the dark where others had gone before.

My torch sputtered, sending me into a moment of panic. Soon it would go out and I truly would be in the dark, perhaps right up to my dying moment. I thought that I could hold it together as long as that flame burned but the moment it shuttered out...

Stepping carefully over the uneven surface was challenging but at least the torch illuminated the rocks and boulders that littered the path. I didn't know how much farther I had gone before I saw her, or I assumed that those bones had once belonged to a woman. They lay scattered across the path as if they had been kicked, possibly by accident. I hesitated, running the torch back and forth over the broken bits of human finger and one recognizable femur, my heart in my throat. Saying a little prayer, I stepped over them and continued.

In the myth, Ariadne had offered her lover string to help him find his way back to her. Clever, clever Ariadne, I thought as I continued winding out the twine. And what did the great Athenian hero do to thank his brave lover? Abandoned her on a rock, helpless and brokenhearted. And what did the ancient storytellers create for her salvation? They sent the god

Dionysus to rescue her with his love, the ultimate happy ending: male rescues female because he decides she's worthy of his love.

But I'd rather have had Ariadne rescue herself and become twice the hero that Theseus had ever been, somebody honorable who never abandoned friends for a better offer. No words existed for the intensity of my anger toward Noel just then. He was Theseus without the heroism, a slippery, gaslighting bastard who would send anyone to hell if there was something in it for him. He had orchestrated this, used Sebastian's fervent love for all things ancient Grecian to set up this charade. Torturing me was part of his plan as was stealing whatever of Sebastian's he could get his hands on. It was all so clear to me. Why couldn't anybody else see it?

And then I tripped, tumbling down a sharp incline before I grasped what was happening. Startled, the torch went flying, sputtered briefly, and then went out.

"No!" I scrambled on my hands and knees to where I saw the torch land against a rock. The thing still smoldered, red and smoky. Lifting it up, I tried waving it about hoping the air would reignite the flame but no luck. Shit! Back on my feet again, I retrieved the ball and continued on my way still waving the torch in hopes that the thing might revive, but after a few minutes, the smoke made it too difficult. Tossing the thing down, I felt my way along.

In total darkness now. The full impact of my predicament hit. Before then I could while away my progress with musings, but something about the dark seemed so impenetrable that it filled my mind with fear. Panicking, I started running, dropped the string, picked it up, tripped again, pitched myself back up, and was just about to bolt again when a sudden insight hit.

Drop the string.

I stood frozen to the spot, listening. The dark felt alive around me, though I couldn't sense any one thing that proved that. My senses only felt cold, saw dark, but still something else seemed to surround me. Some deep-down part of myself said that I had to make a choice: either let fear rule or let the dark be my guide. I dropped the ball of twine and kept on moving, more confident with every step.

That may have been the single bravest thing I'd ever done. At that moment I knew that I could never go back, only forward, always forward, that as dark as the world grew around me, the strongest light shone within. I needed to *feel* to listen, listen to feel with my heart and soul, no matter how hokey that might sound to anybody else.

Not an easy path but a surer one. The way was stony, often with jagged bits that scraped my legs and feet, shredding the robe as I went. It grew colder with every step, and somewhere along the way, the ground began to climb as if the dark leaned upward. The air felt cooler here but fresher, too. A whiff of the sea teased my nostrils. Heartened, I trudged on, thinking of the last Pythia.

Who had she been? Chosen among the priestesses devoted to Apollo at Delphi, she reportedly spoke of the future to her supplicants while inhaling fumes that emitted from a crack in the ground above the Castalian Spring —a drug by any other name. Rumors of the Artemis Key emerged only later, in approximately the sixth century BC. In those centuries when the Byzantines took hold and a new religion began spreading across the Mediterranean, she supposedly escaped with the key in hand.

The Pythia believed that the Artemis Key was sacred. If I feared that something treasured would fall into the wrong hands, what would I do? Wouldn't I be terrified that whatever was in my care would either be destroyed or put on display to be gawked at like a curiosity by millions of disbelievers? How horrible a sacrilege was that?

Our museums brim with objects once sacred to other civilizations but now relegated to the status of curiosities. The Pythia predated museums, as we know them, but the thought of a sacred object being melted down to be turned into baubles for the enemy or, even worse, to fund an army to kill more of her people, must have been unbearable. What would I have done?

I had climbed so far by now that my arms ached, my hands bled, and I could barely catch my breath. Cold fresh air blew down from above but I was too tired to notice. A shelf of rock was dimly visible a few feet over-head. If I could just reach that, I could rest. With what seemed to be my last burst of energy, I hoisted myself up and leaned against the wall to catch my breath. Much more climbing ahead but why bother? Maybe I'd just die here, quiet and peaceful in the dark. So much easier...

My gaze caught some lighter-than-dark gleam on the ledge nearby, not wondering on how I could see anything. Reaching out, I touched something dry and brittle. And stared. A bone? I pressed myself back farther against the rock face. Oh, my God! Not another skeleton keeping me company here, too? Small and comparatively child-like in size, the skull gleamed as a faint luminescence washed the bones with the palest of light.

She was huddled into a fetal position, the curve of her spine seeming to shelter something among bones so brittle they might crumble to dust if touched. I had no doubt as to who she was.

"Pythia," I whispered. "You arrived."

The hairs pricked at the base of my neck. I swear on all that is true and real that she had led me there, that she had urged me to drop the string, that she was with me still. She had no intention of ever going backward, either. Her time had ended, heralded in by a formidable decree that all that she had once held sacred must be banished from the earth forevermore. Gone in the dawn of a new age.

I began to cry, choking back water I couldn't afford to waste. Carefully, I reached between the bones and tugged out something that gleamed golden in the half-light. The bones disintegrated as I held up a chain with a small object dangling at one end. A roped belt, maybe, with a single plain key—not an ankh or a jeweled-encrusted anything, but a plain gold key. I knew without knowing how that this had been the key to the temple where the Pythia had once been high priestess. Without a second thought, I dropped it over my head, letting it fall cold against the skin under my robes. I knew exactly what she wanted me to do as if she'd spoken the words right into my ear.

Go.

Overhead I saw stars twinkling in the dark. Funny how I hadn't realized how close I'd come to my escape. Gripping the wall, I struggled to my feet. An easy climb up. She could have made it but decided to join the goddess instead. That wasn't my path.

I shoved one foot into an indentation in the rock and began to climb.

𝕾 2 0 𝕾

I t couldn't have been farther above than three yards. I pulled myself out through branches into a cold silvered world. Waves crashed far below while ahead the moon was slipping behind an island across the sea. Artemis was going home. Above, at least four more yards of uninterrupted cliff, but here there was light, there was air—I was alive!

Perched high up on a cliff with no visible way down or up and no light to see by, I was no farther ahead, short-term. To make matters worse, the ledge where I clung seemed to be no wider than two feet with nothing but a scrubby bush keeping me company.

But morning would come eventually. Maybe if I wedged myself in among the branches of that bush that grew with maniacal tenacity, I could catch some sleep. That shrub might even hold me. Shivering, twigs scratching the skin through my robes, I tried to spread my weight evenly along the ledge while wrapping my limbs through the branches. Unable to relax enough to truly rest, the best I could do was convince myself that I wouldn't topple over the edge—yet. Somehow an uneasy sleep must have overcome me because the next thing I knew, light filled the sky.

I blinked at the bands of a glorious sunrise pouring molten gold through flying hills of purple cloud and thought it the sweetest, most glorious sight I had ever seen—hope in full color. Ahead the dark outline of an island I thought must be Mykonos increased the drama. Forget my ripped skin, hunger, and thirst—even the throbbing headache retreated. I was alive!

Leaving my cloak and chiton bunched inside the thicket, I clutched a branch with one hand and leaned over the ledge. My enthusiasm plummeted. It was a straight fifty-foot drop ending in crashing surf. No handholds or anything to break that stony face—nothing. The only way to get down was by rope, which I didn't have, and my fraying gown wouldn't help me here. I pulled back, my heart thumping. *Trapped.*

The sun rose higher on the horizon while I sat huddled against the bushes, my legs tucked underneath me, wrapping what was left of my chiton and robe close. Something flickered in the back of my mind. Where did these cliffs come from? I'd seen nothing that matched this topography when studying the Delos geography. I recalled that the low, rocky island had hills no higher than sixteen feet, so where was this?

Staring ahead unfocused, I didn't notice the bird flying around the edge of the cliff at first. In the rising sun, it was nothing but a black speck. When I finally caught the movement, I thought I was watching a bird that should be swooping and wheeling but instead made a steady path in my direction. Too odd. Stiffening, I watched the thing growing closer, tracking straight for me. Well, damn—no bird but a drone! I began waving my red cloak in the air. I'm here! Here!

Blessing every hair on every head who had employed this ingenious way to locate the missing, I struggled to stay calm. If Evan or Peaches were behind this and got me off this cliff, I'd hug them one by one—maybe extralong for one, especially. My red robe must have attracted the drone's camera because it swerved closer.

No need to keep flapping my arm, so I stopped, waiting for it to sail up to me as I hunched over wearing nothing but my loincloth and bandeau. Whoever was operating this thing had to be nearby but how did my team even know I was here? I didn't even know I was there until a few seconds ago. So, if this wasn't Delos, how did they find me? I stilled, watching the thing approach.

As drones go, this model was about the size of a toaster oven with four propellers and a camera mounted before the housing. Having the thing hover before me without knowing who was looking back was unnerving. If it was Evan, I knew he'd be there to rescue me within minutes, but if it was... Then I spotted the Poseidon logo on the housing. No damn way!

I grabbed whatever loose stones I could find on the ledge and began firing them at the thing while it ducked and swooped like it was all some kind of joke. One good-sized rock hit one wing and knocked the techno-beast sideways. Recovering, it came back at me. This time I hit the camera, cracking the glass. Yeah, take that, bastards!

I was shouting myself hoarse by then, hoping the monsters had audio capabilities to catch my curses. Still the drone hovered. It was looking for something, I realized, and in a flash I knew that *something* hung around my neck—the Pythia's key. They must be able to see it since I was practically naked. They'd assume that I'd found the Artemis Key—idiots.

"Come get me, you bastards!"

And then vertigo hit with sudden force. I clutched the bush with one hand as my legs flew out from under me and I began skidding over the edge. One of the branches broke away as I clung to the other with a death grip. Now I was just hanging on with one arm, the other trying to clutch the rock beneath me. What a spectacle my rear view was making; as if I had time to think about that stuff but that's where my mind went.

I could hear the drone hovering behind me but now I caught the unmistakable throb of a helicopter somewhere. That had to be the Sebastian-Noel delegation on the way to retrieve the Artemis Key. Perhaps they wanted me to smash on the rocks below so they could send down a team to pick the key from my ruined body. As if I'd make it that easy.

Inch by inch, I managed to crawl my way back up the ledge. By now the bush had broken away altogether, leaving nothing but a stump to cram myself between that and the cliff. There I waited as the drone hovered and the helicopter grew closer. I couldn't bring down a helicopter—hell, I couldn't even down a drone—but if they wanted me, they had to pluck me off this ledge and hope to hell I couldn't figure out a way to crash the bastards while they were at it.

Two things happened next: the drone operators must have noticed the helicopter at the same time that the helicopter noticed the drone. The flying toaster suddenly dropped from my sight, but based on the path the helicopter now took, a chase had begun.

I watched in fascination as the helicopter started firing at the cliff wall below me, the ping of bullets hitting stone. The copter swerved close enough for me to see Peaches hanging out the door firing with an AK. I tried waving but the stump lurched between my legs. Maybe they hadn't seen me, maybe they were going to zap the drone while I skidded off the edge. I could see Evan at the controls. I tried shouting my lungs out but of course nobody could hear.

For a horrible instant I thought I'd smash to the rocks while they played seek and destroy with the drone. But something changed. Peaches looked up, saw me, and started shouting. The helicopter swerved back to hover about twenty feet away. Peaches stared at me while I stared back, everybody calculating. Suddenly the chopper lifted and I watched with my heart in my throat as a rope ladder dropped from above.

No way could I reach that thing and I sure as hell couldn't jump that far, either. Peaches began climbing down, swaying wildly on what looked to be a flimsy rope. It was windy enough to make this kind of rescue risky if not plain nuts.

"Jump!" Peaches called.

"It's too far!" I cried back.

I stared at the rope swaying back and forth, watching as Evan attempted to maneuver closer by lifting the chopper high enough to avoid hitting the cliffside. The rope now dangled no farther than six feet away but the bottom rung was still above my head. I'd have to jump to reach it.

"Jump, Phoebe!" Peaches cried. "I'll catch you!"

"How?" Just like me to ask for specifics when nothing but faith would do. And faith could do a lot. The ledge shifted beneath me. I sprung into the air as Peaches leaned over to grab me.

⚜

SHE HUNG ON TO ME WHILE I CLUTCHED THE BOTTOM RUNG. I DIDN'T think I had it in me to hoist my bottom half far enough up to secure my legs let alone hang on that long.

"What the hell are you wearing, Phoeb? I have nothing to grip!" Peaches yelled.

I was ignoring the waves racing away below me while she clutched me by one arm and the back of my bandeau as I tried to hoist my body weight up. The ladder was simultaneously pulling in—one of those automatic things—and Zann was leaning out of the door cheering us on. The moment the ladder reached the top, Peaches yanked on the bandeau while Zann fixed some kind of sling under my arms and within seconds I was hauled inside. Minutes later, I sat huddled in one of the chopper's seats, buried under blankets shivering my teeth off.

"Here, drink this." Zann was passing me a thermos. "I've got your phone and backpack here. You need to put on some clothes, Phoeb. What aren't you wearing?"

"Phoebe, I'm so relieved you're alive!" That was Nick. I stared at him over the back row of seats. He was there, too?

"Your father's a blind fool," I told him between chattering teeth.

"My father?" Poor guy looked stunned.

"He's d-down there now...dressed up like an ancient G-Greek. He owns that island, right?"

He almost couldn't speak. "Probably...I mean, maybe. He owns islands all over the Aegean." Realization widened his eyes. "Oh, my God! He's behind this?"

"P-partially."

"Turn your back, Nick," Zann said, waving him away. "Got to get her dressed."

"My father's behind your kidnapping?" he said over her shoulder, his expression stricken. "I didn't know he was after you. I had no idea! And I led him right to you."

"He would have found me e-eventually," I said. "He was a...l-lurker in your ancient civilization th-theorist group while c-considering all those members to be loonies. He's a user and abuser."

I could tell that he was still trying to get his head around that. In fact, he probably thought I was still referring to his father.

"Phoebe!" That was Evan up front.

"Evan!" I called.

Peaches was ordering Nick to avert his gaze again while plucking out the extra set of clothes I always crammed into the bottom of my backpack. "Here, put these on. I'll hold up the blanket. Hurry!"

But all I could do was sip and shake, my limbs trembling so badly that I needed both Peaches and Zann's help to don my leggings and sweater while gazing at the back of Evan's head and my friends' faces one by one.

"You've been scratched to bits," Peaches exclaimed. "Did you climb up the cliff or something?"

"Through a l-labyrinth," I told her through chattering teeth. "*The* labyrinth. Follow that drone!" I cried, one leg in the air.

"Following it now. Ev, what's the drone status?" Peaches called while pulling my leggings on over my knees.

But he had earphones on.

"Looks like it's heading over the top of the cliff," Zann called while looking out the window.

"Watch that thing!" Nick called, diving for the side window.

"Where are we?" I looked over my shoulder down at a formation of white peaks rising from the sea like a fistful of broken bones.

"A tiny uninhabited island called Polydomos, east of Naxos," Evan shouted while passing back earphone sets. "Put these on. Only way to talk here."

I put on the ear set, now dressed, at last. The tea was unlocking my brain and soul. "How'd you find me?"

"I had a hunch," Zann said. "I met Nick after you disappeared, and while a search team combed the island, we went up to the dig on Delos. Turns out that those tunnels end at a beach on the other side with evidence of recent boat activity. They found two more bodies up there."

"The cult of Artemis involved boat processions traveling across islands to the secret temple. Artemis was associated with water crossings," Nick explained into my ear. "We knew they'd taken you off Delos and I knew it had to be somewhere nearby, so checking all of the islands within a reasonable radius was a place to start."

"Noel was behind this," I said. "He roped your father into a bit of ritual playacting so I would fetch them the key. When was the last time you saw your father, Nick?"

"Long ago, after I realized he'd been poaching Grecian art, but I had no idea just how far he'd go."

"Further than anyone could imagine," I said. "He and that arms-dealing art-thief bastard were behind this whole thing, even the tarot cards. Noel's been hiding out with him!"

"Noel!" That was Evan, his voice husky with emotion. "I was tracking him in France before I flew here."

"Probably a bloody wild-goose chase planned in advance," Peaches grumbled.

"Noel's down there?" Zann cried. "Let me at the bastard!"

"Yeah, he's down there. Decked himself out like the Magician from the Rider-Waite tarot deck and participated in a ritual to sacrifice me to the labyrinth. There's a labyrinth down there, like I said, the original one, the one they thought was on Knossos. They sent me down there to find the Artemis Key."

Evan swore with more venom than I'd ever heard uttered from a good man's lips. "I'll kill the bastard!"

"No, he'll try and kill you first. I couldn't bear that to happen. That would be his ultimate punishment—for me to lose everything and everyone I care for. That's what it will all be about now: tracking me to lost treasure and then watching me suffer."

"We'll kill him for you," Zann wailed.

"Damn right!' Peaches added.

"Did you find it?" Nick was asking. "Did you find the Artemis Key?"

"Yes and no," I said. "More later. It's a long story."

Peaches gaze swerved to the long gold plaited rope hanging around my neck. Our eyes locked. "I'm so damned relieved that you're alive," she whispered. "If we hadn't caught sight of you—"

"But you did!" How I wanted to hug them all right then. "Guess who else is part of this show? The Drs. Bergognones and the Roses! Seriously. Long story short: the secret temple of Artemis is buried intact deep inside the cliffs below—on Polydomos—and those four were behind my abduction all along."

"The two doctors and the Roses?" Peaches gasped. "My God, I'll throttle their scrawny little necks!"

"The lost temple of Artemis—seriously?" Zann exclaimed. "What's it like?"

"Intact?" Nick exclaimed. "You mean that it truly does exist just as we've always believed? Oh, my God! I must see it! Describe every detail!"

But I had other things on my mind. "Noel—" I practically spat out his name "—is down there playing dress-up with your father, Nick. It's some kind of bizarre version of the ancient Pythia ceremony mixed with the Eleusinian Mysteries and whatever occult rituals they could cobble together to feed their egos. I'll tell you more later. Let's just get the bastards."

Like I had to ask. Evan was already hell-bent on tracking that drone, but one look out the window proved how hard that would be. The thing had disappeared.

"Where'd it go?" Zann asked. She was looking out one window, me out the other. Peaches had climbed back up front with Evan leaving Nick in the rearmost seat. The chopper was flying low over the cliffs as the sunrise spilled its glory over the Aegean. We were all buckling up our seat belts.

"Can't see it," Evan announced. "It may have landed. There's no place to bring a helicopter down but plenty of places to hide a drone—or a person. I see a boat, though. They must have operated that thing from the deck."

"Three boats," Zann called.

"Five boats, ten boats. I'm losing count!" Nick cried.

We all peered through the closest windows. Multiple speedboats and cabin cruisers were zooming away from the island in a circular formation, each heading in a different direction. "No!" I gasped,

"Boats on this side, too!" Zann called. "Boats everywhere!"

"The bastards had to have an escape plan," Evan said. "They are dispersing in all directions!"

A sharp pang hit my gut and chest simultaneously. "Pull up, Evan! The island's going to blow!"

Evan pulled back on the wheel and swerved the chopper high to veer away over the water. We hadn't made it more than a few hundred yards when the cliffs below shook and shattered as if something had combusted from within, the impact knocking the chopper sideways.

🦋 2 1 🦋

"They blew up the island?" Zann cried, clinging to a handhold while the helicopter lurched and tipped through the billowing smoke.

A cold realization gripped me by the throat: he'd had his contingency planned in advance. Should I not retrieve their key, should the location of the temple be breached in any way, everything would be destroyed. Just like that—boom!

"They blew up the secret temple of Artemis?" Zann wailed. "What kind of monsters destroy an ancient intact Grecian temple? Who does shit like that?"

"Noel," I shouted back. "Noel does shit like that and you can believe he's run away with some of the treasures while he's at it!"

"Oh, my God, let's get them!"

Forcing the truth into my brain provoked bouts of burning rage alternating with frozen grief. How could he? This seemed low even for him and how could Sebastian claim to revere the ancients on one hand while destroying one of the greatest discoveries in the modern world on the other?

I fell back in my seat, processing the loss, wresting with rage, while vaguely aware of Evan struggling to level the helicopter. Peaches called out from beside him. "There are, like, twenty boats down there! How are we supposed to know which one the bastards are on?"

"That's the idea," Evan called. "I'm in touch with the Greek authorities now. The police will attempt to round them up but—" He broke his sentence to speak to someone on two-way radio.

All those boats taking off in multiple directions. Which one carried Noel, Sebastian, the treasure?

"My father has ferries and ships all over these waters. Look for a ferry!" Nick called. "There are ways to pluck a boat out of the sea right under everyone's nose!" But no ferries were in sight.

While Evan held a terse conversation with somebody on ground control, we dropped and banked back and forth over the Aegean. I was trying to keep an eye on the dispersing flotilla but part of me was too numb to do much other than to sit and stare. Then a sudden thought had me reaching back to clutch for Nick's hand. "The island where your father hides all his treasures, do you know where that is?"

He stared. "No. There's an island? I'd always suspected there was such a place but never knew where. After we disowned one another, I was kicked way out of the loop."

"Any ideas?" I squeezed his hand. "You said he owned islands all over the Aegean. One of them has to fit the description of a seemingly uninhabited islet with huge cliffs dropping straight to the sea. Ring any bells? *Think!*"

"That describes three-quarters of the Greek isles," he said. "There are six thousand islands and islets in Greece!"

"Your father has an alternative universe staged on this islet—pseudo ancient Greece decorated by his haul of looted art combined with a helipad. How can you hide that?"

"Easily," he countered. "It could be anywhere."

"But it's not anywhere," I insisted. "It has to be within a boat trip away from Polydomos. They knocked me out at around nine o'clock at night, and several hours later, I was on Polydomos."

"That doesn't prove a thing," Zann said, listening in. "You could be in London by plane in a couple of hours."

I met her eyes. She was right. "From what I recall, I'm guessing they used at least one boat and a helicopter. The islet is nearby somewhere and I'm guessing they're heading straight for it."

"Not straight," I heard Evan say. "Too obvious. My bet is that the bastards will go island- and boat-hopping to throw us off the scent. To make a straight line for the hideout is too risky. They'll divert."

"In the meantime, look for a ferry," Nick called. "Look for any ship labeled *Diamandus*. All his ships are marked with his surname."

"Sebastian Diamandus?" Peaches asked. "The ferry I took to Mykonos was named *Diamandus*."

"The surname you refused to take," I said, my admiration for Nick growing.

"On the day he left my mom and me, I took her name and refused to bear his ever after. He tried to get me to accept my inheritance but I refused that, too," he called. "I refuse to be his son! I didn't want anything of his then and still don't. The last time I laid eyes on him was five years ago at my mother's funeral. He dared to make an appearance."

Evan had leveled the helicopter by now and we were zipping across the sea following the wake of multiple boats, but the likelihood of tracking down the ringleaders seemed impossibly slim. The people who'd participated in that charade were probably ignorant of where the main players were heading. Or, at least, that's what I would have done—played a shell game from start to finish. Noel and Sebastian had to be hiding elsewhere.

"The police have boarded two of the larger boats," Evan called. "Look below."

We all gazed out to where multiple sets of flashing red lights broke the serene dawn glow. I knew without knowing that neither contained our quarry but maybe those on board had crucial information.

"We're heading back to Mykonos to refuel and question whoever the police round up. It's a place to start," Evan added.

It *was* a place to start, I acknowledged grudgingly, but it was equally a monumental time-waster. I guessed that none of the actors corralled that morning had the answers we so desperately needed.

In the police car later, on our way from the helicopter to the station, Evan and I sat together at the back holding hands. We'd barely spoken a word but we didn't need to. I could tell by the grip of his fingers how grateful he was that I was alive and my gratitude to him was equally bound-less. There'd be time for words later.

Forty minutes later we were all crammed into a white blue-shuttered building on Mykonos that reminded me of a Greek version of a western sheriff's office. There was barely space to breathe and Covid protocols had each interview restricted to two police officers, two escapees, plus Evan and myself, at a time. The only ones on the first two captured boats I wanted to interview were Maria and Roberto, the only two I recognized. The others were mere bit players.

"Who are you? State your names and addresses," the police officer said in English.

Time wasted, time wasted...

"Dr. Maria Christina Lucretia Bergognone," Maria stated in an expres-sionless voice after which her husband added his full name plus their address in Milan. This was going to take forever.

"Why did you drug, kidnap, and participate in this conspiracy of greed?" I demanded, half rising from my chair. Evan placed a hand on my knee. Any other time and I would have loved that but...

"Sit down, please, Ms. McCabe. I'll ask for your assistance when need-ed." Got it: the officers, a young, serious-faced guy and an older man both in blue masks and black uniforms, were in control of the interrogation. I was to speak upon request only. How Evan even managed to get us this far was amazing. Until Interpol arrived, our hands were tied, yet these guys didn't know a fraction of what was going on here.

After more question and answer time, all of it preliminary and no doubt following the interrogation code of a small police station, after listening to Maria and Roberto demanding a lawyer based on their rights as citizens of Italy, I'd had enough.

"They're stalling," I exclaimed, getting to my feet, "and while you ques-tion them, the ringleaders are getting away!"

I left the room, slamming the door behind me, the sense of time-frit-tering futility overwhelming. I stepped into the washroom and splashed water on my cheeks. Moments later I was staring in the mirror at a pinched face framed with corkscrew curls and some kind of elaborate topknot. One gold earring dangled from my ear. For a fleeting second, my face reminded me of an ancient Roman funerary portrait only with blue eyes, red hair, and a murderous expression. Pulling away, I strode through the crowded station and out the side door.

Outside, I found Peaches, Nick, Zann, and about thirty others dressed in ancient Greek garb sitting outside on a whitewashed wall guarded by two armed officers. I scanned everyone's faces. No Thalia, no Peter or Heather Rose, no Noel or Sebastian, either. The ringleaders had escaped. I wanted to scream.

"Did you check yourself out in a mirror when you used the loo, woman?" Peaches asked mildly, joining me in my pacing back and forth.

"Yes, why?"

"Because you're wearing one earring, a really old, interesting earring. Hey, Zann," she called.

Zann scrambled over to join us.

"Take a look at what Phoebe's got dangling from her ear."

Zann peered so close I could smell her suntan lotion. "Well, damn, if it isn't Artemis running away across the sea, or at least I assume those wavy things at her feet mean water."

They helped me unfasten the wire hook closure and studied the exquisitely detailed golden earring as it lay in my palm. I expelled my breath in a whoosh. "That wave formation is actually based on the symbol of the meandering path or the Greek key design," I whispered. "They believe one is derived from the other."

"And the Greek key symbol also represents the labyrinth." Nick had arrived on my right-hand side.

I looked up at him. "I need a map of the Cyclades," I said.

"Here." Peaches plucked her tablet from her bag.

"Let's find a table."

In minutes we had all tromped back inside the station past more ancient Greek bit players crowding up the waiting room into an empty office. Everybody official was too tied up to stop us. Apparently, someone had blown up an island.

"Nick," I said, staring down at the Google map app open on the Greek islands, "*think*. Try to remember yourself as a child when you and your father were still speaking. Do you remember any time when he might have said something like 'one day all this will be yours, son'?"

"Ha," he said, digging his hands into his curly hair as he paced around the tiny space, "I'm trying to think. I remember plenty of boat rides—always boat and ferry rides with lots of islands passing by. He'd say, 'I own this one, I own that one,' but I don't remember which islands they were. I couldn't have been older than six or seven."

"No plane rides?" Peaches asked.

"I hated planes and helicopters back then. They gave me the jitters. I was always crying. There was this one time when—" He stopped.

"When what?" Zann prompted.

"When my father took me up in a helicopter..." he said, his eyes glazed with memory. "I was screaming at the top of my lungs; he was trying to comfort me. We were flying low over all these islands and he was saying, 'This will be our sanctuary someday.'"

"Where?" I demanded.

"I don't know where," he said. "It was all so long ago! We took off here, from Mykonos, I remember that much."

Unfastening the pen from Peaches's tablet case, I took a screenshot of the map of the Cyclades before making a red mark using the tablet's photo program right over Mykonos. I then proceeded to draw several Greek key patterns radiating out from one direction after another, always intersecting Delos and the tiny speck that was Polydomos.

My Greek keys meandered in multiple directions like a geometric accordion. Nick would pinch open the live map to see which islands were captured in the design. We did this for several minutes before Nick's finger came down in the middle of the Aegean. "There. Perpendicular to the last right-angled key."

"Pinch it farther out," Zann demanded.

He did until we were staring down at a tiny speck of an island too easy to miss at first glance.

"That must be it," I whispered. "That's his sanctuary."

"Does it have a name?"

"It must but it's not labeled on this map. At least we have the coordinates."

Evan had arrived at the door. Our eyes met. "We need a helicopter fast."

22

R eturning to the helicopter required a fifteen-minute ride back to the airport following a heated discussion between Evan and the police until Interpol intervened via phone call. When we finally lifted off, another hour had been wasted and I was almost jumping out of my skin.

Below, the Aegean zipped by, mesmerizing blue streaming with the wakes of boats and broken by islands for as far as the eye could see. The trip to the islet would take at least fifteen minutes, according to the map. I had been reunited with my phone by then but, strangely, my pleasure in its company had waned. It was as though somewhere in the labyrinth I had been reunited with my own internal GPS. Sometimes there's so much ambient noise, we lose it.

"What happened on the *Sylvan Seas?*" I asked no one in particular as we sat in our seats, earphones on, me in front with Evan, the other three in the back. Evan's profile against sky and wispy clouds was enough to quicken a marble Aphrodite's pulse. It certainly worked on mine. He caught my gaze in a sideways glance and smiled. For two seconds all was right with the world.

"Captain Adamos went ballistic when you disappeared," Nick replied, "and held me accountable, of course. He was still yelling when Peaches arrived and took the phone from my ear."

"We didn't have time for that shit," Peaches explained. "I was looking for the real culprits. Guess what I found in Peter and Heather's cabin? A pack of tarot plus a copy of our keycard. So Giorgi and I took off to follow your trail back up the hill where the docs had whisked you off to the medical facility."

"Only there is no medical facility on the island," Nick added. "Susan and Renate and some of the others tried to follow you but they were ordered back by a couple of guys dressed up as security guards. I'm guessing they were all part of the sham. I trusted those doctors. I thought they were real physicians, and when Roberto insisted that you'd had a stroke, I thought that could be true even though you're too young."

"Not a stroke, but a drug-induced collapse," I told him. "Maria doused my water somehow. Roberto and Maria are real doctors but also conniving believers in your father's alternate Greek universe."

"And probably being paid megabucks, too," Zann muttered. "Money never says 'it's all Greek to me.'"

I turned to look at her. She shrugged.

"And then there were the Roses," Peaches continued. "They were my first suspects since finding the tarot pack but they'd disappeared, too. By then, we knew who we were looking for but the place was chaos. The Mykonos police had arrived and ordered everybody off Delos."

"I landed just minutes before," Evan said. "They arrested me for refusing to leave but a call to Interpol headquarters nixed that. A bloody frustrating waste of time. Every second counts in a kidnapping case and I couldn't bear to think what they had planned for you."

"Plenty, as it turns out," I said.

Zann picked up the story. "So while the local cops had Evan in handcuffs and Peaches was arguing with them to free him, Nick and I took off for the Delos dig when no one was looking. Like I said before, I had a hunch that they may have taken you there."

"It was a joint hunch," Nick added.

"Yeah, it was." She grinned at him. "So we scrambled up to the dig and guess what? The gates were wide open and one of the real security dudes had been shot along with that George Baros character. We ran the length of the Processional Way—man, those frescoes are something else—and it ended at a beach with signs that a boat had recently been launched."

"But not recently enough," Peaches said. "Maybe twenty minutes earlier, long enough for the bastards to get away. That's when Ev brought in the helicopter."

I rubbed my temple, surprised to find my corkscrews had turned to ringlets. Meanwhile, my headache came knocking again. "Okay...so I missed plenty of fun and drama. Is there anything left in that thermos?"

"Sure. Filled it up at the station." Zann passed me her flask.

"Thanks."

"You smell fishy," she remarked.

"They tried to wash most of it off but that stuff sticks around," I told her.

"Are you all right, Phoebe?" Evan asked, shooting me a quick glance.

"Fine," I said with a smile. "I'm just boiling mad and ready to spit nails. I want to see Noel behind bars so I could visit him and spit in his face. Or dead." That stunned me. Had I really said that? Yes, and the shock was in just how much I meant it.

"We'll get him," Evan promised.

"But maybe not soon enough." I already had that deep gut chill telling me that he'd escaped,

Five minutes later, I recognized the islet below, the zing of my excitement tempered by the sight of numerous ships within miles of the outcrop, including a mammoth cruise vessel sailing south toward the Mediterranean. Evan dropped the chopper's altitude until we were staring down at the islet's gnarly top, then we could see the lookout promontory, and even the vacant helipad.

"The good news is that that's the right islet," I said.

"And the bad news is that the empty helipad with no visible boats moored on that jetty could mean that they've been and gone," Evan added.

I nearly choked on my heart when the chopper landed. I couldn't wait until it was safe to unbuckle and climb outside.

"We should spread out!" I called as I ducked below the beaters and headed for the metal stairs. The garage door was now shut.

"I'm with you!" Peaches shouted.

"Me, too," Zann said as I pounded up the metal stairs.

"We'll stick together!" Evan ordered, and I let him take charge based on his experience in these matters. When he raced up behind me and gently pushed me behind him, I went along with that, too. Don't quibble when a good man is on your side. Besides, by then I was exhausted and a bit strung-out.

Of course the metal door was locked, but Evan had it open in seconds after which we all piled into a series of dark, empty rooms. No computers anywhere and it seemed no source of power, either. The place had been abandoned.

My heart pounded in my ears. "The bastard's cleaned the place out." I gazed around, using my phone to illuminate the barren shelves with the occasional dangling plug. "There has to be a door connecting to the pleasure half of the property somewhere."

We found it several minutes later—another of the steel variety once secured by an electronic lock but now held closed by a standard padlock that Evan easily severed with his laser app. Beyond that, a corridor with stairs leading straight up. At the top, a door opened onto the outside back corner of the building. I recognized the path up to the promontory to the left but bolted around the corner, across the tiles, past the pool, toward the gymnasium door. Inside, the sense of a building abandoned was increased.

But once inside the atrium, all I could do was stand and stare. I had expected anything but this. Everything stood exactly as I'd seen it last, including Aphrodite guarded by Medusa's gnarly head at her feet and every piece of pottery on every marble pediment table in between. "Why hasn't he taken his collection?" I gasped.

"Look at this place!" Zann exclaimed, dashing past me. "That statue looks like the real deal and that mosaic—wow! Third maybe fourth century BC."

Nick didn't say a word, only gazed around with his mouth half-open.

"This is only part of it," I told them. "Every room in this place is filled with art of this caliber. He couldn't have been able to move it in time."

"Where would he have taken it?" Nick asked, turning to me. "Father claimed never to have loved any place as much as he loved Greece. If escaping with his art meant bolting to another country, he'd never do it."

"Let's not assume that the property is deserted quite yet," Evan warned. "First we need to turn this place upside down. Interpol is en route but it could take hours before they get here. Let's comb this place inch by inch but stick together. I'll go first and run my explosives detector. I don't trust these bastards not to blow the place up and take us with it."

"But he'd never destroy these precious artifacts!" Nick cried. "He loved art over anything, even me."

Peaches turned to him. "Remember the Temple of Artemis? Does blowing up that island sound like a man who puts Greek art over everything? We're just lucky he didn't blow up Phoebe while he was at it."

"That wasn't Sebastian," I said with startling conviction. "That was Noel. Noel Halloran, one of the most ruthless art thieves on the planet, expected me to die in that labyrinth. The ritual playacting was only to appease whoever he had working for him—I guess the Roses, among others. Unlike him, they really believed the rituals they were enacting. If the treasure is still here, it's because Noel couldn't figure out how to move it in time."

"So, maybe the bastard's still in here. Maybe he didn't get away, after all. Come on," Zann called.

Evan wielded his bomb-detector app as I led my companions to the banquet area where the wall gaped open on the courtyard pool, the smoky scent of smoldering braziers suffocating. This was the spot where Noel had appeared before me only hours before. Why did it feel like eons ago?

"Dining couches, seriously?" Zann exclaimed, striding among the furniture. "And amphora and kylixes, like genuine ones?"

"Are you frickin' kidding me?" Peaches muttered. "They really did get into the whole lost-world thing, didn't they?" She peeked under a pottery bowl. "Stuff's still warm."

"I'm starving." Zann plucked a roll from a basket and bit down while Evan prowled every corner of the room.

Nick stood gazing around, his expression both stunned and sad. "I didn't realize he'd go this far."

"You haven't spoken to him since you were a teenager. How could you even know who he is now?" I asked, touching his arm. "Let's try upstairs next."

We filed upstairs, investigating every room, the offices, the lounges. Everything appeared more or less intact, the one exception being the jewelry case on the second-floor landing with its glass case hanging wide open and half the contents gone. I stood before it, staring. One hand strayed to the single earring dangling from my ear. "This is where they must have taken all the jewelry for the ritual last night."

"Is that how you got the gold girdle around your neck?" Zann inquired. "You haven't told us about that yet. Can I look at it more closely?"

I clutched the key hidden beneath my sweater. "Not now. Let's continue scouring this place. I need to find that bastard." But deep in my heart, I knew that Noel had gone, and that knowledge hardened me to the core. I almost didn't care about anything else.

Evan stood in the middle of the second-floor corridor. "No sign of explosives anywhere."

I walked right up to him. "He's escaped, Evan. Noel's slipped right out of our fingers again!"

"He won't get away with this, Phoebe. If I have to chase that bastard to the ends of the earth, I will." The phone buzzed in his hand. "Hang on."

He turned away to give orders or take orders or whatever was going on between him and whoever was controlling operations. That left me standing alone in the hallway feeling a tiny bit broken, or maybe cracked right down the center. I couldn't explain the feeling. It was as if all my rage had dissipated into a cold well of exhaustion and pain, the kind of deep bruising that makes the soul ache from the inside out, the kind you think will never heal.

Peaches and Zann were dashing down the hall checking every room one more time.

I just stood there.

"Phoebe."

I turned, surprised to find Nick's eyes moist.

"I didn't expect it to hit me this way. I thought anything he did was so separate from me that nothing could affect me but..."

"He's your father," I whispered. "Of course you're hurting. Your life and his are entwined by blood and memory. I'm so sorry, Nick."

"I—wait. Did you hear that?"

"Hear what?" All I could detect were the beat of footsteps on the tiles as my friends ran from room to room, calling to another over the sound of Evan's deep baritone arguing on the phone.

"What did it sound like?" I asked.

"Like glass breaking."

"Glass... The observation deck! This way!" I dashed across the hall to the side door half-hidden behind a potted fern. I had forgotten about the damn observation deck!

I half ran up the steps hoping against hope that I'd find Noel up there trying to make his escape. He'd have a hoard of ancient gold on his back with some complex rescue plan that involved plucking him from the platform by helicopter or some damn thing and Evan would come up behind me and zap him with his phone, maybe stand over him repeatedly shooting pulses into his heart until he was gone, finally gone, the forever kind of gone. I wouldn't feel a twinge of remorse. I'd stand by and watch in my goddess-given right to see the world rid of vicious heartless bat-shit bastard scum like him.

I practically flung myself into the light-filled dome, spinning around, scanning the circle in every direction. "Noel?" I called, holding my phone aloft and set on the red end of the sliding scale.

Nick dashed in behind me and stopped. "Father?"

I followed his gaze, focusing on the hunched-over form of a robed man sitting on a bench, shattered glass at his feet.

The man lifted his head. "Son? Is that really you?" he whispered.

Nick took a step forward. "Father, what have you done?"

Sebastian, pale, his face slicked with sweat, seemed to lack the ability to hold himself upright. "I have left all this to you, my boy...to do with as you will... Give it to our people. Share it as you see fit... Everything is yours now."

"What have you done?" Nick cried again, his shoes crunching on glass as he crouched at his father's feet. "You destroyed the Temple of Artemis? You tried to kill my friend? What kind of monster are you?"

"That wasn't...me," he whispered. "I had no knowledge of the explosives... That was...him."

"Noel," I said.

His filmy eyes met mine. "Yes...and the others, Peter and Heather. I didn't believe they would do it. I believed Phoebe...that you would find the key. Did you?"

"Where is Noel?" I demanded.

"Gone," he gasped. "Took the cella of Artemis with him. Peter and Heather, too, all gone. Escape planned in advance. I didn't...know."

"Gone where?" I demanded.

"No idea. Did you...find the key, Phoebe? Does it exist?"

His desperate pleading tugged at my heart. How can one deny a dying man? I pulled the braided gold from under my sweater, vaguely aware of Evan, Peaches, and Zann arriving behind me.

"Yes and no," I said. "The Artemis Key was not an object but an ability, a powerful gift that once belonged to only a few people on earth at a time when the world's population was much smaller. It was the gift of second sight, to see what others couldn't, to foretell the future, even locate lost objects. She used it to help and guide people, the honor of being an oracle at Delphi passed down according to this ability for hundreds of years. Today the gift is spread thinly among thousands, maybe millions, of us, diluted. I have but a small amount but maybe more than others. But maybe we all have a bit of the Artemis Key. We call it ESP or any number of names to describe an ability that was once respected and revered as sacred, now not so much. The Pythia had this ability in abundance."

Sebastian's gaze seemed filled with wonder. One hand gripped his stomach and spittle frothed on his lips. "You found it, then!" he gasped.

"No," I said. "I found *her*. Try to understand. The last Pythia died in that labyrinth the way you knew I might. She could have climbed free but didn't because there was no world left for her to climb back into. It was gone." Tears rolled down my cheeks. "She died there alone remembering her goddess, who she believed would take her to Mount Olympus upon her death."

"How do you...know that?" Sebastian managed to ask.

"Because she told me," I sobbed. "Right there in the labyrinth, she told me the truth. Don't ask me how. You'd never understand but she gave me this." I dangled the key. "The key to the last temple at Delphi, which she knew lay in ruins even as she took her last breath. It was her gift to me and I promised to wear it always."

"Thank you, Phoebe," he whispered. "You do the...goddess a great honor. I have honored no one but my own folly. Look what he...placed in my hand." He dropped the Fool and the Devil cards onto the tiles as he curled himself over the bench. "Time to go now." Convulsions racked his body. He reached for Nick's hand. "Forgive...me," he whispered.

"Dad! What did you take?" Nick cried, taking his father's head into his lap. "Don't tell me hemlock!"

Sebastian tried to smile. "A fitting...end."

<hr/>

I SAT BESIDE NICK ON THE PROMONTORY BENCH, HOLDING HIS HAND, both of us staring out to sea, mourning in different ways. Below us, ships encircled the islet with smaller boats traveling back and forth. Interpol had arrived along with a medical crew and a team from the National Archaeological Museum, plus the police and other officials stomping through the complex in various states of amazement.

Evan had suggested that I escape the chaos and the inevitable questioning, which I did, taking Nick along with me. There'd be time to answer the questions, provide our statements, and the rest. Just then, we needed time to breathe.

"I can't believe that he chose to die by drinking hemlock," I whispered. "It's such a horrible way to go."

"Father would think it noble. The ancient Greeks always used hemlock as the poison of choice."

"As in Socrates."

"Yes, the most famous hemlock poisoning of all."

I needed to distract him. "You're a rich man now, Nick," I said from that numb place where I currently resided.

"Yes." He spoke softly as if trying to focus on something far in the distance. "And Adamos demanded twenty minutes ago that I return to the ship immediately and, in a roundabout fashion, informed me who owned the *Sylvan Seas*—my father. Adamos still doesn't know that I'm his son."

That made me smile. "Which means you now own the *Sylvan Seas* and probably twenty-five percent of every boat on the Aegean, too."

"But I don't want all that money and power," he said, turning to me. "What would I do with it?"

"Something good," I said, squeezing his hand. "You'll build a museum for this collection, maybe donate millions to a hospital, help orphans, or purchase masses of vaccinations for struggling countries. You'll be a philanthropist art-preserver extraordinaire. You might even find Atlantis. That's who you are—one of the good ones."

His smile reached his eyes. "What about you, Phoebe? You're one of the good ones, too."

"Not me." There was iron in my voice. "I have too much hate in my heart right now. I need to fill that dark cavity back up with love, something that feels like I may have lost. I don't want to be bitter and twisted but that's how I feel now. Those aren't the words of a good person."

He squeezed my hand. "Those are the words of a good person deeply bruised. This Noel fellow masquerading as the Magician is the probable orchestrator of the labyrinth madness and ultimately responsible for all these deaths. Maybe if he hadn't played on my father's weaknesses, none of this would have happened. Your agency will catch him and do the world a big favor. In the meantime, you need to heal and let the light back in."

Footsteps sounded behind us. I turned to find Evan stepping up to the promontory.

"Nick, they're deciding what to do with your father's collection. Maybe you need to get down there and introduce yourself," he said.

"You're right." Nick got to his feet and sighed. "It's time I stepped into my father's shoes so I can walk them in a new direction." Shooting us both a quick smile, he turned, and dashed down the stairs.

My heartbeat picked up its pace as Evan took a seat beside me. "So, what's happening?" I asked.

"Peaches is minding Zann in case she tries to post something to the media; the museum and antiquities crew are assessing the art bounty; Interpol and the local police are arguing over jurisdiction; and the ambulance boat just took Sebastian's body away. Oh, and, Phoebe, they found two bodies identified as Heather and Peter Rose floating in the Aegean."

"How—?" I began.

"Shot. I'm guessing Noel no longer needed them. In any case, they'll be sorting this mess out for months to come. You don't need to be in the thick of it until you're ready."

He put an arm around my shoulders and brought me close. I rested my head on his chest and closed my eyes. "I'll wade back in soon enough. I just needed to get my thoughts straight and wrest this rage of mine to the ground. My anger...makes it all so dark inside of me." I began to cry.

"You're the Artemis Key," he said softly. "You follow the light. Leave that bastard to me."

"But I should be the one who nails him, shouldn't I? You're not the one he sent into the labyrinth to do or die and you're not the one he's been using to track down priceless art for years. And even though my recent ordeal ultimately resulted in me gaining a great gift, maybe the task of ending Noel is mine alone."

"Not alone, never alone. You never need to be alone, Phoebe. Don't darken that light inside you with thoughts of revenge. Leave that to me."

I gazed up. "But I feel so much...hate."

He drew me closer. "Look at me and tell me what you see."

His eyes were the kind of deep hazel brown that flickers green in certain conditions and at that moment the conditions suffused them with an illumination all their own, an illumination focused completely on me. "Think of the opposite of hate, Phoebe. Let me shine the light on those dark, aching places of yours to remind you what you stand for and who is on your side always."

What followed was the kind of long delicious kiss that wipes everything from one's mind except the deep connection that can hold you together from the inside out. Believe me, Noel Halloran wasn't in the picture and everything that had once been dark swirled with color, light, and hope, waves and waves of sparkling hope.

We could have continued for longer, maybe hours, days, even, but his phone began ringing imperiously.

"Ignore it," he murmured.

I snuggled deeper into his arms...until my phone started, too. Now we had dual phones ringing, one after the other, each stopping only long enough for the other to start up again.

"Damn it," Evan muttered, pulling gently away. "That's Rupert's tone. I've already spoken to him twice today."

I held up my phone and pressed the green Talk button. "We'd best get it over with."

Rupert's face came into view. "Phoebe, are you all right? I truly expected you to call by now. Must I wait indefinitely? What have you done to your hair? I can't say that I like it, though I dare say a little styling was in order."

"I'm a bit busy right now, Rupert. What is so important that it can't wait?" I asked, smiling into the screen.

"Pardon? Yes, well, I promised to send the new banner image as soon as I received it from the graphic artist, which I now have in hand. Therefore, I have just dispatched it to all members of the team. Do open your email. Phoebe. Whose arm is around your shoulders?"

"Mine, and I have the image here," Evan said, holding up his phone so I could see the banner and leaning forward so Rupert could see him.

I gazed at a graphic gold coin emblazoned with the image of Medusa's head in a fiery vortex.

"Allow me to introduce you to the new logo of the Agency of the Ancient Lost and Found," Rupert announced. "The ancient head of Medusa being a universally recognizable symbol once emblazoned on the shields of Roman and Grecian warriors alike that will now symbolize our mission to protect lost, endangered, or stolen art."

"It almost looks like me," I whispered.

"There is a certain resemblance admittedly," Rupert agreed, his bushy eyebrows seeming to wiggle above his eyes, "especially now with that interesting hairstyle of yours. Are those curls? However—"

"However—" Evan leaned over and removed the phone from my hand "—we're signing off now, Rupert. Medusa and I are busy at the moment. Talk later." And he pressed End.

THE END

Be sure to follow Phoebe's next adventure into French history and the mystery of the missing tapestry in

The Thread of the Unicorn Due June 2022

The Agency of the Ancient Lost & Found

Book Five

THE THREAD
OF THE
UNICORN

JANE THORNLEY

AFTERWORD

Though the influence of the ancient Greeks permeates Western society, there's so much we don't know about their rituals, especially those associated with Artemis, the oracles, and any of the "female mysteries." Scholars speculate that even in a civilization so verbal and literate, some things just wouldn't be disclosed in print. That suits me just fine. The life of females, goddesses or otherwise, have been portrayed through men's eyes long enough. I'm relieved that male notables like Herodotus found other topics on which to chew.

As for Artemis, she appears to have become the goddess of all things mysteriously feminine and left the thinking part to her sister Athena. The moon doesn't think, the moon *feels*, and it's the power of instinctive thought that rules her silver glow. The designers of the Rider-Waite tarot deck understood that along with countless other ancient symbolic references. Of course, any powerful symbol can fall into the wrong hands. Consider the swastika, once a symbol of divinity and spirituality that became corrupted by an evil force.

There is no such thing as the Artemis Key historically but of course it exists. You probably have a touch of the key yourself. Phoebe certainly does and she invites you to follow her into book 5, *The Thread of the*

237

Unicorn, where medieval history, the Cluny tapestries, and a long-ago story of courtly love unravels before her eyes.

ABOUT THE AUTHOR

JANE THORNLEY is an author of historical mystery thrillers with a humorous twist. She has been writing for as long as she can remember and when not traveling and writing, lives a very dull life—at least on the outside. Her inner world is something else again.

With over twelve novels published and more on the way, she keeps up a lively dialogue with her characters and invites you to eavesdrop by reading all of her works.

To follow Jane and share her books' interesting background details, special offers, and more, please join her newsletter here:

NEWSLETTER SIGN-UP

ALSO BY JANE THORNLEY

SERIES: CRIME BY DESIGN

Crime by Design Boxed Set Books 1-3

Crime by Design Prequel: Rogue Wave e-book available free to newsletter subscribers.

Crime by Design Book 1: Warp in the Weave

Crime by Design Book 2: Beautiful Survivor

Crime by Design Book 3: The Greater of Two Evils

Crime by Design Book 4: The Plunge

Also featuring Phoebe McCabe:

SERIES: THE AGENCY OF THE ANCIENT LOST & FOUND

The Carpet Cipher Book 1

The Crown that Lost its Head Book 2

The Florentine's Secret Book 3

The Artemis Key Book 4

The Thread of the Unicorn (pre-order) Book 5

SERIES: NONE OF THE ABOVE MYSTERY

None of the Above Series Book 1: Downside Up

None of the Above Series Book 2: DownPlay

Printed in Great Britain
by Amazon

26583401R00136